JAHQUEL J.

Second Chance Christmas

MEDIA

WWW.BLACKODYSSEY.NET

Published by
BLACK ODYSSEY MEDIA

www.blackodyssey.net
Email: info@blackodyssey.net

Library of Congress Control Number: 2023919225

First Trade Paperback Printing: October 2024
ISBN: 978-1-957950-49-5
ISBN: 978-1-957950-50-1 (e-book)

10 9 8 7 6 5 4 3 2 1

Manufactured in the United States of America

Distributed by Kensington Publishing Corp.

Dear Reader,

I want to thank you immensely for supporting Black Odyssey Media authors, and our ongoing efforts to spotlight more minority storytellers. The scariest and most challenging task for many writers is getting the story, or characters, out of our heads and onto the page. Having admitted that, with every manuscript that Kreceda and I acquire, we believe that it took talent, discipline, and remarkable courage to construct that story, flesh out those characters, and prepare it for the world. Debut or seasoned, our authors are the real heroes and heroines in OUR story. And for them, we are eternally grateful.

Whether you are new to Jahquel J. or Black Odyssey Media, we hope that you are here to stay. We also welcome your feedback and kindly ask that you leave a review. For upcoming releases, announcements, submission guidelines, etc., please be sure to visit our website at www.blackodyssey.net or scan the QR code below. We can also be found on social media using @iamblackodyssey. Until next time, take care and enjoy the journey!

Joyfully,

Shawanda Williams

Shawanda "N'Tyse" Williams
Founder/Publisher

Prologue

I KNEW THE DAY would come.

A day when I would be pulled out of bed because of my mother's recklessness. The day that I would have to toss on my clothes and run down to the police station and promise them that I would get her home safely. It was usually my father who was doing the promising and apologizing. Instead of practicing how to kiss a boy in the mirror, I would practice how apologetic I would look when it was finally my turn to pick her up. I had watched my father do this same charade at least half a dozen times. The other half, I was too young to comprehend why Daddy picked Mama up from the police station. These days, the police were so tired of Mama's bullshit that they didn't want an explanation or promise. They just wanted her out of their building as quickly as possible. Daddy would grab my mama by the arm and pull her to the idling car where I was waiting. He'd reach across her, strap her in, and then take one long look before slamming the door to walk around the car.

That man was tired.

Tonight, I wasn't pulled out of bed. It was the night of my senior prom, and I was supposed to be heading to the hotel room that Rome booked for us. It was going to be our night. We had done plenty of other things, and as much as I enjoyed doing those things in the backseat of his mama's Lexus, I was excited to be sharing a bed with him tonight.

Or so I thought I would be.

"She probably just passed out at the bar in town or something." Rome tried to cheer me up about the situation. He knew Mama's and my relationship wasn't the best.

I already felt low because I was supposed to be having a special night with my boyfriend, and here he was, driving me to the hospital because my mama had drunk too much.

"This isn't the bar, Rome. We're heading to the hospital. What if she's hurt or something?"

When Principal Miller called me into the hotel hallway where the prom was taking place, I didn't know what he wanted. I was the top student at Sageport High, so I knew I couldn't have been in any trouble. He told me that my mother was in the hospital.

New location unlocked.

As angry as I was with my mother, I was scared too. Wringing my hands, I tried to busy myself by counting the trees that passed by the window.

One. Two. Three. Four.

God, what if something happened to her? My relationship with my mother was very strained. I was a reminder of the life she never had. The living, breathing regret that she had to be reminded of every single day. I knew I was the reason behind Mama never making it out of Sageport.

It didn't help that she constantly reminded me.

"Fay, she probably just needed to be escorted home. Remember when you fell down the steps near the General Store?" Rome reminded me.

I smiled. I loved it whenever he called me Fay. That nickname was reserved just for me. He grabbed hold of my hand and continued to drive.

"It's hard not to think the worst. She promised me she would stay in the house tonight. She knew how important tonight was."

"We can still make it to the hotel after she's settled in the house." Rome was always so optimistic.

He always saw the bright side of things. I guess you would when it wasn't your mama that you had to pick up on prom night.

"When does your father come back? You have to call him and tell him about this, Fay."

I refused.

"No. He will try to rush and book a flight to get back home. I can handle this on my own . . . I can handle my mom," I confidently told him.

It had been months since my uncle called and told us that my grandmother was sick. Living in a different state made it hard for my father to drop everything and be at her side. When you owned one of the most popular restaurants in town, you couldn't just pick up and leave whenever someone needed you. My father also felt torn between maintaining a relationship with his family and choosing his wife. As I became older, I wanted to prove to my father that I could carry some of the burden he had been carrying alone all these years.

When Rome pulled into the parking space and killed the engine, I felt a somber feeling in the pit of my stomach. The lights from the emergency sign illuminated both of our faces. We sat in the car for a few seconds before breaking our silence.

It was embarrassing.

Having everyone pity you because your mom is an alcoholic always made me feel low as if I wasn't good enough to exist in the same places as these people. Even being with someone like Rome felt wrong, as if I wasn't worthy of his love.

Rome never made me feel like that, though.

I hated having to hear stories about how she was tossed out of a business because she was belligerent drunk. This town was far too shallow not to patronize one of the most popular restaurants in town because Kimba Stone was the town's alcoholic.

Rome turned in his seat and grabbed my hands. "Tonight, will still be everything that we have ever wanted. This is just a small bump in the road."

"There's always going to be a bump in the road when it comes to my mom," I whined.

Rome had been accepted into Georgia State University. He knew what life would look like after high school. Our lives after school were going to look different. While he was chasing his dreams in Georgia, I would attend a community college here.

It would be selfish to leave my father here alone with her. He couldn't possibly run the restaurant and manage my mother at the same time. How would he be able to continue to follow his own dreams while having to micromanage Mom? He needed me here, and despite him encouraging me to leave Sageport, I would stay.

"You should reconsider the scholarship, Faith. Columbia is a big deal, and not many get scholarships there. This could be big for you."

The day I received the acceptance letter and scholarship from Columbia University, I sobbed. Not because this was something I had always wanted and had accomplished it. I sobbed because, in my heart, I knew there was no way that I could leave my parents behind. My father would never verbally admit it, but I knew he needed me here.

Instead of jumping for joy like other students did when they received their letters, I folded mine and put it in the back of my diary. At best, it would make for a great conversation starter when I was older. People who were accepted into Columbia could have bragging rights . . . right?

"I have considered it a million times. My family isn't like yours, Rome. I don't have a mom who attends all my games, bakes cookies because she loves me, or is fully present to hear me vent. These are the cards I was dealt, and I need to deal with them."

Mrs. Atkins was the definition of a supermom. She was on every committee there was for the school, and she still managed to be a great wife and mother to her boys. Mr. and Mrs. Atkins were prom king and queen and were considered a success story around Sageport. Mr. Atkins owned most of the car dealerships in town, so their family influence ran deep. Everyone loved them, and a few people wanted to be them. Both their boys—a year apart—played football for the local high school, and talks were circulating that there was a spot waiting for Rome's brother when he was ready to start touring colleges.

Rome didn't understand my life because he had never had to live it. My parents were happy once upon a time. It was probably before I was born because I had never seen them happy. Mama was discreet with her drinking for a while. Then she stopped caring.

She stopped caring about everything.

"What the—?" Rome dropped my hands and stared out the window.

We watched a panicked Mrs. Atkins run past the car and into the hospital. She hadn't even noticed that we were in the car when she rushed past. Rome was out of the vehicle and behind his mom before I could close the door. I trotted behind him, holding my dress up to step onto the curb. We saw Mrs. Atkins talking to the front receptionist when we entered the waiting room.

"Mama, what's going on?"

"It's Allen . . ." She was trying hard to catch her breath. "They called and said he was in a bad wreck . . . I came as soon as I got the call."

When she finally turned around, I saw her face was wet with tears. She had probably been crying since she received the call.

"Do they know anything?"

"She's getting the doctor no—Romeo, why are you here? This is your prom. Did they call you too?" You could tell she was just processing that her other son was standing in front of her instead of at his senior prom or, at best, having sex with me.

"Faith got a call about her mom too."

I knew Mrs. Atkins wasn't a fan of mine. She hated my mother, so it was natural that those feelings trickled down to her only daughter too. "Hi, Mrs. Atkins," I greeted her.

She looked me up and down, then pulled Rome to the side. I was used to her doing this by now and never cared. Rome loved me and would never listen to his mother's lies.

"Faith?"

I turned around and saw Dr. Thompson standing there with a somber expression on her face. My stomach knew something was wrong before I did. "Is Mom all right?"

Dr. Thompson and my mom grew up together and were even best friends at some point. I heard the story of how they would get out of this town and follow their dreams in a bigger city. Dr. Thompson was the only one to leave and follow her dreams. She ended up falling in love and moving back to Sageport to be closer to her family.

"Come with me, Faith." She tried to quickly rush me toward the back, away from the emergency room, but my feet refused to move. "Faith, come quickly," she ushered me toward the back.

"Nooo! God, no! Not my baby!" I heard Mrs. Atkins start wailing, and Rome caught her as she collapsed into his arms.

Rome struggled, trying to hold his mother, who was tossing her body and arms every which way. The tears sliding down his cheeks indicated how bad the news they had just received was.

"I need to be with them." I quickly got out of Dr. Thompson's grasp and rushed toward Rome. "Rome, what's going on?" I asked, reaching out to touch his back.

Mrs. Atkins was still sobbing in his chest while I rubbed his back. "A . . . Allen didn't make it." Rome's voice cracked while trying to get the sentence out.

I watched as Mrs. Atkins's head rose slowly from Rome's chest. "You!" she pointed at me. "My baby is gone because of you!" she screamed and lunged at me.

Dr. Thompson quickly grabbed me and pulled me toward the back. Everything was happening so fast that I couldn't comprehend it. One minute, I was at prom enjoying what was supposed to be the best night of my life, and now, I had just been saved from Mrs. Atkins attacking me.

"What was that about? Dr. Thompson, what's going on?"

"Come with me in the exam room . . . You may want to take a seat."

I pulled away from her. "No. I don't want to take a seat. I want to know why Mrs. Atkins just tried to attack me, and what happened to Allen? What's going on?"

She heaved a sigh. "Kimba didn't make it either, Faith. She passed twenty minutes ago . . . I called her time of death." I could tell that she was trying to remain professional. However, her personal feelings were slowly creeping in.

My heart pounded against my chest like Travis Barker playing the drums. Did I hear her correctly?

I couldn't have.

No, I wouldn't process what she had just told me. My mom couldn't have been dead. The chilled bottle of bourbon was still fresh in the garage freezer. She needed to finish that.

It was her Sunday ritual.

Not tonight.

She had her spades game tomorrow down at the community center. It was the only thing she looked forward to these days, and the older crowd wasn't so harsh with their judgment.

"No, she's not." I shook my head.

I don't know why I couldn't stop shaking my head. It was like my body was being controlled by someone else. I wasn't in control of my body, which worried me. I was always in control of everything. After growing up with a mom who often lost control, you learned to master having control. It became an obsession since I was in fourth grade, and Rodney Chase told the whole class that my mom pissed in the parking lot of the bowling alley.

"Baby, I spoke to your father, and he will get the first flight out. We both agreed that you should come and stay with me tonight . . . . You shouldn't be alone," she wrapped her arms around me.

Dr. Thompson had this maternal presence about her, and this wasn't the first time she had embraced me with it.

"My mom isn't dead."

I was in denial. Tears didn't fall from my eyes like they did Rome's, and I didn't overreact like people in movies.

What was wrong with me?

I felt numb. This couldn't be my life. How could this be happening right now? My mom had always been selfish, but I never thought she would have been *this* selfish.

"She was drinking and driving, Faith. Caused a three-car accident down on Mural Road. Allen Atkins was one of the drivers. He was ejected from the car upon impact."

Jesus.

Why couldn't she just sit in the house? This day was supposed to be about me, and now look at where I had ended. Now, I was standing in a hospital hallway listening to how my mother not only killed herself but how she killed my boyfriend's younger brother.

"You end things with her now! She's the child of a fucking monster! Kimba Stone murdered my baby. Oh God, nooo!" We could hear Mrs. Atkins scream from the waiting room.

Dr. Thompson pulled me in the opposite direction. "You can wait in the on-call room while I wrap up everything. Your dad thinks you should come home with me tonight," she repeated.

It was like I was watching myself from above with how she pulled me into a room with a few beds, then left, closing the door behind her. My hands were red from the way I had been violently wringing them to help calm my anxiety. It was something I had been doing since I was seven. It started when my mother left me alone at the grocery store.

Standing up, I left the room. I know I was told to do one thing, and here I was, doing the opposite. But I needed to see Rome and let him know that I wasn't a monster, either. I would never get behind the wheel drunk or pick up a drink ever. I wasn't my mother's child, and he had to know that. He had to know that our plans to be together could still happen.

Mr. Atkins had arrived and had taken over consoling his inconsolable wife. Rome was off to the side near the vending machines with his head in his hands. I slid into the seat next to him and sniffled.

"Rome, I'm so sorr—"

"Did you leave the car keys in the house tonight?" He had cut me off before I could apologize to him and his family.

I was always apologizing and fixing my mother's messes. Even with her now departed from this world, I was still left to fix her mess.

"I . . . I didn't think about the keys."

It was true. Tonight was the one night for me. I was allowed to be selfish because I had spent the entire year sacrificing my happiness to achieve academic success. I just wanted to hang out with my friends and boyfriend tonight while enjoying prom. So, no, I didn't think about the car keys.

"You know, once she drinks, she starts to wander, and you allowed her to take those keys and drive, Faith," he accused, sending my heart further into the pits of my soles.

"W . . . Why are you blaming me?" I stammered.

Had I known she would do that, I would have snatched the keys and taken them with me. I hated myself for not thinking about the keys before leaving.

While all my friends were at their houses getting a million pictures taken of them by their parents, I was making sure my mom was satisfied enough to stay in the house and not end up in town at her favorite bar.

"'Cause you should have fucking known better, Faith . . . My br—" he choked. "My brother is dead because of your mother . . . Had you taken those keys, he would be alive."

I tried to hold him, and he snatched away from me. "I'm sorry, Rome . . . I swear, I'm sorry." My eyes were blurred with tears as I stood up and tried to hold him again.

My mother dying didn't provoke tears out of me, but seeing Rome hurt did. Rome had always made me feel safe and had shown me true love.

Seeing him hurt, hurt me.

"Get the fuck off me, Faith." He snatched himself away from me.

"I'm sorry, Rome. I swear if I could do it agai—"

"Do *what* again? This is real life; we don't get any do overs. My brother is dead, and he's not coming back." He started to walk off and then stopped, turning back to face me. "Mama always said that your mom was bad news and that you would end up just like her . . . Maybe I should have believed her."

A heavy flow of tears cascaded down his cheeks as he walked away from me, leaving me to sit in the waiting room of the hospital—alone.

Chapter One

PRESENT

FAITH

GOD, I HATED Fridays.

I stood behind the counter and sipped my coffee while listening to my children bicker about who would ride shotgun on the school drop-off.

It was less than a month until Christmas break, and I was counting down the days until I was rid of the carpool lines and complaints from both kids.

"Daddy said he would make it to my school play tonight." Madison, my daughter, stood on her toes and batted her long lashes at me.

Lashes that she inherited from her father.

Lucky bastard.

Ashton wouldn't make her school play because he never made her plays. He had too many meetings that were always far more important than his family. Madison knew he wouldn't make it, but that never stopped her from believing he would show up with the pink and purple roses she always requested.

"How about we call him on our way to school?" I nuzzled her hair and waited for that look of satisfaction to come across her face.

Once it did, which it always did, I gently ushered her toward the mud room to grab all her things for school.

"Okay, Mommy. We can call hi—"

"I want to call him first." Mayven interrupted her sister and bumped into her at the same time. "Daddy wants me to call him first," she continued.

"No! I'm calling Daddy!" Madison shoved her sister back before I got in the middle of them.

"Mayven, have you packed your things into your backpack?" I crossed my arms and stared down at my daughter, who loved testing my patience.

Especially when we were running behind.

"No, Mama . . . I want to ca—"

"I don't want to hear another word unless you have everything packed and ready to go."

Mayven groaned before stomping off to the mudroom to make sure all of her things were ready for school. Madison stood there with a sly expression fixed on her lips before skipping off to the mudroom to do the very same thing.

Madison and Mayven were eight years old and the most opposite set of twins I had ever met. Usually, twins loved to spend time with each other.

That was utterly false when it came to my set.

Ashton and I even hired a therapist to see if it was normal. Mayven and Madison were just twins who enjoyed having their own things and space. They hated being treated like twins and loved when treated like individuals. If Madison were picking out a purple shirt, then Mayven would go out of her way to find a shirt that was the furthest thing from purple. The only time I got away with dressing them alike was when they were too young to speak out against it.

Every morning, I put out tiny fires to avoid a bigger explosion. The goal was to get out the door in one piece and without a meltdown from either child. Some days, it felt nearly impossible.

"When are you going to call Daddy?" Mayven asked the moment I buckled myself into my car.

I looked in the rearview mirror and heaved a sigh before responding. Mayven was so intense, and at times, her tone didn't feel like it belonged to an eight-year-old child.

"Your tone, May."

She sucked her teeth and folded her arms. Some days, I didn't know how I would survive when the girls turned into teenagers. I remember how I was as a teen, and they wouldn't be anything like me. My daughters had way more attitude than I ever had when I was their age.

They also weren't a big fan of hiding their feelings. Unlike me, whenever they were having big feelings, they would let it be known.

"You never let me call Daddy. It's always Madison's turn, and I'm sick of it," she continued with her sassiness.

Today wasn't the day to go back and forth with Mayven. This morning, it took every ounce of energy to pull myself out of bed and have a smile plastered across my face while making their breakfast. Whoever said divorce got easier definitely lied or didn't like their husband to begin with.

"Jesus Christ, enough, Mayven . . . Shit!" I hollered, losing my shit in the process.

I had made it a rule long before the girls were born that I would never lose my temper with them or raise my voice. I went through my entire childhood always walking on pins and needles because I feared what would set my mother off next.

I didn't want that for my kids.

"Hello?" I heard Ashton's voice come from my phone.

I gripped the steering wheel and lowered my head, wondering how this day could get any worse. Ashton hearing me lose my temper with Mayven wasn't something that I wanted to experience today.

Madison knew that I was irritated, so she just handed me back the phone. I looked back at my girls before getting out of the car to have a conversation I didn't want to have.

"Good morning." I leaned against the driver's door.

"Sounds like a hectic morning . . . Is everything good over there?"

I wanted to scream and remind him of our obligations following our divorce.

No.

I wasn't all right, and I wished he never uttered those five words. Nothing would ever be all right with breaking up our family because we couldn't get it right. I wanted so much out of my marriage.

Maybe too much.

I sacrificed so much to be my husband's backbone, the person he could turn to when things in the outside world became too demanding. I carried our daughters in my womb, nearly dying, while still trying to turn our house into a home. I had given so much of myself to him, and now, I had nothing to show for it.

No. Everything *wasn't* all right over here.

"Ash, your daughter wants you to attend her play tonight." I ignored his painful question and focused on the reason he was even on the phone in the first place.

I could tell from the silence on the other end of the phone that he was about to let our daughter down this morning. The girls were true daddy's girls and loved spending time with their father. Anything that Ashton was doing, they wanted to do the same thing.

"Um . . . Damn. This is kind of last minute, Faith. I'm in meetings all day, and my last one is the biggest one. I'm not sure I'll be able to make it to the school in time."

"This has been on our shared calendar for the past two months. Ash, you even dropped her off to a few rehearsals." I jogged his memory.

Since the divorce, we had a shared calendar for the girls. Both girls were involved in different activities, and I always wanted us to be on the same page when it came to them. Ashton knew this, and I always kept the calendar updated with everything the girls had going on. It infuriated me that he never paid attention to what I set in place to make this transition smoother.

"I know, I know. I've been busy with work, so I haven't had a chance to catch up with everything. Tell Maddie that I'll make it up to her this weekend."

"You're always making something up to someone," I muttered.

"Seriously, Faith?"

"Goodbye, Ashton." I quickly ended the call and stood outside the car for five minutes to catch my breath.

I had to climb back into the car, apologize to Mayven, and then make an excuse about why Ashton couldn't make tonight's play. Some days, I wanted to be honest and tell her that we weren't a priority to Daddy. I also knew that would cause more damage in the long run.

"Hey, Faith, are you going to meet us for drinks after the play?" Sherri Richards, the most annoying PTA mom, popped her head over the shrubs that separated her home from ours—mine.

I knew the drinks were nothing more than an invite to get into my personal business. A few drinks would cause loose lips, and she would eat it right up.

"You know, Sherri . . . I'm not sure I'll be able to get a sitter tonight. Rain check?" I offered an apologetic smile and opened the car door.

My short moment of decompressing was over, thanks to my annoying neighbor.

"Awe, that's all right. I know how hard it has been with the divorce. Let me know anytime you need a break . . . Lolly and I would love to have the girls over to play."

The girls hated Lolly Richards and made sure to show their displeasure each time she rang our doorbell. It was rare for the girls to agree on something together, but when it came to Lolly, they both agreed that they hated her and didn't want to play over at her house anymore.

"Thanks, Sherri. Let me get the girls to school . . . Catch up soon," I lied, knowing I wouldn't be catching up with her and would remember to park in the garage from now on.

The car was silent when I closed the door behind me. I hated how I lost my temper with Mayven and should have been better about it. It seemed like everything was being tossed my way this morning, and I couldn't deal with it.

"I'm sorry for screaming at you, Mayven," I started the conversation. "Mommy shouldn't have taken her big feelings out on you, and for that, I'm sorry."

Mayven smiled weakly. "It's all right, Mom."

Mom. The word I hated the most. While Maddie still called me Mommy, Mayven had commenced calling me Mom.

Just Mom.

It felt so formal, as if the little girl I carried and loved on had vanished, and this little woman had stepped into her place.

"I love you girls with my entire heart. You know how Dr. Vicky spoke to you girls about big feelings?"

They both nodded their heads in unison.

"Well, Mommy had big feelings today. I'm going to do better to check them before lashing out at you . . . okay?"

"It's all right, Mommy." Madison was the first one to speak. "We all have big feelings sometimes."

Mayven remained silent. I reached my hand toward the back and rubbed her knee. "Are you okay, May?"

"I'm okay, Mom." She offered me a smile.

Somehow, I felt like she was saying it just to please me. I looked over at Madison and smiled at her. "Baby, your father has meetings all day today. He's not going to make it, Bug."

The sadness in Madison's eyes spoke volumes without her even having to open her mouth. It pained me to know how much faith my daughter put in her father and how he always found a way to let her down in the end.

"Okay, Mommy."

I quickly turned around before I became emotional. My daughters were my world, and I hated that the one person who constantly let them down was their father. Ashton had always put everything before me, and I always dealt with it. But it was a whole new feeling with him doing it to our daughters.

"Do you think he'll be able to come to my jazz recital?" Mayven finally spoke up, and I stared at my sweet child in the mirror.

"Hopefully. Daddy and I will talk and see what he can attend and what he can't . . . Sound good?"

They both nodded and pulled their tablets out of the back pocket of the seats. I wasn't usually a fan of screen time before school, but after this morning's "festivities," I think we all could use a welcomed distraction. I put on our favorite Beyoncé song and quietly hummed along to the words while the girls became lost in their favorite apps.

Since the divorce, we agreed to put the kids into therapy. They needed someone to talk to help them get through this tough time.

They had always been used to a home that had both their parents. Despite how absent Ashton had been, they were used to seeing Daddy making a cup of coffee before bolting out the door to make it to the office. If we were lucky, he might come home earlier than expected with takeout, so I didn't have to cook.

It didn't matter how inconsistent I thought my husband was. The girls thought the world of him. He was a good father—when he was present.

Ashton had always worked outside the home while my job was raising our daughters. While Ash worked long hours to put food on the table, I had my hands full, raising our two babies. It was a challenge, but I welcomed it. I wanted to prove I could hold down our home while he ventured into the world to make us money. I wanted my kids to look back on their childhood and smile.

Not cringe like I did.

My parenting style came from the home I wanted as a child. I wanted my mother to be soft, apologetic, and comforting. However, she was the opposite of all of that, and I had trauma that I refused to deal with as an adult.

I never wanted my daughters to look back and have to pay endless amounts of money to unpack some childhood trauma in therapy. That was why I held onto my marriage with their father for as long as I did. I wanted our children to witness a healthy marriage, which I had never witnessed.

They deserved that.

I deserved that.

Chapter Two

FAITH

I RUSHED INTO MY favorite restaurant in town and plopped across from my best friend. She stared at me for a second, then raised her already-filled wineglass and tapped the side, mouthing "bottle" to the waiter. These were the times I appreciated having a best friend who could read my body language without me having to utter a single word.

"Thank you, Tierra." I finally let out a breath and plopped my bag beside me. "Today has been a long day," I confessed.

The girls' usual sitter was able to meet me at the school and take the girls home after Madison's play. My baby girl did wonderfully, and I was there waiting with a bouquet of pink roses.

Apparently, you needed to put in a special order for the purple roses.

I held back tears during the entire play because I knew how much it would have meant to Madison if her father had shown up. He couldn't put his daughter first and his job second. Not even once. Watching every daughter run into her father's arms after the performance was hard. Madison looked around before her eyes landed on me, and she rushed into my arms.

It was hard.

I didn't think I would have been attending my child's school play alone at thirty-two. When I held my daughters in my arms when they were born, I envisioned a different future for us. I was determined to give them everything I never had.

"How did our superstar do with her play?" Tierra had accepted the bottle from the waiter and filled my glass nearly to the rim.

"Um, I still have to drive home after this," I giggled but accepted the glass when she handed it to me.

"Girl, your face tells me everything I need to know about your day. Drink the wine and worry about getting home later." Tierra waved me off.

The funny part was that Tierra used to be Ashton's personal assistant. At one point, we spoke more than my husband and I did. Tierra would remember to send flowers on anniversaries or important dates that Ashton had scribbled on their calendar. Half the gifts I received were because she picked them out with Ash's credit card. Tierra played a vital role in our life for the three years she worked for him.

When Mayven had a fever, and Ash was away on business, she rushed over to my house to watch Madison so that I didn't have to take her with me to the emergency room. Tierra always went above and beyond for the girls and me.

Even when she didn't have to.

Over the years that she worked for Ashton, we formed a bond. On the days I had a sitter for the girls, we would have dinner together and have girl talk. She became my only friend and one who understood how lonely I was in my marriage.

"Ashton didn't make it to her play tonight." I slumped further down in my chair and sipped the wine.

"Please don't tell me that's why you're all disheveled tonight?"

I silenced the call I had received and then turned my attention back to Tierra. "She was so hurt. All she wanted was for her father to be there holding roses for her."

Tierra took a sip of her wine while shaking her head. "I hate this for her."

"He misses nearly all of the girls' events, and *I'm* the one who has to make an excuse and wipe their tears."

"How about you stop making excuses for him? I understood why you did it before . . . He was your husband. Just like you have a duty to be the best parent to those girls, he needs to have the same duty."

I desperately wanted to stop making excuses for Ashton. He made it all too easy to stop making them when he didn't show up for our children the way that he was supposed to. He was a hero in our girls' eyes, and I didn't want to be the person who tarnished that image for them.

Gulping some wine, I cut my eyes at her. "It's not as easy as you're trying to make it. Not making excuses means I have to explain more, and the girls will start to hate him."

"Not hate him . . . They will see that he's breaking his promises with them. You can't shelter them from reality, Faith. Eventually, they're going to figure out things on their own."

As much as I wanted to disagree with Tierra, I knew she was right. Since the girls were born, I always made excuses for their father's absence. I often felt guilty about complaining because he was trying to earn a living for us. As an investment banker, it was his job always to be available to his clients. For so long, I tried to be the understanding and supportive wife who stood by her husband.

At first, it was after this promotion, and then he could be more present and not work so many late hours. However, after that promotion, he needed another one so we could take a big family vacation.

When was enough ever going to be enough?

"It's hard."

"Only because you didn't want this divorce. I, more than anyone, know how much you loved your husband and would have fought to keep your family together."

I would have.

My happiness meant nothing if it meant keeping my family under one roof. I wanted to be the success story that everyone boasted about. All I wanted was for my husband to choose me for once.

Choose *us*.

Instead, he continued to put his career before our marriage.

Before his children.

Before everything that he ever cared about.

When was it enough?

"I wanted us to work so bad." I sniffled and took another sip of wine.

Maybe it was the wine that caused me to be more emotional than usual. I wanted my marriage to last, and I wanted my husband.

"I know, baby. I know." Tierra reached her hand across the table and grabbed my hand. "I also know that you were unhappy in that marriage, and you deserve to be happy."

The thing about friendship was that you bared your entire soul to that one person. Tierra had witnessed me at my best and worst. She had front-row seats to the destruction of my marriage. I wished it was as easy as Ashton having an affair and leaving me for a younger woman.

That would have been easier.

I almost wished another woman was the problem in our marriage. Maybe then, I could sleep at night knowing I wasn't the problem within our marriage. As much as I placed the blame on Ashton, I stopped trying. Our sex life had always been the star of our relationship, and it died. The only conversations we had revolved around the girls.

We both stopped trying, but Ashton had stopped way before I did. It seemed like he didn't care to keep me. All the late hours sure didn't help our situation either. All I wanted was for my husband to care.

To love me.

Show me that I meant the world to him.

After having two babies at once, I knew my body didn't look the same as before. I changed because having children did that to you. We both knew that by having kids, things would change and wouldn't be the same.

We went from living in a skyrise to moving to the suburbs of Atlanta. Our usual dinner dates were put on pause because we had two babies to take care of. When we did have a sitter, I spent all my time wondering what the kids were up to. I had become so wrapped in motherhood that I didn't make time for him.

I blamed myself for a while.

As the girls became older, I tried to step back into my role as a wife. It never felt the same. I always felt like I was trying too hard, or maybe he wasn't trying enough. Our date nights were filled with both of us asking useless questions until the check was paid. Even the car rides home were filled with silence.

Not a flirtatious laugh or a touch on my thigh while we waited for the light to turn green.

Nothing.

Ashton couldn't wait until we walked through the door so he could retire to his office. Work was always the excuse for why he didn't come to our bedroom until after I was asleep. I would feel him climb into the bed and shove a pillow between us before drifting off to sleep.

Of course, I was never actually asleep.

It was a different feeling when you realized that your husband was no longer in love with you. Ashton didn't desire me as he once did, which pained me. His eyes used to light up whenever he laid eyes on me. Of course, things weren't the same as they used to be.

I used to wait up for him in lingerie and couldn't wait to hear about his day while I slowly undressed him.

That wasn't realistic with two kids who had so many afterschool activities. I could have tried, though. Life was chaotic, trying to juggle two children while attempting to keep our marriage afloat. If I had to take the blame for one thing, it would be not trying enough for my husband.

"God, I wish he would stop calling me," I snapped out of my emotional trance and silenced the call—again.

"Who?"

"My father."

Tierra took another sip of her wine and stared at me before she spoke. She knew my relationship with my father was a complicated one.

One I avoided talking about at all costs.

"Maybe there's an emergency."

"He always calls around this time . . . with the holidays approaching. He wants to ask me to come spend the holidays in Sageport."

"Is that such a bad thing, Faith? Ashton is taking the kids to New York to visit with his parents . . . You'll be here alone."

"I don't want to spend any time in Sageport. There's a reason I haven't been back in fifteen years."

My father had met the girls a handful of times since their birth. Anytime he came into town, he would call and arrange some time so he could see his granddaughters. I could always expect birthday cards in the mail whenever their birthdays arrived. I appreciated the effort he put into maintaining a relationship with them. I didn't want to face him and explain why I was divorced.

I felt like a failure.

All I had was one job: to keep my family together, and I couldn't even do that. I had failed to give our children a two-parent household, and I wasn't ready to admit that to my father.

"You should spend some time with your father. He's only becoming older . . . You're going to regret not spending that time with him."

I should have been more active in knowing about my father's life. As far as I knew, the restaurant was still doing well, and he had even opened a coffee shop in Sageport. He always sent me pictures via text messages to keep me updated. I hated how he reminded me how all of it would be mine one day.

Nothing in Sageport belonged to me.

When I left there all those years ago, I promised myself that I would never return. There was so much pain, anger, and resentment back in that small town . . . all things that I worked hard to cut out of my memory.

"Not a chance. I was actually thinking of tagging along with Ashton and the girls for the holidays."

Tierra gasped. "Girl, no. You are now divorced . . . Spending the holidays together is something in the past. His parents don't want the reminders of their son's failed marriage in their home."

"Ouch." I held my chest.

"I'm just being honest. Ashton would likely have a problem with it too. You're divorced, and you both agreed to split the holidays for a reason. Call the girls on Christmas morning and then allow him the time with them."

It was a bitter pill to swallow.

"I've spent every holiday with them . . . never missing one. This may be too much for them."

"The girls are smart. You and Ashton have been splitting custody, so they know what's to come. Sit down and have a small follow-up conversation with them . . . *Don't* go to New York."

I groaned and drowned my sorrows with more wine. Tierra decided that we both needed to get some food on our stomachs, so she ordered us a bunch of our favorite appetizers that we loved.

"This is all my fault. I'm the one who wanted the divorce, and now, look at me. Sitting here stupid while my husband moves on with his life."

"*Ex*-husband," Tierra corrected me. "You wanted the divorce because your marriage was like beating a dead horse."

I wanted the divorce because I thought it would trigger something inside of Ash. Trigger something that would make him want to put forth the effort to fight for our marriage. It was a heavy burden to carry when you were doing all the fighting in your marriage. It took two people to make things work, and I was the only one doing the heavy lifting while he got to take the easy way out.

"Something I'm still trying to get used to."

"I'm not saying you need to get out there and date, but I'm also saying that you should consider his offer and move into something smaller. A fresh start for you and the girls, and you don't have to live within the walls of your marital home."

Ash asked if I wanted to sell our home. I refused and was so angry that he even brought it up. This was the home where we brought the girls after their birth at the hospital. Every inch of this home had memories of our girls growing up. The etches in the wood near the pantry told a story of how big our girls had grown over the years. I could have been painted over the crayon marks I kept hidden behind the family room's couch years ago, but I held that small memory close to my heart.

We would never have these moments with them again.

Why would I want to sell our home? He shouldn't have wanted to sell our house either . . . Didn't it mean *anything* to him? We were happy there once upon a time, and it was those memories that I tried desperately to hold onto.

Ash knew how much our neighborhood meant to me, so he found some houses a few miles away so the girls could remain at their school. I stomped out of his office, angry the day he showed me the listings. The house was the last piece of *us* that I had.

The one thing that hadn't changed.

"I'm not moving."

"Maybe you should."

The thought of starting over frightened me. Having to start over as a single, divorced mother was the last thing I wanted.

"Girl, drop the subject."

"Eventually, you'll have to stop living in the past and move into the present. You and Ash are divorced, and *you* need to move forward."

Although I was the one who wanted the divorce, it didn't hurt any less. I knew I would eventually have to stop living in the past. Things didn't work out for Ash and me, but that didn't mean I couldn't push forward and find love again.

I deserved to find love again. One that would cause me to glow from the inside out. The thought of dating again scared me. However, I knew that I needed to get over that. The girls deserved a happy mother, and I was determined to stop pretending for them and actually *be* happy.

Chapter Three

PAST

FAITH

SICK WAS AN understatement for how I was feeling at the moment.

My father held my hand as we walked into the church and sat in the first pew. This was the most interaction I had with my father since he returned to town. When he found out that my mother passed, he never sobbed or blamed himself. He pulled out a thick binder with all their information inside and started making calls.

He closed the restaurant down while he planned to put my mother into the ground. Every night, I tapped on his office to bring him food, and every night, my knocks were left unanswered.

The silence in the house was unbearable.

All I thought about was how Rome stared at me at the hospital. The look was one I never wished on anyone, not even my worst enemy. When I reached out to talk to him at his house, they hung up the phone on me. Rome didn't want anything to do with me, and now, my father was giving me the silent treatment.

If my mom wanted me to feel alone in the wake of her death, she certainly accomplished that.

The funeral had to wait until the Atkins had their funeral. The only reason the church allowed my mother's funeral was because my father had been attending their church for years. He attended every Sunday alone. My mom had stopped attending years earlier and spent her Sundays drinking on the couch.

The church was empty.

I didn't understand why my father didn't cremate her and let us move on with our lives. Things were already tense, and the whole town either felt sorry for us or hated us. I couldn't show my face at school because everyone hated me.

It was hard to focus on finishing out my senior year when I was referred to as "the girl whose mom killed Allen Atkins." Thankfully, I was allowed to finish my studies at home, which was no better. The silence was so loud that I found it impossible to concentrate on my schoolwork. The only sounds I heard were my father's office door opening and closing. He never came out to check in on me or make small talk.

I lost a parent.

Shouldn't *my* mental well-being be a concern too? I never received a hug or kiss on the forehead while promising me that things would be all right. All I got was slammed office doors and small sticky notes for things Dad needed me to do.

"I'm so sorry for your loss, Carl." Mrs. Brenda came and touched my father's hand. "I have a casserole that I will bring over later this evening."

It was far too late for a casserole. My mother had been dead for two weeks, and *now*, she wanted to bring a casserole over? It was a nice gesture, but I couldn't help but think how many she had sent over to the Atkins's home.

"I appreciate it, Brenda." He patted her hands back and offered a weak smile.

The funeral was a waste of the church's time and our money. Nobody showed up, and I knew that would be the outcome. My mother, Kimba Stone, caused a young boy to lose his life because she decided to get behind the wheel of a car drunk.

Drinking had always been more important to her than anything else. Especially me. I was the constant reminder of her never being able to exit out of Sageport. I used to beg my mother to love me and show me that I meant something to her, and she never could.

It was like she was physically blocked from showing me any love or caring for me. She left the responsibility to my father to handle everything that had to do with me. It was the reason I overapplied myself for everything I was involved in.

If I got good grades, maybe then she would love me.

Maybe if I cheered on the cheerleading squad, that might open up her heart to me. In my heart of hearts, I tried more than my mother had. It was how she stared at me, as if trying to figure me out. It wasn't how a mother looked at their only child. It was how a reverend stared at a demon spawn.

"Why did we even have a funeral for her at the church? Mom hated the church and hadn't attended for years." I broke the silence the moment we stepped into the house.

Daddy tossed his keys on the foyer table. "Your mother was raised in the church . . . So she should go out being blessed in one."

"Blessed in a church? We're lucky it didn't burn to bits with all the sinning she has done. Did you forget Allen lost his life? The Atkins had to bury their youngest son because of her."

He clenched his teeth as if this was something that had been replaying in his head the moment he found out about my mother dying. I watched as he walked into the kitchen and poured himself a glass of water.

"You don't think I know that? I sent my condolences and flowers to their home. I feel horrible for what Kimba did. Sitting here pointing the finger won't bring either of them back."

"Rome won't even talk to me. They told me to stop calling their phone."

"Maybe you should."

I was too stunned to speak. How could he sit there and say that I should stop reaching out to the love of my life? Rome meant the world to me . . . more than this stupid small town did. I wanted forever with him, and it was something we were once determined to have together.

"I'm glad she's dead!" I screamed.

My father's head snapped toward me, and he gripped his glass of water tightly. "Watch your words, Faith."

"No. Nothing has ever been mine since the day I was born to that fucked-up woman. She has resented me since the day I was born, and you allowed it. Rome was someone for me . . . someone that I loved, and she had to rip that away from me!"

"You selfish bitch."

I gasped and stared at my father.

"Guess I get it from the woman you married, huh?"

"I'm . . . I'm fucking trying, Faith. I'm trying to put together these pieces your mother left behind. Everything is in jeopardy—everything!" He slammed the glass onto the table, and it shattered, cutting his hand in the process.

I abandoned the counter I was leaning on and rushed to the kitchen drawer for the first aid kit and rubbing alcohol. Reluctantly, he allowed me to take his hand and clean out the glass before bandaging it up.

"I'm sorry, Faith." He apologized.

"It's all right, Daddy," I replied. "We're both feeling a lot of emotions and unsure of what's next. I can work at the restaurant if you need me to."

He stopped my hand and stared me in the eyes. "When you graduate, get out of here . . . Go live your life far away from Sageport, Faith. You don't deserve to sit and clean up the mess your mother has made of our lives . . . This is not your fault." He used his free hand to touch my face.

Tears fell down my cheeks as I held onto his wounded hand. From the expression on his face, I could tell that this discussion wasn't up for debate. "I can't do that . . . I can't leave you here to clean up her mess. When is enough going to be enough? You've always been the one cleaning her messes."

"And I knew that when I married her. What I won't allow is for you to put your life on hold to do the same. There's so much your mother and I wanted for our lives, and I got what I wanted . . . my restaurant. She never got what she wanted, and I blame myself daily for holding her back from that. I refuse to do the same to you, Faith. Promise me that after graduation, you will move away from Sageport."

"I . . . I promise," I stammered and stared into my father's eyes.

The doorbell pulled us away from our moment. "Can you get the door . . . I'm not in the mood to have any company right now."

"Okay."

I watched as he went to his office and closed the door. Putting the first aid kit back, I kicked off my heels and walked toward the front door. Peeking out of the side curtain, I was shocked when I saw Mrs. Atkins standing there.

My heart started racing, so I swung the door open quickly. "Mrs. Atkins, is everything all right with Rome?"

My heart couldn't take something happening to Rome. I wanted to be there for him because I knew how much his brother meant to him. Allen and Rome were as thick as thieves. They always spoke about how they would both play for the NFL, and everyone would know the Atkins brothers.

"Rome is fine. I came here to speak with you."

I stepped outside and closed the door behind me. "Okay."

What could she have wanted to talk to me about? Why wasn't Rome with her? I hadn't seen him since that night at the hospital, and I desperately missed him.

"Stop calling our home for Rome. He doesn't want anything to do with you or your family. His baby brother was killed because of your mother. Faith, you're a constant reminder of that, so please, give us space to grieve. You should be doing the same as well."

"I . . . I love your son, Mrs. Atkins."

She had to know I loved Rome with every inch of my body. I don't think I ever loved anyone the way that I loved that boy. How could she expect me to stop contacting him? I felt like I needed him to breathe, and being without him for the past few weeks felt miserable.

"If you love him, then give him the space he's requesting, Faith." She shoved her purse up on her shoulder and turned to walk down the steps. "I came over here to give you that warning. If you continue, we will press charges against you. Focus on your own family."

I stood on the porch gasping for air while holding onto my chest. Rushing back into the house, I grabbed the house phone and dialed Rome's cell phone. The disconnection message played in my ear.

"*The number you have reached is no longer in service. Please hang up and try your call again.*"

Chapter Four

ASHTON

"*W*HEN DO YOU think you're going to tell her? We've been dating for six months, and you haven't mentioned anything about me to her," Francis, my girlfriend, said. She stood with her arms folded. "Does she *know* I'm going with you and the girls to your parents' house for Christmas?"

This was my weekend with the girls, and I planned on introducing them to my girlfriend. It was a delicate subject, and I was trying my best to approach Faith with ease and understanding. Although she was the one who wanted the divorce, I didn't know how she would react to knowing I had a girlfriend.

"I plan on telling her."

Francis wasn't convinced. She had been trying to get me to tell Faith about her for the past two months. Each time, I had a brand-new excuse for not telling her. The recent excuse was that our anniversary had passed. I would be an asshole to bring up my new girlfriend around a sensitive subject for both of us.

I loved my ex-wife.

Did I want to be divorced?

No.

Faith had never experienced a healthy relationship with her parents. When we met, she spent many drunken nights crying over her relationship with them. Her one goal was to have a healthy relationship that her children could grow up admiring. She wanted to set a standard for the girls, which I respected.

I tried to be everything for Faith for so long until I couldn't anymore. Things changed, and while we both knew they would, it felt like we were clawing at trying to get back to us. It seemed like we tried everything, and nothing worked. I checked out of our marriage, and I take full responsibility for that. Faith fought tooth and nail to keep us together and to make this marriage work, and I failed her.

Being too much of a coward to ask for the divorce myself, I shut down on her. Forced her hand at times, and then she eventually couldn't take it anymore. How much longer could a woman take not being desired by her husband?

Faith was a strong one. She held on for longer than I would have, which was my one regret. I should have opened my mouth, spoken to her, and tried to fix things like she had been trying to do. She held the burden of our failing marriage on her back while trying to raise our daughters. Every day, I got to escape to work and not think about my home life for eight to ten hours. Meanwhile, she was stuck in a constant mental hell, worrying about things she could have done or said to make my morning smoother.

When Faith asked for the divorce, I didn't fight her on it. She deserved to be happy and have a relationship with someone who would give her the world and reinstate that smile that could brighten up an entire county. It had been so long since I saw that smile that I was starting to forget what it looked like. I drove her to doubt herself as a mother and a wife instead of just being open with her.

It was something I would never forgive myself for.

When it came time to decide how to split up things, I let her keep the house and agreed to pay spousal support. Faith had given up everything to become my wife and the mother to our girls. Pushing her back into the workforce felt wrong on many levels. The girls were used to their mother being around often. The divorce was a lot of change for them, and I didn't want to add more to their plates. My lawyer tried to convince me to reconsider since it was Faith who filed for divorce.

I refused.

This woman had given up everything to become my wife and support my career. She wasn't a random woman I met at the bar; she was the mother to my daughters. The person who would raise my daughters to be the epitome of class like she was. I worked hard to afford to keep my ex-wife and daughters in the lifestyle they were accustomed to.

The private school that Faith loved for the girls.

A safe neighborhood where the houses sold for over half a million dollars.

These were important to me and the things I wanted my girls to have. It was hard not being under the same roof as them, so if I kept them in a safe neighborhood, it would help me sleep better at night. Paying for two separate households was stressful at times, and there were a few times when I asked Faith to consider selling the house. We never needed a house as big as the one she was currently living in, and it wasn't necessary with just her and the girls.

I lived in a two-bedroom condo with enough room for the girls and me. They shared a bedroom, although they complained every time they came over. Since I traveled often for work, I didn't need an outrageous-size house for three people.

"When is that going to be? I'm tired of being a secret, Ashton." Francis continued speaking, plopping onto the couch with her arms still folded.

I plated our food and set it on the kitchen table. "You want me to rush and drop this bomb on her?"

"It's not a bomb, Ashton. You've been divorced for almost a year. Does she not think you're going to move on?"

I felt I owed Faith way more than just dropping that bomb on her. There was no way to ease her into knowing I had a girlfriend and had already been dating. Francis was right, though.

It wasn't a bomb.

It was my life.

As much as I wanted to protect Faith's feelings when it came to living my life, I knew she wouldn't do the same for me. Had she been dating, she probably would have tossed it into my face already. The girls were far too nosy not to let it slip that their mom was dating, so I knew she wasn't.

"Babe, having her find out that we've been dating for six months and that you're going to meet the girls is a lot."

The thought of telling her that Francis was coming with us to my parents' house for Christmas was another conversation. I went back and forth, often trying to decide if I even wanted to tell her that part. I also knew that if the shoe were on the other foot, I would have wanted to know if she had her boyfriend around the girls.

"I just don't want to always feel like a secret because of your ex-wife." Francis sauntered over toward me and draped her arms around my neck. "We're not in the 'knowing each other' phase anymore . . . We're really together."

Francis and I had gone from the "testing the water" phase to now having real conversations about a future. For the first time in a while, I felt excited about this new start and couldn't wait for my girls to experience their father in a new relationship. I wanted them to understand that both Mommy and Daddy were happier apart than together.

"I know. You won't always feel like that."

"I hope so. Did you talk to her about possibly moving to New York?"

"One thing at a time."

I was offered a better position and salary at a bank in New York City. My parents lived there, and I had a ton of family there too. Everything was leading me to accept the position because I knew it would benefit the girls. The more money I made, the better life they would have. The only thing stopping me was living a long distance from my girls. I knew I missed out on a lot of their day-to-day life and activities, but I loved being able to pick them up and spend time with them when I could.

Living in New York, I wouldn't be able to do that often. Faith wouldn't uproot her entire life to move there for me.

Not with us being divorced and me having a girlfriend.

I quickly glanced at my watch and started eating because I had less than an hour to meet Faith to pick up the girls. Today wasn't the day to bring up Francis. It would be better to do it when we meet back up to do the exchange.

Chapter Five

THE CONSTANT RINGING of my phone from across the room was tap dancing on my nerves. The kids were with Ashton, and I didn't have to wake up early to pack lunches or prepare breakfast. It felt nice spreading out in the bed, knowing I didn't have to adhere to an alarm clock this morning.

That was . . . until my phone started blaring from across the room.

Shuffling out of bed, I crossed my bedroom floor to make it to the dresser. The size of this master bedroom was the thing that made me fall in love with this home. A private oasis for my husband and me was all I thought about during the entire home-buying process. When I stepped into this room, I almost didn't want to leave. Ash tried to convince me that this was too much house for us, but I wouldn't listen. This house was enough space for us and the babies we were currently pregnant with.

It was no secret that I wanted more children. Ash turned down the idea before the girls were six months old. He told me we needed to focus on the fact that we had been blessed with twins. For the longest time, I considered him to be correct. In my eyes, he was always right.

Now, I wasn't so sure he was right. With the girls getting older, I missed the baby stage and desperately had baby fever. The thoughts always seized the moment I thought about my life at this stage.

"Hello?" I answered, not recognizing the phone number.

It bothered me that some random person decided to interrupt my morning sleep. Didn't they know it was rare for a mom of two to sleep in?

"Hi, is this Faith?" a woman asked.

I prayed hard that this wasn't a "Hello, Shirley, this is Barbara" call. Ash and I were divorced and were moving on with our lives.

"Yes. Who is this?"

"This is Marie. Your father and I have been dating for the past two years . . . I've been trying to reach you from his pho—"

"Dating?"

I was stuck on the fact that she mentioned the words "dating" and "my father" in the same sentence. He and I didn't talk often, but he never mentioned having a girlfriend when we did catch up.

I never mentioned getting a divorce.

Touché.

"Yes. Your father wanted to wait until you visited for the holidays to break the engagement to you."

This woman was filled with surprises.

"Engagement?"

"I'm sorry, Faith. This is not how I wanted you to learn about this information." She quickly apologized. "Your father had a mild stroke, and I figured you needed to know."

My heart dropped, and I held onto my dresser for support. "I . . . Is he all right?"

"He's home and resting. The doctor wants him to take it easy and take time to recover. Although it was mild, it was a warning that he needs to slow down."

"I told him that he needed to start taking it easy. He works way too hard when he doesn't have to."

Though I didn't talk with my father over the phone often, he always sent me pictures and text messages of everything he did.

He didn't have to work as hard as he used to. With a full staff, he didn't have to come in if he didn't feel like it.

Not my dad.

He was so used to being a workaholic that he couldn't sit down. Sitting down was worse than death to him. I knew his doctor had probably given many warnings, and he ignored them. My father was the only parent that I had left, and I didn't want to lose him too.

Sure, our relationship could have been better.

When I left Sageport, I branded my entire life into a new one. All things that reminded me of Sageport had been blocked out. No matter what, my father still tried to be a part of my life despite my not welcoming him into the folds of my new life.

"Carl doesn't listen to anybody. He's truly the most stubborn man that I know."

I felt compelled to ask why she called. Was there another reason why she called me?

I decided against it.

Maybe that would come off way too harsh and insensitive for his daughter. "Sounds like my dad."

"Well, he will be out of the restaurant for more than a few weeks. The doctor isn't playing around with him anymore. I was wondering if you could fly in and help with the restaurant and coffee shop. I know he would be happy to have you around for the holidays too."

My words were caught in my throat while I tried to find an excuse mentally to get out of this. "Um . . . me? I don't know much about the restaurant or the coffee shop," I stuttered.

"Honey, this would mean the world to your father. I think he could use a familiar face around here . . . and we could use the help at the restaurant."

The name Marie sounded slightly familiar. I believe my father mentioned that she made the best cakes in Sageport. He rambled on and on about her cakes, promising to send the twins one for their birthday.

Seems like he was getting more than cake with Ms. Marie.

"I would need to check with my hu . . . husband," I choked out, forgetting that Ash was no longer my husband, and I needed to remove that word from my vocabulary.

"Oh, sweetie, I don't want to rearrange your life, and I understand you may have had other plans for the holiday."

"It's not a problem at all. My girls are due to get out of school next week, so I can come then," I assured her.

Since the girls were in private school, their holiday schedule differed slightly from public school. I could visit with my father to make sure everything was on the up and up, then make it back to Atlanta to see the girls off to New York with their father. Did I want to spend outrageous amounts of money on plane tickets around the holiday season?

No.

But it was my dad's health, and I needed to at least check in with him. As his only child, it would look selfish on my part if I didn't show up. I'm sure the entire town of Sageport knew that he had a mild stroke. I knew he wouldn't have told me because he hated anyone making a fuss over him.

"Are you sure, sweets?"

"Yes. I'll save your number and keep you updated," I promised her.

"All right. It was nice briefly speaking with you. I'm sorry it was under these circumstances."

We quickly ended the call, and I shuffled back to my bed, stunned that I had found out that my father had a stroke and a fiancée—all in one phone call.

It wasn't like I had been completely honest with him about everything happening in my life. So I felt like I couldn't be too upset with him about not being upfront about his own life. There was probably so much that had changed about him that I had no clue about. I wondered if he renovated the house or even sold it.

He always talked about not needing the house after my mother passed. He only held on to it because she loved the house. It was the one thing he figured would make her happy, and it never did.

The same house she loved, she constantly escaped to get drunk in the local bars. I don't think anything my father did would have made her happy. I damn sure didn't make her happy. If anything, I was a pest that lived within the same small walls as her.

I hated my mother so much that I never told the girls about their grandmother. They knew all about their Pop-Pop from Sageport, but nothing about the woman that gave birth to me. She wasn't worth mentioning to them. As far as I was concerned, the only grandmother they had was on Ashton's side.

"What are you trying to tell me, God? Going back to Sageport . . . Why?" I spoke out loud and tossed myself across the bed.

When I left Sageport, I promised myself that I would never go back. There were too many bad memories and not enough good ones. I never wanted to relive the pain that I had all those years ago. When I graduated, I bought a one-way ticket to Atlanta, Georgia. Columbia used to be my dream when Rome was very much still a part of my life. I knew I had to push him out of my head and move on with my life.

He hated me.

My father wanted me to get out of Sageport to have a better life. He didn't want me to live in my mother's shadow constantly. He knew I would never be able to step into my own had I stayed back in Sageport with him.

Hey. We still on to make the switch at noon?

Fuck.

I forgot that quickly that I was supposed to meet with Ash around noon to get the girls. Apparently, he had to fly out of the country earlier than expected and couldn't take the girls to school.

Yes.

I tossed my phone onto the nightstand and stood up, preparing myself to get ready for this exchange.

Our meeting spot was always Starbucks inside Target.

The first few times, the girls would get so emotional because they had to leave their father that I needed something to bribe them with and an expresso to help my frazzled nerves. So now, our meeting spot was a table toward the back of Starbucks. If I was lucky and got there early, I usually cruised a few aisles and picked up some necessities Target told me I needed.

Today wasn't one of those days.

When I walked into Target, I spotted the girls immediately. They were having their usual decaf coffee. My babies loved to feel like little adults with their little coffee cups in their hands. Mayven was eating her favorite, a croissant.

"Mom!" She abandoned her croissant and ran over toward me, hugging me tightly. This was the best part.

It felt amazing to feel how much they missed me while they were with their father. At times, I felt like they didn't miss me at all. Maddie noticed, ran right over, and gave me the same tight hug I had missed over the past few days.

"Hey, sweet peas, how was your weekend with your dad?"

"It was fun. We got to meet Daddy's new girlfriend."

"She's nice." Mayven piggybacked off her sister's statement.

I kept the smile on my face, but my heart was officially in my throat. Did they just mention that their father had *a girlfriend*?

Ash was sitting down at the table and smiled when he noticed me walk up. Ashton was so handsome that it hurt. How a man could have the look that God gave him but couldn't communicate his feelings was beyond me.

His mocha-chocolate skin, high cheekbones, and narrow-shaped eyes always made me feel honored to be his wife. If Tyson Beckford had a twin, Ashton would have been him. When I was pregnant with the twins, I became so self-conscious because I had a husband who looked like him, and I was sporting cankles and a swollen nose.

"Hey, Ash," I greeted and sat across from him.

From how he fidgeted with his watch, I knew he wanted to have a conversation. The girls were sipping their coffees, wondering what was about to happen.

"Hey, Faith . . . um, girls . . . How about you pick out a toy or some makeup? It's on Daddy."

Both girls jumped up with excitement. "Stick together, girls," I called behind them as they rushed off holding hands, which surprised me.

"How have you been?"

He didn't need to beat around the bush. Ash didn't care how I was doing when we were married, so I knew he didn't give a damn now that we were divorced. He could spare me the wealth-fare check and just lay everything out.

"I'm good." I kept it short, not revealing the details of my father or the fact that I had been looking at flights in traffic on the way over here.

"That's good."

"What's going on, Ash?"

"I introduced the girls to my girlfriend that I've been dating over the past few months." It was a mouthful.

I was bitter about it.

How dare he introduce *our* girls to *his* girlfriend without at least talking to me about it first? I would have never done anything like that to him.

"Wow."

"Faith," he sighed.

"The fact that you didn't think to introduce her to me first before shoving her down our kids' throats . . . I don't care how you live your life or what you do with it . . . I *do* care when it has to do with our kids."

He regretted his decision. I could see it all over his face, but he was here now and had to deal with it. "I know. It was a bad call on my end."

"We both agreed that we would be on the same page regarding the girls. I've held up my end of the bargain even when it was too painful."

He had a girlfriend, which meant he was able to make time for her. Yet, he could never make time for our daughters and always came with some excuse for them. The girls were just happy to be around their father, so they never thought of any of this. As long as Daddy was around, that was perfect enough for them.

"I'm sorry."

I stood up and gathered the girls' half-empty coffee cups. "Is that all you wanted to tell me?"

"Yeah. I would love for you to meet her—"

"I don't want to meet her." I cut him off.

Why would I want to meet her? She was *his* girlfriend, the woman that would replace my role in his life. He could try with her but couldn't make the effort with me.

"Okay. Whenever you're ready to meet her, just let me know."

"The girls and I are going to Sageport to visit my father next week," I decided to inform him. Since he was heading out of the country, I had no choice but to bring the girls along before their trip to New York.

I couldn't ask Tierra to watch them for all that time. She had her own life, though she would step in without hesitation.

He was confused.

I had told him so many times I never wanted to return there. "Sageport? Is everything all right with your father?"

"He had a mild stroke. I'm going to make sure everything is good with him. We'll be back before the trip to New York."

"Oh God, I'm sorry, Faith. I can move some things around and come wit—"

"We're not married anymore, Ash. I don't need you to move things around or try to insert yourself into my life any further. I can handle it, and I *will* handle it."

The girls rushed over toward us with huge smiles on their faces. Madison had a bunch of makeup, while Mayven had four books. They were so different and unique in their own ways. The girls had grown out of playing with toys long ago.

Shows how much he knows about our daughters.

As promised, Ash paid for the girls' items, and we headed back to the car. He hugged and kissed the girls while helping them into the car. I closed the door and leaned on it, waiting for him to make some lame-ass apology for going over my head and introducing his girlfriend to our girls.

"Please give your father my blessings. I know this trip is hard for you, and I really wish I could be there for you."

"Ash, you haven't been there for me in a long time. Don't start trying to be now." I opened the car door and slammed it behind me.

A lone tear slid down my cheek as I started the car and drove to Olive Garden. Tonight, I wasn't cooking a damn thing.

Chapter Six

ROME

"**HOW IS SHE** doing today?" I asked as I set my keys down on the foyer table.

The home care attendant nodded toward the kitchen, and I followed her. I could always tell from her facial expressions what kind of day Mama was having. From the look on her face today, I knew that it had been one of those tough days when Mama fought everybody on everything.

"She screamed in agony for four hours," Pia, the home care attendant, informed me. This wasn't out of the ordinary for Mama, though. A few nights a week, I would jump out of my sleep because she released a bloodcurdling scream that almost always woke the neighbors.

Luckily, the police station knew our situation and always called before having squad cars show up at the house in the middle of the night. From the look on Pia's face, I could tell that today was one of those days that she considered quitting on me.

It wasn't like she was the first. Finding good care for my mother had been my biggest challenge. She ran off every person that I found because she was too much to handle. Some of them even suggested that I put her into a nursing home so that she would have around-the-clock care.

I couldn't do that to my mother. She had given up her entire life to be there for me and my brother. I watched her never miss a school event or game when we were growing up. Some women were born to be mothers, and that was precisely my mom. It was like God handpicked her perfectly to become my mother and my father's wife. A nursing home wasn't something I was ready to consider.

"Did you give her some medicine to calm her down?"

"Rome, she refused to let me get near her. She kept screaming for Allen to come downstairs, or they would be late for school."

Fuck.

It had been fifteen years since I lost my brother, and every year that passed never got easier. I often sat and wondered what our lives would have looked like had he not been killed. Would Mama be suffering from dementia, and would Pops still be here? These were questions that plagued my mind almost daily. Every time I walked into my house and saw my mother sitting in her recliner, looking spaced out, I questioned if Allen's death brought on this dementia.

"Did you try to talk her down from it? When I show her pictures, it always helps to calm her down."

Pia was becoming irritated with me.

She would never say it, but her facial expressions and body language told a different story. "Maybe you should consider the nursing home, Ro."

I never wanted to consider the nursing home. My mom deserved to be with family, and as her only living child, I was determined to make this situation work.

Was it difficult at times?

Yes.

Did my personal life suffer because of it?

Of course.

If that meant I needed to hold off on meeting the one, then that's what I would do for my mom. After all the things she had sacrificed during my childhood, I was willing to do the same for her.

"I'm not ready for that."

"I love you and your mom, but I'm not sure how much longer I can do this alone. She hits, screams, and bites."

Pia was around five foot four and probably weighed no more than a hundred and fifty pounds. She was in her early forties and came highly recommended by the home care agency I hired. After dealing with aides who would quit with little to no warning, she was a godsend for us. My mother loved Pia and would sit talking her ears off for hours on a good day.

It was the bad days . . .

The days when she became violent and didn't want to hear a word anyone was saying to her. I had a few of my own battle scars from dealing with her on those bad days. I knew this job was a lot, so I always hit Pia with a little extra on top of her regular wages. She put up with a lot with Mama, and she cared about her too.

It was hard finding people who worked for you to care about something other than their pockets. Pia was one of those people who would do this for free if she could.

"I understand." I took a seat at the counter and watched her resume cooking dinner. "Whenever it becomes too much, let me know so I can make other arrangements."

Pia propped her hand on her bony hip. "You know, I just pop my gums out of frustration. You couldn't get rid of me with a tree branch. I love Mama Atkins . . . She just needs to stop hitting."

I blew a sigh of relief. That was one crisis averted and a problem that I didn't have to solve . . . right away. "Thanks, P."

"How was work?"

"The same as yesterday." I loosened my tie and set my phone down beside me. "Another day, another dollar, right?"

Every time that Pia looked into my eyes, she became sad. She never spoke about what made her sad, but I could see the change in her eyes almost instantly.

"Well, I'm going to finish up dinner before I leave. She's asleep in the living room, so just sneak on past and wash that long day off you."

I stood and did a big stretch. "Thanks . . . You didn't have to cook. I would have grabbed something to eat."

"You need a break from takeout. That's all you got in the fridge, and I'm sure that's not helping her out either."

Pia didn't cook every day, and I didn't know how to cook. It was something that I wanted to learn and kept putting off. With the state-of-the-art kitchen in this house, you would have thought I already knew how to throw down in the kitchen.

Just like Pia said, Mama was sleeping peacefully in her chair. I quickly crept by and made it upstairs to my room. But it was like she had a Rome radar, and her eyes would pop right open when she even thought I was home or near her. Out of all the things that she forgot or was confused about, she never forgot me. She knew I was Rome the minute she laid her eyes on me, and that always brought me some comfort.

Fifteen years ago, our lives changed for the worse. It was something I wished I could go back and alter. If I had one wish, it would be to change the outcome of that night. Having to hold onto my mother while watching my baby brother being lowered into the ground was something I could never forget. As debilitating as dementia was, I was glad that my mother didn't remember *that* memory. To her, Allen was still a teenager who was slacking on time as usual.

We always joked that he would be late to his funeral and he was too early. Allen wasn't supposed to be in that casket. He was so young with so much more to accomplish in life. A piece of all of us died when Allen did.

Nothing was ever the same for the Atkins family.

It didn't matter how much I prayed or tried to be a good person. My family constantly suffered from my brother's death. Mama went into a deep depression. The bubbly Southern woman who could whip up cookies in under ten minutes was gone. She barely got out of bed some days, and on the days she climbed out from under her covers, she remained in her pajamas. My father tried everything for my mom to get back to herself.

She lost her baby boy.

Even as a teen, I knew she would never be the same again. Hell, I wasn't the same anymore, and trying to be strong for everyone was hard, especially when I just wanted to crawl under a rock and disappear. My father worked long hours at the dealerships to avoid coming home and seeing my mother in the state that she was in.

He used any excuse to get away and block out the loss that we all suffered. The dealerships had become his primary focus while Mama withered away in her grief. As a teen, there was only so much that I could personally do, especially because I was grieving on my own. Not only did I lose my brother, but I also lost my first love. Everything had gone from sugar to shit in a matter of seconds that night.

It was clear going away to college while my family was suffering wasn't the right call. I needed to be here for both of them. Who else would make sure Mama ate or got out of bed for the day? Family only stayed around until after the funeral, and then they all returned to their own lives. It was up to me to look out for my family, so college wasn't a priority anymore. This was my family, and it was up to me to pick up the pieces so we could continue with our lives.

I couldn't lie and say it wasn't tough every time I drove past Faith's house or the restaurant. It took me a solid four years to even step foot inside the restaurant without wanting to knock over everything. My anger was misplaced because it wasn't Faith or her father's fault. Kimba was a grown-ass woman who decided to climb behind that wheel, knowing that she was impaired. Carl spent so many years putting out the fires that Kimba set ablaze everywhere she went. His only fault was that he loved his wife a little too hard and didn't get her the help she so desperately needed.

It didn't take long for the news of Faith moving away after graduation to make its round. I was crushed knowing that our last encounter was the one she would always remember. Every time I got the urge to go to her house, anger stopped me. While my brain knew she wasn't at fault, I just needed someone alive and breathing to blame. I couldn't help but be pissed that she left the keys in the house for her mother to find. It was that small piece of information that left me bubbling with anger and prevented me from making things right with her.

I always tried to keep up with her, but Carl didn't talk much about Faith. If you were new in town, you probably wouldn't have known he had any kids. Faith never returned for holidays and wasn't registered at Columbia University. In the age of social media, she wasn't anywhere.

Or maybe I wasn't searching hard enough.

When life felt like it was starting to let up on us, my father was diagnosed with colon cancer. We barely recovered from Allen's death, and now this had come knocking on our door. Mama wasn't herself, but she was getting better every day. The constant calls for Allen should have been a sign for all of us. My father's diagnosis prevented us from giving that attention. We were more concerned and focused on him than on my mom's confusion, which she seemed to suffer from constantly.

Colon cancer moves quickly, but my father's moved rapidly. He died six months after finding out. Another person we loved was now gone, leaving just my mother and me. Mom couldn't live alone. Some days, I had to drive to the house and pull her out of bed. After losing her son and husband, she needed to be around her family, and that was me.

I moved her into my town house and was determined to be there for her. Despite having everything on my shoulders, my mother was my priority. My girlfriend at the time couldn't understand that.

Or wouldn't understand that.

It was up to me to take ownership of the dealerships while trying to be there for my mother. I tried therapy with her, but nothing seemed to help. She had given up on life, and there wasn't anything anybody could do about it. As much as I believed we could get through this, I slowly started losing faith.

Mama was diagnosed with early-onset dementia a year after my father passed. It was a relief to know that there was something actually wrong, and it wasn't just related to grief. It wasn't until after she nearly burned my house down and blamed it on Allen heating pizza bites that I knew she needed to be checked out.

This was more than grief.

Although the doctors all recommended that she move into a facility, I refused to put her into one. I was her son, and it was my job to protect and care for her, just like she had done for me when I was a child. Mom lost two of her greatest loves early on in life, and she needed to see a familiar face.

After my shower, I sat on the edge of my bed and checked my phone. Dating these days was useless. Nobody wanted that real genuine love anymore. It was all about hooking up and seeing how much a man could offer. As much as I enjoyed sex, that wasn't what I was looking for anymore.

I wanted somebody that I could come home to. A familiar face to smile at after dealing with the roughness that life provided. They had to accept my mother fully, not because they thought that was what I wanted. She was a part of my life and would always be, so the person needed to accept that or keep it pushing.

What Faith and I had was what I craved. We were both so young and probably had no clue what love meant then.

I felt it, though.

Since she has been gone, I haven't felt a love like the one I had with her. It was so intense that my heart formed its own rhythm whenever I came around Faith. There hasn't been another woman who has made me feel that way again. I had to stop asking Carl about her when I stepped in to grab takeout. It wasn't like he offered much conversation about her anyway. He was always pleasant, always unsure about how to act around me.

When my father passed, he had the restaurant send a huge spread to my house along with flowers. When I tried to thank him, he stopped me and handed me another bag of food for my mom. He knew how much she loved their meat loaf and had stopped eating it because she refused to support his business.

That spoke about what kind of man Carl truly was. He had always been faithful to his community, even after all the pain Kimba caused. It took him a while to regain the town's trust. I know times were tough, but no matter what, he showed up with a smile on his face. Sageport was forgiving, especially to someone who wasn't to blame.

"All right, the beef is in the oven. Leave it in there for about twenty more minutes. I have to run to the pharmacy before they close." Pia put on her coat and grabbed her bag. "See you tomorrow, Rome."

"Thank you, Pia." I smiled and held the front door open for her.

She quickly jogged to her car and waved as she pulled out of the driveway. The smell of the beef caused my mouth to water, and I couldn't wait to dig in. Hopefully, tonight was one of those nights where Mama had an appetite.

Chapter Seven

FAITH

A GIRLFRIEND.

That was all that went through my head during my entire flight. I couldn't believe that Ashton had a girlfriend.

For six months!

Six whole months, and he had a girlfriend but didn't tell me about her. I wasn't expecting a full report on their relationship together. Just a heads-up to let me know so I didn't feel blindsided by the news. My heart ached that this woman would spend time with my daughters and husband.

Ex-husband.

Could I really be that upset? It was my fault that we were divorced in the first place. I couldn't keep him from living his life and moving on with another woman. I just wished he had put more effort into our own marriage like he did getting a new girlfriend. He must have been an amazing boyfriend if she stuck around for six months. I couldn't help but question what was wrong with me.

Why didn't he try hard enough with us?

Was I broken?

The pilot's announcement about the plane descending brought me back to reality. I had spent the entire hour and a half in my thoughts. Flying had never been my favorite. In fact, I always made a big fuss out of the whole ordeal. From the moment I pushed my bags into the overhead compartment and buckled my seat belt, I had been in my thoughts heavy. The main thought that continued to run through my head was that I was on a plane heading back to the very place I swore I would never return to.

It's for Dad.

That was the one thing I continued to tell myself as I waited to deplane. I would be a horrible daughter if I sat back and never came to at least check in on my father. A stroke wasn't something to take lightly. Since this would be a quick trip, Ashton and I decided it would be best to leave the girls behind.

Because Ash had to fly out of town for work, he arranged for his mother to stay at his place to watch the girls. The last thing I needed was my ex-mother-in-law snooping around my home. Clara had always been nosy when I was married to her son, so I knew that would only continue well after.

It made me wonder if she had met his new girlfriend yet. Was I the *only* one he decided to keep in the dark about this? Ashton treated me like I was this fragile flower that couldn't handle a simple conversation. It was me who wanted the divorce in the first place, so I think I could handle a conversation about him dating someone other than me.

Would it hurt?

Of course. I never wanted to be divorced in the first place, but he forced my hand. Seeing him happily in love with someone else would hurt me to my core, especially because I loved Ashton and wanted my family together—not apart.

I also knew that our getting back together wasn't right either. There was a reason I asked for the divorce and a reason Ashton never stepped up to the plate once I asked for one. Some days, I regretted being the person to ask for the divorce. I felt like I had made things easier on him, which I had always done. It was clear

Ashton had wanted a divorce before I even mentioned it to him. Instead of being a man and pulling up his big boy pants to ask for one, he sat back and waited for me to become fed up.

It took me forty minutes to deplane, grab my luggage, and take the shuttle to pick up my rental car. No matter where I traveled, I always got a rental. My worst fear was depending on someone else for transportation, including the rideshare apps. They were also so inconsistent, and if I was ever in a situation where I wanted to storm out, I needed to have my own set of wheels.

Once I retrieved the keys, found the car, and took a minute to decompress behind the wheel, I started the vehicle to make the two-hour ride to Sageport.

God, I never thought I would be returning to this place. Every time I became comfortable with the idea of returning to Sageport, my anxiety crept in, and all the memories I had spent years burying resurfaced. I purposely wrote that place off years ago, and now I was forced to return.

Sageport was a small coastal town located two hours from Orlando, Florida. It was only a two-hour ride from Orlando International Airport. While I pulled out of the car rental parking lot, I grabbed my phone to call the girls. It had been so long since I traveled without them.

It felt foreign to me.

Before the girls were born, I used to travel all the time. Ashton and I loved doing weekend getaways. We would pick a state we had never visited and stay the entire weekend as tourists.

That was when we tried.

When we were happy and wanted to make each other happy.

I took a deep breath because I knew Clara would have that smug attitude she usually had. My mother-in-law and I never got along. She was very clingy when it came to her precious baby boy.

It was like Ashton could do no wrong in her eyes. That was part of why man hated confrontation and often ran from it.

He always had his mama to handle everything for him.

"Hello?" she answered.

"Hey, Clara. I just landed and wanted to speak to the girls really quick . . . Are they around?"

"Thank God for the safe flight," she smacked her lips.

I rolled my eyes and merged onto the expressway. "Yes. Thank God for that. Um, are the girls around?"

"Yes, one second."

I heard the phone shuffling before Madison came to the phone. "Hey, Mommy. Are you in Sageport yet?"

"Not yet, baby. I'm heading there now . . . I miss you already."

"I miss you too, Mommy. You have to make sure that Pop-Pop is feeling better."

"Yep, that's what I'm going to do. I will be back home before you know it," I promised.

I loved my girls with all my heart and had never been away from them long. Ashton had surprised me with a Mother's Day trip when they were four. That was the only time I had been away from them for more than a weekend. I hated the entire trip because all I wanted was to be with my girls. Some would even suggest that it wasn't healthy.

"Mayven is napping. She has a stomachache from the cookies Nana made for us."

I bit the inside of my cheek. "Okay, baby. Will you put your nana on the phone for me?"

"Okay. Love you, Mommy."

"Love you more, sweetie."

Clara was the kind of grandparent who felt like she didn't have to listen to the rules I put in place for the girls. This had been a problem since the day the girls were born. She constantly argued that she knew better how to raise kids since she raised my husband.

"Yes, Faith?"

I could hear in her voice that she was annoyed that she had to get back on the phone with me.

"Did those cookies have dairy in them?"

She chuckled. "Of course. Who makes cookies that don't have dairy in them? . . . It's not a real cookie without some milk or butter in it."

I gripped the steering wheel so tight that my hands started to cramp. "Mayven has a sensitivity to dairy, Clara. It's on the laminated papers I gave you."

"A little milk or butter won't kill her, Faith. The girls always have dairy whenever they visit me in New York."

"Yes, that was before we discovered Mayven has a dairy sensitivity. I asked you to read over everything I prepared before I left."

"I don't need an instruction manual to watch my grandchildren, Faith. She told me about her stomach, and I gave her some medicine to make her feel better."

Clara always acted like this.

She acted as if *I* was the one who overreacted when, in reality, I just wanted her to respect the rules I set in place for my kids. Ashton was no help because he never put those boundaries in place, so Clara walked right on over him with no remorse.

I was different.

I think that was why our relationship was so strained. Where Ashton would wait until we were home to complain about something his mother did, I would speak up and tell her that what she did made me feel uncomfortable or angry.

She didn't like that.

I was accused of being combative and confrontational because I was open with my feelings. Holidays together were spent with me doing everything in my power to hold my tongue in order for us to have an enjoyable time. I kept my mouth shut for years because I wanted those good memories for my kids.

Memories that I never had.

All the holidays that I can remember were quiet. Filled with silence because Mama either had a hangover or hadn't gotten up for the day. Daddy was always gone before we were awake because he needed to get the restaurant together for the holiday dinner rush.

My girls deserved to have everything that I never had. A loving home, happy family, and holiday memories that they could always look back on with a smile. Because of that alone, I always bit my tongue when it came to Clara.

"I asked you to read that paper because it has a lot of information about girls' allergies. What if she had been allergic to dairy, Clara? Then what would have happened?"

"I . . . w . . . w—"

"Exactly. When it comes to *my* kids, you will do what *I* want. I don't care who you raised and how you raised them . . . These are *my* kids, and they are to be raised how *I* see fit when I'm not in their presence."

Clara may have been speechless right now, but I knew Ashton would be calling me tonight to ask my side of the story. He knew his mother could be difficult, so we never disagreed on that.

His unwillingness to set boundaries with her was always the problem and topic of our arguments. He acted like that scared little boy afraid to talk back to his mother.

Clara had nothing else to say, so she ended the call. I shook my head, ready for the conversation I would have with Ashton about his mama. I wasn't her daughter-in-law anymore, and I refused to allow her to do whatever she wanted when it came to my kids.

The only reason I hadn't turned this rental around and was headed home was because I knew Mayven would be all right.

Whenever she had dairy, her stomach became queasy, and she would get the runs. Other than giving her fluids and allowing her time to rest, there wasn't much I could do.

The entire ride, I drove without any music, just my anxiety and fear collaborating on the thoughts that were running through my head. I wasn't nervous to see my father as much as I was nervous to drive through Sageport. It had been so long since I had been back, and I had a lot of questions.

People always said small towns never changed. I wondered if that was the case for Sageport. I became more nervous as the car inched closer to the exit sign labeled Sageport.

My hands were clammy, and my heart sped up.

In fifteen short minutes, I would be entering the town I swore I would never return to. Was everything the same as before, or did things actually change? It wasn't like my father had updated me on what was happening in Sageport.

I didn't know what was there besides the restaurant and the coffee shop. I didn't want to know about anything going on in Sageport. All I wanted to do was forget about the town that had taken so much from me.

I'd be lying if I said the Atkins didn't cross my mind every year on my mother's birthday. I couldn't help but think of the tragedy she caused on a day that was meant to celebrate her. There wasn't anything worth celebrating when it came to Kimba Stone. She was a piss-poor mother and an even worse wife.

Ashton didn't even know when my mother's birthday was because I refused to celebrate or acknowledge the day that she was born. To me, it was a regular day that neither my husband—*ex*— or children needed to know about.

My father . . .

My sweet father continued to celebrate her birthday. He would have her favorite cake on the menu at the restaurant and play all her favorite music softly in the background. Nobody knew that the cake served on that particular day was Kimba Stone's favorite cake or the soft Aretha Franklin playing was because she was her favorite singer of all time.

If they knew, they probably wouldn't have come in to eat on that day. My father loved my mother more than anything, so much so that he always tried to protect her even though he was so fed up with her drinking. His love did more harm than good because he enabled my mother in so many ways. Instead of getting her the help she needed, he continued to make excuses and made it easier for her to be the hot mess she was.

He should have left.

Should have taken me and moved out of the house to force her to get her act right. She never had to get her life together because she knew my father would always be there for her.

I let out the breath I wasn't aware I had been holding in. As the wheels of the car crept down the exit lane, I took slow and small deep breaths. The Chick-fil-A was a sure sign that small towns did change. The booming Chick-fil-A used to be a gas station where my mother would buy her cigarettes and beer—before her alcoholism got in the way.

I would sit in the car while she argued with the clerk about her change. He always tried to shortchange her, and she always got in his ass about it. I think the whole town complained about him shortchanging them on their change. His cigarettes, gas, and beer were always the cheapest out of the whole town, so it was a small price to pay to get everything cheaper.

I had to keep reminding myself to keep my eyes on the road because my eyes couldn't believe what I was witnessing. Sageport still had the small-town vibe with a modern twist. There were more restaurants, stores, and fast-food places than I remembered.

When I was growing up, we had to go to the next town over to get McDonald's because Sageport didn't have one. Not only was there a McDonald's now, but it was also one of the new modernized establishments. I hadn't fully gotten over Chick-fil-A being in Sageport, and now I had to come to terms with the fact that there was a McDonald's here too. The small coastal town I knew and grew up in was not what I was driving through.

We had always been a slight tourist town because of the proximity to the coastline. We had some of the most beautiful beaches and beach houses. My father bought our home more inland because of Florida's unpredictable weather. Mostly everyone in Sageport had property inland except the Atkins. They owned a beautiful house right on the water. I always teased Rome about being privileged enough to wake up to a view like the one his bedroom had.

I turned right and entered a traffic circle near my old elementary school. A traffic circle that wasn't there before. Even the elementary school had gone through some renovations. The bright jumbotron had a list of birthdays they were celebrating today.

Our . . .

My father's house was a few streets down. I pulled down our block and observed the houses that didn't look like they changed much. Even my childhood home remained the same. Other than freshly painted shutters, the craftsman bungalow had not changed. I pulled into the driveway and killed the engine.

This felt surreal.

I kept trying to figure out how or when it would sink in that I was back in Sageport. When I left here, I promised myself I would never return or even think about this place. For the most part, I had followed through on those plans.

I never took into account the fact that I would have an aging parent. My father's health was the only reason that I was here. The minute I laid eyes on him and knew he was fine, I would be on the next plane back to Georgia.

Snatching my purse, I slowly exited the car and walked up the pathway. The same path that I had watched my father lay one summer. My father bought this house as a short sale, so he did most of the work whenever he had the time. The landscaping was all done by him, and I knew he probably was the one who kept it up.

The man had a green thumb, something I didn't inherit from him. I held onto the railing and took each stair one at a time. My heart was beating too fast, and I needed to calm it, or I would end up sounding out of breath. Finally, I pressed the doorbell and waited.

"Faith Stone?" I heard a voice, and I peeked down over the porch.

Mrs. Browning was standing there with a small basket filled with squash. Her thinning gray hair was pulled back in a tight bun, her lipstick was bright pink, as I remembered, and her smooth chestnut skin had wrinkles, a sign that things did change in Sageport.

"Greene," I corrected her.

Her eyes widened as she held onto the basket. "Oh, you got married?"

I couldn't bring myself to reveal that I was divorced. "Yes, I did." I smiled. "You look amazing, Mrs. Browning."

She blushed. "Oh, shush . . . I look like an old dirty lady who has been digging in her garden."

"Well, if I could look like that in my garden, I would be so lucky."

We both shared a laugh.

"It's good seeing you, Faith. I always ask Carl about you, and he always gives the same answer."

The door opened behind me, and a young Angela Bassett peeked her head out. "Hi, Brandy," she waved to Mrs. Browning.

"Hey, Marie. I will be picking those zucchinis tomorrow . . . Perfect for some bread, huh?"

"Bring 'em over, and I'll make you a few loaves to hold you over."

"Sounds good . . . It was great seeing you, Faith. Please don't be a stranger," she winked and then hobbled up the three steps to her covered porch.

"It was great seeing you too, Mrs. Browning," I smiled and pulled my purse up on my arm.

"Hi, Faith . . . I'm so happy that you could make it," Marie smiled. "Carl has no clue you're coming, so this will be a great surprise."

She held the door open, and I stepped in. The moment I entered the house my voice was caught in my throat. Everything looked just as I left it, without any change.

Not a changed curtain.

Or couch.

Or the sneaker rack where my mother's house slippers rested. The more I tried to speak, the harder it became. I was embarrassed because Marie was staring at me.

"Do you need some water?"

Instead of replying, I nodded, and she rushed to the kitchen. Why did he keep everything the same? He should have tossed everything out the moment I left.

I didn't want *any* of these memories.

They were all too painful to relive. How could he truly move on if he was still living in the past? Everything about Sageport had elevated and changed, and this was the one place I desperately wanted to see change in.

"Here you go, sweetie . . . Come sit in the kitchen. I have a fan in there."

The house was built in the 1900s, so there was no central air installed, and since he didn't bother to remove the shoe rack with my mother's fifteen-year-old house slippers, I knew he didn't install central air in the house.

I sat on the rattan dining chair where I had done my homework for years. My favorite thing to do was to lean backward, which always drove my mother crazy. The creaking from the chair didn't pair with her withdrawal headaches. Marie was in the middle of cooking when I arrived.

The shock from seeing the time capsule of a house deterred me from the delicious aroma that floated in and out of my nose. Marie stood by the stove, staring at me to make sure she didn't have to use the landline hanging on the wall.

"I'm sorry," I apologized after I finished my water.

"You don't need to be sorry. Your father has told me so much about what the two of you went through. I know it wasn't easy for you to come back here."

"It's not," I cosigned.

"I can only imagine the feelings and emotions going through you." Marie abandoned her post at the stove and sat across from me.

"He didn't change anything," I whispered.

Marie made me feel welcome, as if I could talk to her about anything. I was very closed off to people I didn't know. With Marie, I felt a sense of safety and peace, something that I had never experienced when it came to having a relationship with an older woman.

"Yeah." She paused. "Everything in his life has pretty much changed except this house. He refuses to renovate or sell," she sighed.

She seemed just as stressed as I was with the situation. If my father was healed enough to move on and become engaged, what was so hard about tossing out those old, raggedy slippers, slapping some paint on the walls, and removing these ancient, shaggy curtains that never let any light in?

The home was dark.

My mother hated the brightness in the house, so she kept the curtains closed. Any part of the house that she frequented was kept dark. The only place that I enjoyed the sunlight shining in was my bedroom or my father's office.

Those were two places she never visited.

"I can't believe he still has those on the fridge . . . That was my junior year report card," I said, removing myself from the table and going to the fridge.

The crinkled and faded paper had signs of wear and tear. I felt like I was in a museum of my past, which made me uncomfortable. The work I had to do to block all of this out of my memory over the past fifteen years was hard. In a matter of ten minutes, all the work I had done in fifteen years was undone.

"He has never forgotten about you, Faith." Marie offered a weak smile. "He loves talking about you and his grandbabies . . . He even has their school pictures up there too."

I picked up Mayven's picture and smiled. Out of both girls, she resembled my dad the most. From her expressions and perfect eyebrows, I saw so much of him inside her.

"He loves spending time with the girls when he visits."

Whenever my father visited us, he always made time with the girls. They enjoyed going to museums with him and trying new restaurants. I always joked that he was turning them into miniature Gordon Ramsays because of how picky they were when it came to restaurants. They always bragged about their Pop-Pop owning a restaurant.

It broke my heart that I made excuses about why we couldn't visit Pop-Pop and eat at his restaurant. Sageport had too many bad memories, and I refused to bring the pieces of my life that brought me true happiness there.

"Before all of this happened, he wanted to take a trip to visit you guys. We were going to tell you about the engagement then."

I spotted the small emerald-cut diamond ring on her finger. "Congratulations, by the way. I'm sorry I was so distant on the phone . . . My father and I don't talk often, so I was caught off guard about the engagement."

She waved her hand. "Faith, please. This is new to all of us. I just want you to be comfortable here . . . I changed the sheets in your old bedroom and opened the windows so it won't be so stuffy."

"I planned to stay at the hotel in town . . . Is it still there?" I didn't know how I could stay in this house without having minor panic attacks from reliving my memories.

The trauma I experienced in this house was horrid. No child should have gone through the mental turmoil that I went through when it came to living here.

"It's a quaint bed-and-breakfast now . . . overpriced too. Faith, it would mean a lot to us both if you stayed. This is your home too . . . Why waste money on an overpriced bed-and-breakfast when you can be with your father?"

I smiled. "Okay."

"Your father is taking his midafternoon nap. He can't sit still to save his life and keeps bothering everyone at the restaurant."

"How is the restaurant?"

She plopped back down on the kitchen chair. "We're swamped, but we have some extra hands with the college kids returning home for the holidays. Your father has been doing it all for so long."

"Sounds like my dad."

"We can use the extra help while you're in town. Our manager is out because she's high risk with her pregnancy."

"I've never run a restaurant in my life . . . What makes you think that I can do her job?"

Marie smirked. "Your father showed me the pictures of you at the restaurant. Faith, I *know* you know something about the restaurant business."

My father has had a restaurant for as long as I've been alive. I spent my childhood running in the kitchen, refilling the salt-and-pepper shakers while trying to do whatever I could to help my father out. I was always in the way and causing more work than I was doing, but he never said it to me. He loved seeing me in the restaurant and always reminded me that it would be mine one day.

When I became a teenager, I started to stray away from the restaurant. I was more interested in my studies or chasing behind Rome Atkins. Taking over the restaurant was never my dream, and I made sure to remind my father of it every time he mentioned it to me. He lived for the moment the restaurant was short-staffed, and I would step in to help.

"I don't know, Marie."

She waved her hands around. "Listen, tonight, let's enjoy the dinner I prepared and worry about all that other stuff once you're settled."

I didn't know how much more "settled" she wanted me to be. I packed three days' worth of clothes and didn't plan on extending my trip. Marie showed me down the hall to my old bedroom, and I took slow breaths. When she opened the door, I didn't expect to smile.

Everything was exactly the same as I had left it. The queen bed was pushed against the window with bright white, fluffy linen. My Beyoncé posters and pictures of Rome and me were still plastered all over the walls.

"I'll give you some time to freshen up and decompress. I know this trip has taken a lot on your mental," Marie smiled before closing the door behind her.

I walked over to the picture wall and touched the picture of Rome and me. We were at the football game, and he stopped midgame to come over to kiss me. Everyone shouted and was angry, but that was Rome.

He never cared.

Whenever he stared at me, it was like I was the only person in the world. Rome had always made me feel seen and showed me that I mattered. It didn't matter how unimportant something was.

Rome always made me feel like it was the most important thing in the world.

I smiled at the picture of Rome, Allen, and me. Although Allen was younger, he was very protective of his older brother. Rome was a softy and let people get over on him.

Allen was the complete opposite.

You could always count on Allen to speak his mind, which I loved. He didn't have a date for the spring formal, so he tagged along with Rome and me. The entire night was filled with so many laughs and good times. We took many pictures that night, but this was the only good one. Allen had forgotten to take off the cap of the Polaroid we were using.

When I noticed that we only had one picture left and needed to make it count, we all squeezed in together, and I angled my hand up to snap the perfect selfie for us. Allen said it would be a waste to get them developed because he forgot to remove the cap, and Rome agreed.

I was so glad I never listened to them because I had this picture. Touching the picture, I smiled briefly before moving on to my dresser. When I left, I wanted no memory of the last year of my life. I told my father he could toss it out, and I wouldn't have cared.

I was wrong.

This picture meant more to me than anything else in this room. I could never retake this picture again, and that was why it was so special to me. Allen was gone, and Rome was off living his life far away from Sageport. He was probably married with children and had the best career.

The jewelry box my father gifted me for my sixteenth birthday caught my eye. I reached for it and opened it, not expecting it to play the soft melody that chimed the moment you lifted the case.

When the soft song started to play, I pulled out all my jewelry pieces. Most of it was junk or fake costume jewelry I swore I couldn't live without.

Funny how life works.

I picked up the small golden beaded necklace that I wore to prom. Rome picked me up with flowers, this necklace, and a corsage. Instead of having doting parents snapping pictures of us, we both stood on my porch and attached flowers to each other while being too excited. Then he pulled the velvet box from behind him and showed me the necklace.

It was beautiful.

I had never had a boyfriend give me a real piece of jewelry before. The small kisses he placed on my neck after he put it on me still sent chills down my back. I held the necklace close to my nose and envisioned smelling the cologne he wore that night.

It was so woody that I could still smell it on my dress two weeks after prom. I spent so many nights after prom sleeping with my dress because it smelled like Rome.

After prom, this room became my private hell that I couldn't escape from. My friends had abandoned me, my boyfriend hated me, and my father ignored me. The silence was so loud that it didn't matter what music I played. The silence overpowered the music. I couldn't go anywhere in town because my mother's reckless decisions made everyone hate me.

My senior year of high school was ruined because my mother was selfish. The decision she made, she had made on her own, and because of that, my father and I had to suffer the consequences.

I plopped onto the bed while holding the chain in my hands. Losing Rome was my greatest regret. After the incident, I prayed that I could go back in time to change things.

No matter how much I prayed, whenever I opened my eyes, reality was staring me right in the face.

Chapter Eight

FAITH

"*I* CANNOT BELIEVE THAT you pulled this off without me knowing. I know everything," my father laughed, exposing that missing tooth on the side of his mouth.

He was too excited and tickled not to laugh without exposing it. It was an insecurity of his, and he always laughed just enough so you wouldn't see it.

"Dad, you need to sit still and let Marie help you." I reached across the table and grabbed his hand.

When he came down to dinner, he nearly had another stroke when he noticed me sitting at the table. After making sure he wasn't hallucinating, he came over and gave me the biggest hug that his frail body could muster.

He had lost weight.

A considerable amount where it would be alarming. If I lived closer, I probably would have noticed right away. Since we didn't talk often, and he chose what he wanted to share with me, I didn't know just how much my father's health had declined.

"I will sit down when I'm dead. The restaurant and coffee shop need me right now." He insisted on being stubborn.

I used to hate how stubborn he was. This man was so stuck in his ways that it was a headache to try to tell him otherwise.

"Well, you'll be there soon if you don't sit down." Marie came over and set down the banana bread she had made for dessert.

He broke out into laughter as he cut himself a piece of the loaf. "The reason you fell in love with me was because I'm so stubborn."

"No, I fell in love with you because you were consistent and sweet. Now, that stubborn part was something we were supposed to work on."

I giggled. "How did you meet?"

It was different witnessing my father in love. I had never seen him or my mother affectionate toward each other. The only reason I knew he loved her was because, without fail, he always showed up with flowers on Mondays. In my young brain, I thought that meant he loved her.

My mother hated flowers.

No matter how much she expressed how much she hated flowers, he always showed up with them. He would bend down and place a kiss on her forehead, even if she was passed out drunk on the couch.

It was like a breath of fresh air now witnessing him being loved back. I always have known him to have a big heart, but it was never reciprocated.

"Well, she swept me off my feet with her butter pecan loaf. She dropped it off at the restaurant for a retirement party for Earl."

"Earl retired?"

"About two years ago," he confirmed, making me feel guilty for not knowing these small pieces of my father's life. "Marie dropped off the loaf and promised that she wouldn't be staying long . . . but I changed that."

"Your father kept me talking and eating the entire night. By the time I looked at my watch, I had stayed the entire party."

"You had a good time . . . didn't you, baby?"

Marie blushed. "I sure did. After the retirement party, he invited me on a real date. He took me to Pier 3, where we had the best seafood. I told myself that I never wanted to be without him because people treat you better when you visit a restaurant with Carl Stone."

They broke out into laughter and kissed each other. "I believe you . . . He has turned my girls into quite the restaurant snobs."

"The girls just know good food," he said, waving his fork at me. "Why didn't you bring them with you?"

"They're spending time with Ashton's mother. She flew in to see them," I quickly replied, not wanting to get too deep into my life story.

My father smiled at the mention of his granddaughters. I had no complaints when it came to the relationship he had with the girls. They loved spending time with him and always questioned why he couldn't live closer to us.

"How is Clara doing?"

I bit the inside of my cheek. "She's doing well."

I wanted to tell him how much of an annoying bitch she could be but decided against it. As far as he knew, I loved my mother-in-law, and we had a great relationship.

"Ashton is busy with work, I bet, huh?"

"Always."

I hated having to lie to my father about my life. The divorce had happened nearly a year ago, and I still struggled with saying I was divorced. I still caught myself calling Ashton my husband more times than I should have. Telling my father that I was divorced would make it real.

Not that it hadn't been real before.

Ashton had a girlfriend and a new life that didn't involve me. I hated thinking that my daughters might have half siblings and a life that had nothing to do with me one day.

"I always liked that man for you. He's a hard worker and takes care of his family."

Ashton was like my father in more ways than one. He was a hard worker and provider; it was something that they both had to do. I guess they didn't feel all macho if they weren't providing for their families. They also always hated confrontation.

The reason my mother got away with so much was because my father refused to deal directly with the situation. He would make smart remarks under his breath and complain when she was far too drunk to comprehend, but in the end, he never confronted the situation head-on.

Ashton was the same way.

He mumbled under his breath and then covered it with a yawn. He probably complained about me to his friends too. Instead of coming to me to fix the problems in our marriage, he ran away and pretended they didn't exist.

"He does work a lot. However, he's younger and has the stamina for it . . . You need to sit still, sir."

"Who else is going to help me run the place, Faith? You live in Georgia, and I know you'll never move to Sageport."

I scoffed because the sound of it sounded insane. "Maybe we can hire some new help while I'm in town . . . I can help you with that."

He smiled. "You're going to help me hire work at the restaurant?"

"Dad, I can't lose yo . . ." my words trailed off while I quickly gathered myself.

Having young kids, you learn how to keep your emotions in check. Anytime I broke down in the pantry, and one of the girls found me, I learned to be quick on my feet. We used to pretend that the onions in the pantry caused me to cry. Now they were older and knew that was a bunch of bullshit.

"I'm not going anywhere, Faith. That was a minor setback, and I came back swinging."

I wiped the tears that escaped my eyes. "What happens when you don't come back swinging?"

"She's right, Carl," Marie agreed with me.

I didn't expect to become so emotional while discussing my father's health. We didn't speak much or have a close father-daughter relationship. Despite all of that, I still cared for my father and never wanted something to happen to him. It didn't matter how much I pushed him away. He always tried.

That was more than what my mother did when she was alive.

My father touched Marie's hand on his shoulder, then reached across the table and grabbed mine. "My girls." He smiled, exposing his wrinkles and laugh lines.

Had he been laughing more?

My father was a somber man; well, that was the version I had known. This affectionate, laughing, and joyful man in front of me wasn't the father I remembered.

"Da—"

"Let me speak, Faith." He paused for a brief second. "I know we haven't spent many holidays together, which is one regret I will always have. It's this Christmas that I want . . . I don't ask for much, Faithy. This Christmas, it would mean the world to me if you, Ashton, and the girls could spend it with us."

I smiled when he used my nickname.

God, I hadn't heard that name in years. Whenever he wanted me to clean my room or do my chores, he would always call me "Faithy."

My mother hated that nickname. She always made fun of him whenever he used it. "Dad, Ashton and I are divorced."

I had no plans to talk about my divorce or even reveal that I was actually divorced. Seeing the emotions behind my father's eyes told me that I needed to be honest. Maybe this was healthy for me. I needed to stop hiding the fact that I was divorced and embrace it.

Ashton and I had no plans on ever rekindling our marriage, so I needed to rip the Band-Aid off and start living in my truth, no longer hiding it. I guess that was something I inherited from my mother.

Keeping secrets.

I expected my father to gasp and act surprised by my news. Instead, he rubbed the back of my hand and smiled. "Was it something that you wanted?"

"Yes. I asked for the divorce."

"Then I trust your judgment. I just want you to be happy, Faith . . . truly happy," he winked.

Was he hinting that he knew I wasn't happy in my marriage? Anytime my father visited, which wasn't often, I made sure to turn on a switch. I became supermom, superwife, and any other superperson I needed to become to show him that my life was perfect away from Sageport.

"It never matters who wants the divorce; they're never easy. I divorced my husband nearly five years ago. We were together for fifteen years, and I worked hard to keep it together," Marie said.

I touched my chest because that was how I felt. I worked so hard to keep things with us together, and it never seemed like it was enough. I wanted my marriage, and I never wanted it to end in divorce.

I wanted to beat the odds that were stacked against me. My parents' marriage wasn't one I ever wanted to become, so I figured if I worked hard and became the perfect wife and mother, that was all I needed to keep our marriage afloat.

Children came into play, and we grew further apart because our kids needed me. He needed me too, but I focused more on the children's needs.

I knew I had a part to play in our marriage going downhill. However, I was also the one doing the damage control alone. Ashton never gave me half the effort that he claimed to have. If he had, we probably wouldn't be spending the holidays apart.

"It's tough . . . This is the first Christmas we're spending apart . . . the first Christmas I will miss with my girls," I whimpered.

"It sounds like you might need a Sageport Christmas after all. A new start to this journey you're on." Marie cut me a piece of the loaf cake and smiled.

"Maybe."

My usual alarm pulled me from my slumber as I tussled with the blankets to grab my phone from the window ledge. It felt surreal waking up in this room after fifteen years.

As surreal as it felt, I happened to get the best sleep in my life. Since the divorce, I hadn't had a good night's sleep unless my night was accompanied by a glass or two of wine.

After dessert last night, I sat on the porch, scrolled through the unanswered emails from the girls' school, and soaked in the nighttime breeze. The smell of salt water wrapped its arms around me as I swung on the porch swing in complete bliss.

I hadn't felt bliss in a long time.

The familiar smell of ocean water, the cool breeze, and the sound of crickets were like a sound machine to me. I cracked open the window in my room and fell into a deep sleep while listening to the familiar sound of crickets I loved.

Who says sound therapy doesn't work?

I silenced my alarm and leaned up in the bed. The sun was already crashing into the room, and I didn't mind. For years, I had slept with blackout curtains, and now, here I was, welcoming the sun into my room before noon. The smell of bacon ran through my body, nudging me out of bed and into my house slippers.

Creeping down the hall, I found Marie in the kitchen with her back turned. "Good morning," I greeted and poured a cup of freshly brewed coffee.

"Good morning, hon. How did you sleep last night?"

"Surprisingly, great."

"First time in a long while, huh?" Marie clocked exactly what I didn't say.

"Yes. Sleep used to be my favorite thing. Now, with twin girls and a divorce, it's hard to do the one thing I loved to do."

When I had my twins, I couldn't sleep because they were up nearly every hour to feed. Once they became old enough that they didn't need to wake every hour, I finally got my sleep schedule back. Now, with a divorce under my belt, sleep never came.

"When I was going through my divorce, I didn't sleep for almost two years. Catnaps were what pushed me through."

I took a sip of coffee. "Great. We're approaching the one-year date . . . You mean to tell me I have another year of this?"

Marie smiled. "I have a feeling you won't go through it like I did . . . You're more put together than I was." She winked at me.

"Being put together is all I have left. My girls won't allow me to fall apart how I need to." I watched Marie grab my mother's favorite mug from the cupboard. "Do you ever get weirded out living in this house?"

"All the time . . . The bathroom still has all her things in it, so I use the bathroom down here. I want to be respectful because I know you lost a mother, and he lost a wife."

"Yeah . . . fifteen years ago, Marie."

This house was a constant reminder of the memories we needed to let go. While my father probably still mourned the loss of my mother, I never did. You couldn't miss someone that you truly never knew.

"I just want to be respectful when it comes to his boundaries." I loved how she was so respectful and never wanted to force her way into my father's life.

However, she was living in a house that he shared with his deceased wife. It wouldn't have been a problem, except he still had my mother's things in this house as if she were alive. This was no longer a home but a crypt.

"If he wants me to spend the holidays with him and visit with the girls often, then we need to do something about this house. It's so dark and dreary . . . like I remembered it."

"Good morning, ladies," my father hobbled into the kitchen.

He took a seat at the kitchen table beside me. "Coffee, love?" Marie asked.

"Yes . . . splash of cream and two sugars . . . if you don't mind." He smiled, reaching up to kiss her on the cheek.

"I never mind, sweets."

"Dad, I was thinking . . . Maybe we should do some decorating around here."

"What's wrong with it?"

I sighed. "Mom is *everywhere* in this house. You're engaged, and it's unfair to Marie to live in another woman's shadow."

Marie remained quiet while fixing his coffee. "Another woman's shadow? Come on, Faith. Let's not cause any fuss when it's not needed . . . I got that brand-new TV last year on Black Friday."

He was missing the point, and I think he was missing it on purpose. Parting with my mother's belongings meant he was truly letting go of her. He had held onto everything for years because it felt like she was still here. It wasn't healthy for him to continue living like this, especially because the marriage he had with my mother was far from healthy. It was a codependent relationship between the two of them.

There was never any happiness, and now he had found some with Marie. It was unfair of him to expect her to live in Kimba Stone's shadow. "I almost had a panic attack when Marie first welcomed me in yesterday."

He grew concerned. "Why didn't you tell me about that yesterday? Are you feeling all right now?"

"I'm fine now. This house is what caused my near-panic attack. You were never home, so you don't share the same memories as I do. Living in this house was torture for me. I've spent so many years trying to forget the memories in this house. It's unhealthy for you to hold onto so many of her things." I reached out and touched his hand. "You lost your wife, and I understand that. However, you have to let her go so that you and Marie have a chance at a healthy marriage . . . something you've never experienced before."

I could tell having this conversation was hard for him. He didn't want to let go of all of the memories he had, though some of them weren't all that great. More than anything, Marie didn't deserve to have to live in this house while he held onto pieces of his ex-wife.

"Okay," he spoke lowly.

It made sense why he kept the house in the same exact way. Although our family was dysfunctional and had many problems, the last time the house was this way, he had his family together. It didn't matter how dysfunctional or flawed we were. He had his family together under one roof.

"I know you wanted me to go to the restaurant and help out, so I will go before the lunch rush."

He gave me a weak smile. "Thank you. You don't know how much it means you're here with me, Faith."

I planned to get in and out. I didn't want to stay and spend the holidays here. That quickly changed upon seeing my father. He needed my help, and I couldn't turn my back on him. He was the only family that I had, and I needed to stop pushing him out of my life.

Ashton had his family and could fly to spend the holidays with him. The only family I had was my father and the girls. I didn't grow up having a grandfather who could teach me things and spend time with me.

My father never knew his dad.

The greatest gift that I could give my girls was their grandfather. They adored one another, and I needed to stop keeping them apart because I was too scared to deal with my past. They didn't deserve that.

It wasn't fair to them . . .

And it wasn't fair to me.

Chapter Nine

ROME

MAMA HAD A rough night last night, so I decided to work from home today. After talking her down, she allowed me to get a few hours of sleep before Pia rang the doorbell. Since I was younger, I have always been obsessed with getting nine hours of sleep.

I needed a good night's rest to perform my best as an athlete. Whenever I didn't get enough rest, I was always grumpy. To spare my employees, I decided working from my home office today would be best. Whenever Mama had a rough night, she was usually too exhausted to do anything the next day, so she slept the day away.

"Morning. Tough night?"

Pia could always tell what kind of night I had when she stepped through the door. I usually came into the kitchen dressed in a suit and ready to leave moments after she arrived. Today, I was sporting my favorite flannel pajama pants and a hoodie.

I'm sure she could tell from how I loaded my cup with black coffee. I hated black coffee, but today was one of those mornings that I needed it straight. Black coffee would get me through the day of work that I had to do.

"She screamed for my dad for two hours. I had to talk her down and give her some tea to calm her."

"At least it's not Allen. Whenever she wails for Allen, it's almost impossible to calm her down."

Pia was right. My mother rarely called out for my father, but whenever she did, I was always able to talk her down from it. When it came to Allen, you couldn't calm her or talk her down. She was irrational when it came to Allen, which always made me sad.

How could I grieve and move on fully when my mother was stuck in the past? It wasn't her fault that she was stuck back there, but it was hard for me to create a future whenever I had to hear her screaming for two of the people we had lost.

"She may not eat breakfast. When I got her back into bed, she fell fast asleep. She may sleep for most of the day."

"Good. She needs some rest. Have you spoken to her doctor about prescribing something to help her sleep through the night? I know it will help you a lot too."

"I don't want her all drugged up. The meds they give her for the dementia already keep her loopy."

Pia flipped the pancake in the pan. "I love how much you want the best for her, Rome." I knew there would be a "but" somewhere in there. "You have to think of you too. As caregivers, we often forget to take care of ourselves. Your mother will be fine if she takes something to help her sleep."

I felt the guilt.

What kind of son was I that I wanted to give my mom sleeping meds so *I* could have a peaceful sleep? I had never been a person who slept lightly. It would take a train to wake me up. These days, I haven't slept too hard because I needed to listen for my mother. We had babyproofed her room and made it where she couldn't get out of her door. But it wasn't her body that escaped the room. It was the screams for her dead son that constantly escaped.

"It's something to consider."

Pia sighed and placed a perfect pancake onto a plate. "Can you at least put some food on your stomach?"

On cue, my stomach started to growl. "Put four pieces of bacon on that plate, and you got yourself a deal."

She quickly scooped two additional pieces of bacon and added them to the plate, then slid it across the island. "Deal."

I quickly ate breakfast and showered to prepare for my day. Today was payroll day, and I liked to get those issued before doing any other task. The family dealerships were left up to me to run, and I couldn't allow my father's dream to dwindle down the drain.

Since childhood, my father always told Allen and me we would take over the dealerships when he was gone. I didn't think that would mean he and Allen would both be gone at the same time. Atkins Family Dealerships were throughout Sageport. There were a few other dealerships, but AFD had been around for years, and we had a relationship with the community.

Before passing away, my father had put the majority of the kids from my high school in their first cars. Everyone trusted Dale Atkins. He was everyone's family, so AFD were the first and only dealerships most of Sageport went to when they wanted a reliable car.

Since he passed away, it was up to me to fill his shoes as being the trusted and reliable Rome Atkins. Football has always been my dream and something I had wanted since childhood. I had big dreams of going away to college and then making it into the big leagues. I wanted to stand on TV and shout how Sageport and my family made me the man I am today.

Then the accident happened.

Life was never truly the same after that. I stepped up in a major way because I knew both my parents needed me. Allen was gone, and I couldn't bring him back, but I could be the best son possible for them. Deciding not to go away for college was one of the hardest decisions I ever made.

Deciding between what you wanted and what needed to be done was difficult. I wanted to go away to college because I knew Allen would have wanted me to. He would have wanted me to continue with our dreams and do everything we always talked about.

How could I even fix my mouth to tell my parents that college was still my plan when they were falling apart? It would break their hearts to know they had lost one son and were about to lose another one to college.

That was hurt that I didn't want to inflict on them.

They deserved none of it.

While my father was alive, I worked at the dealerships during the day while trying to keep my mother from falling apart at night. I learned everything that I possibly could from my father.

I often thought about if he knew he was going to die next.

As much as I wanted to learn more about the dealerships, he desperately wanted to teach it to me. At the time, I chalked it up to him just wanting to spend more time with me.

Now that I am older and wiser, I realize he wanted me to be prepared. If he could have, he would have fought harder to be here with us. His last words were:

Protect her.

My mother had always been his pride and joy, and he protected her with everything when he was alive. Their marriage was one that I always wanted for myself. A wife that would do any and everything for her family, and I would return the gesture by providing for our family.

That had been their family dynamic for years. Neither my mother nor father grew tired of it. Every night, she would have his dinner warm and ready for him. Even if she had eaten, she would sit at the table while they filled each other in on their days. I used to sit on the steps and listen to my mother telling him how difficult Allen or I had made her day, and my father would validate her feelings.

He never made her feel like she was "just" a housewife. He always sympathized with her and validated what she felt. My mother always made her role as mom and wife seem like a piece of cake, but when I listened to how she broke down to my father about it, I realized she was carrying a heavier load than he was.

And he knew it.

After their talks, he would finish his food and send her to their bedroom to soak in the bath. He would take control of the bedtime rituals and ensure my brother and I were showered, read for thirty minutes, and were ready for bed. Then he'd give me a pep talk about being the oldest and setting the example.

God, I prayed for a marriage like that.

I wanted to come home to a warm body in the house. My wife didn't need to cook. I could bring home takeout. I just wanted someone I could share a meal with. Someone to cuddle with at night and not the empty side of the bed I despised.

My life didn't turn out how I envisioned it, and I could have sat back and hated Kimba Stone because of it. Lord knows how many nights I sat up resenting the fact that I had ever crossed paths with Kimba Stone. Then I took it back because had I not met Kimba, I would have never met Faith, and I never regretted Faith.

I could never regret what I shared with Faith. The look on her face at the hospital still haunts me to this day. She didn't deserve that from me. At the time, so much was happening that I needed someone to blame. The one person I wanted to blame was dead, so I needed someone else at that time.

It was never Faith's fault.

Every day that passed, I regretted that I blamed her. Especially because she had always been so vocal about feeling responsible for her mother's messes. I was always the one who made sure she knew that her mother's mistakes were her own. She couldn't take responsibility for another woman's life.

Then I went ahead and blamed her for something her mother did. Faith was selfish for once and was living her life at prom. How would she have known her mother would get drunk, get behind the wheel of the car, and drive? She wouldn't have known, and I spent years wishing I could take back those words.

I hated myself for it.

I had lost Allen, and she had lost her mother that night. Instead of worrying about her mother, she just wanted to ensure I was all right. Instead of comforting her back, I lashed out at her.

Her face . . .

The way her bottom lip poked out while tears fell down her face was something I never forgot.

Faith Stone was the reason I could never truly move on. Every relationship I've had after her never worked because none of those women were Faith. I continued to put imaginary pressure on these women to be someone that they weren't.

My last girlfriend couldn't handle the pressure of my mother. It was all too much for her, and as much as I respected her honesty, that shit hurt. It made me feel like I would never find a woman who would accept my situation. Most of the people I went to school with were either married or had children.

I had neither.

It was hard not to compare my life to my peers' when I was the person selling them their family vehicles.

They felt pity for me.

Here I was, working at my father's dealerships and still single, while they celebrated their first anniversary and were welcoming a new bundle of joy.

I would sit and watch how the wife would smile and then reach her arm out to tell me she was praying for my mother.

Pity.

I hated anyone to feel bad for me, and that's what they felt. Anytime I went into a restaurant or picked up some dry cleaning, I would see a discounted price for my food or my dry-cleaning order.

Fifteen years had passed, and Sageport had changed drastically. Yet, they couldn't forget about the tragedy that my family went through.

"Hey, I hate to do this to you, but I have to leave a bit early today." Pia coughed.

"Everything all good?"

"I've had this nagging cough for a few days. My doctor can squeeze me in around five."

"Definitely get that taken care of. Mama and I are good . . . I'll pick up her favorite from Carl's restaurant."

"Are you sure?"

"Pia . . . Go see your doctor. We'll manage just fine."

She chuckled. "All right. She's finally up, so I'll help her get bathed and ready for the day."

I checked my watch. It was already after two. "Sounds good. I think it might be nice to get her out on the porch later . . . We'll eat dinner there tonight."

"How wonderful . . . She'll love that."

"I'll finish here, order the food, and pick it up," I replied.

"Sounds good."

Pia was a godsend. I don't know what I would have done without her. She was slowly becoming a part of our small family. She didn't just look after my mother. She looked after me too, even when I told her she didn't have to.

I could come in from a long day at work, and she would be waiting with food and a little conversation before she clocked out.

Pia didn't realize how much of a blessing she was to both my mother and me. As much as my mother needed her, I did too. Those little conversations we had did wonders for my mental health.

Whenever she did a quick check-in, like she did often, it helped me a ton. It always made me realize that I mattered too and deserved to have a life. As much as I knew I deserved to have a life of my own, I often battled with guilt.

Putting my mother in a nursing home was out of the question. I wouldn't be able to live with myself if I put her into a facility with strangers. She didn't have family other than me, so I wasn't going to put her away to rot in a nursing home to make my life better and easier.

I checked and responded to a few emails before I logged out of my computer and went to call the restaurant for our favorite meal.

Hopefully, her favorite meat loaf meal on the back porch will cheer her up and help her get some rest tonight.

We both needed it.

I killed my engine and sat in the car for a bit. Carl's was always busy around this time. It was right after the lunch rush and just before the dinner rush. I didn't eat here often because I couldn't take the way Carl would stare at me.

He was always cordial and made small conversations, but I could feel the guilt radiating off him. With all the renovations he had done to the place, he couldn't keep an empty seat there. Everyone loved the fresh home-cooked food that Carl's provided.

While all the new restaurants were going for the fancy aesthetic, Carl stayed true to who he was by providing the staple meals we had all grown up on. The new renovations brightened the place, but the menu remained unchanged.

While Mama got the thick double meat loaf meal, I always got Faith's Shepherd's Pie. When everything happened, my mother was the first on the picket line to protest eating at Carl's. I couldn't blame her because she was hurt. His wife was the one who killed her baby boy, so she was angry. Although she loved Carl's food, for years, she stopped eating there. It wasn't until she started developing dementia that she would ask for her favorite meat loaf.

I hit the locks and climbed out of my truck to head inside. They were typically quick with the to-go orders, and I didn't want to heat the food back up when I made it home. The door chimed when I stepped through, and I spotted Trixie, one of the waitresses.

We had gone on a few dates and realized we were better off as friends. Trixie knew the baggage that I came with, and instead of complicating my life further, she wanted to remain friends.

"Hey, Rome! Let me guess . . . the usual?" She pulled out her pad, and I stopped her.

"Already put the order in."

"To-go order and up!" She hollered out the usual lingo they used when someone came to pick up their food instead of dining in.

I leaned on the counter and waited for my food. With all the smells that were going on in here, my mouth was watering to get home and eat. Mom had slept most of the day, so she was wide-eyed and bushy-tailed.

"Order is for R . . ." her voice trailed when she realized who the order was for.

When she looked up, she came face-to-face with me. My breath was caught in my chest, knocking me back a few spaces. Faith Stone was standing and breathing right in front of me.

"Fay," I was the first to speak.

Trixie looked at both of us. "Um, yes, it's for Rome." She gently took the bag from Faith, who had been stuck in place since she read the name attached to the bag.

"Rome," she finally spoke.

"You two know each other?"

Trixie was one of the newbies that didn't know my family's history. All she knew was that my mother had dementia. However, she didn't know anything else about my brother or my father.

"We went to school together," Faith finally snapped out of her trance. "It's been a long time, Rome," she smiled.

"Too long . . . How are you? Are you back in Sageport for good?" I had so much that I wanted to talk to her about.

So much that I needed to apologize for.

"Just in town for the holidays and to help out my father."

"Oh yeah," Trixie snapped. "Mr. Carl had a stroke."

"What?" I blurted.

"Mild stroke," Faith corrected. "Um, please check in on those other orders."

Trixie nodded, put her notepad back into her apron, and headed off. "Sure thing."

I watched as Faith folded her arms. Her pecan-caramel complexion glistened under the fluorescent restaurant lights. That tiny beauty mark sat perfectly by the corner of her eyes. Her hair was pulled back into a perfect, bouncy ponytail. She was dressed down in a pair of faded jeans and a Budweiser graphic T-shirt.

I didn't know how it was possible, but she must have had time in a bottle. How was it possible for her to still look just as youthful as she did when we were in high school?

"Is he all right?"

"Yes, he's getting stronger every day. His doctor wants him to take it easy and, well . . . You know my father."

"Easy isn't in his vocabulary."

We both broke out into laughter. Carl Stone was a hard worker, which was partly why Sageport wrapped their arms around him. Even when everyone refused to eat at his restaurant, he arrived there every day. It didn't matter that he had to pour fresh pots of coffee down the sink at the end of every day. He showed up until one person turned into sixteen.

He never pretended his wife was innocent and took responsibility for her actions. Carl loved his community, and we loved him back. No matter how much Sageport has changed, Carl has always remained the same.

"Exactly. How have you been?" She moved out of a customer's way and nodded toward the door.

I held the door open as we stepped into the breezy afternoon day. We didn't experience real winters here other than the cool winds from the ocean.

"I've been doing good."

"Guess you're here for the holidays too, huh?"

I paused.

Unsure of how or what to say to her response. Carl must have never spoken about me to her. It didn't surprise me because he never mentioned Faith, either. Most of his staff probably didn't know he had a daughter until she arrived.

Trixie quickly opened the door. "Marie is on the phone . . . It's about Carl."

Faith took a deep breath. "It was good seeing you, Rome . . . Don't be a stranger," she winked.

I watched as she rushed inside to the phone. It took me five minutes to become unstuck and make it back to my truck.

Faith Stone was back in Sageport.

Was this some kind of message sent from above? A Christmas wish that needed to happen?

I would have expected many things before seeing Faith come from the back with my order. She was still just as beautiful and poised. Faith had this aura about her that I never found in anyone else.

Her presence made you want to be around her and keep her near. I made the mistake of letting her get away before, and I don't think I could sit back and allow that same thing to happen again.

Starting up my truck, I pulled out of the spot, making mental plans to have lunch there tomorrow. I had—needed—to see Faith again.

Mama sat on the back porch eating her food. She smiled at me before putting mashed potatoes into her mouth.

"This is lovely of you to set up, Rome. The weather is absolutely beautiful today."

She was lucid today.

It was always a good day when she was lucid and we could converse. I used the term "lucid" lightly because even when she seemed like her old self again, she wasn't.

"How's the meat loaf?"

"Delicious. Carl's will always have the best meat loaf in Sageport. These potatoes are so fresh and fluffy . . . Here, try this." She tried to spoon potatoes into my mouth.

"I'm fine, Mama."

She kissed her teeth with a sly smirk on her face. "I forget you and your brother have to eat healthy for football. Speaking of your brother . . . Where is Allen?"

"Probably with his friends," I nonchalantly replied while eating.

I learned a while ago to play along with her. No good would come from me revealing that Allen had died many years ago. Instead, I played along like my brother was alive and we were still teenagers.

"Well, I sure hope his homework is done." She paused again. "Have you done yours?"

"It's been done since earlier," I lied again.

She smiled and patted my hand. "That's my boy."

After seeing Faith today, I didn't have much conversation with my mother. My mind was on how stunning she had looked. Faith had always been thin, so to see how she had grown into a lady curve made me wish I could explore them.

"I saw Faith today," I blurted.

"You and that girl are inseparable. What is going to happen when you're both off to college? Do you truly think the relationship will make it?"

"I do."

My mother kissed her teeth again and waved me off. "Focus on your studies and football, not that girl. She's destined to end up like her mother did."

My mother had never been a fan of Faith. It wasn't anything that Faith had personally done. She had never cared for Kimba Stone since they were in school, so she naturally disliked Faith, too.

I remember having this same conversation with my mom about Faith. She was adamant about me focusing on school and not a relationship with her. Even though she wasn't a fan of our relationship, it meant a lot to me. You couldn't tell me that Faith and I wouldn't be high school sweethearts.

It's funny how life is.

Not only did we not end up being high school sweethearts, but we also lost touch for the past fifteen years. I wanted to know so much about her and what her life had been like.

She never visited Carl.

When he was out of town, I assumed he was visiting Faith. I didn't know anything about her, and Carl never offered up any information about her. From how she was surprised to see me, I could see he never offered her any information about Sageport.

Maybe it was what she wanted.

To have no attachment to Sageport and move on from the tragedy. I wished I had that same opportunity, but instead, I've relived the trauma every other night when I heard screams and sobs coming from my mother's bedroom downstairs.

Did she have children?

A husband?

Maybe even a wife?

Did she ever attend college and get the career she had always wanted?

Faith always joked that she would never be a housewife. She was going to have a career and support mine too. I always countered with a laugh, even though I agreed with her. Faith was never going to be a housewife. We would have a full staff ready to take care of whatever we needed.

How naive we were as teens.

We had our entire life planned out and had no clue that one fatal night would alter those plans. There was a reason that Faith came to Sageport after all these years, and I was determined to show her that it was meant for us to cross paths at the restaurant today.

Chapter Ten

FAITH

ROME ATKINS STEPPING into the restaurant to pick up his to-go order wasn't what I imagined for the day. I had been at the restaurant helping and ensuring everyone was doing their job. I didn't know much about how my father ran his restaurant. However, I raised twins on my own while cooking, cleaning, and making sure they were alive.

This should have been a piece of cake.

And it was—at first.

That was, until Rome stepped through the door, and all the wind was knocked out of my chest. He was still as handsome as ever, only with an added beard. He had put on some weight that looked good on him.

Rome was always a stickler for fitness when we were in high school. Every morning, he worked out, and he didn't eat certain starches because he swore they would knock him off his game.

I always teased him while eating something I knew he would never eat. That had always been our relationship with each other.

Fun and easygoing.

We rarely had disagreements, and when we did, Rome always cracked first and made things right between us.

I was still shocked that we had run into each other yesterday. The way he stared at me was a big difference from how he stared at me in that hospital waiting room.

He was so disappointed in me that night.

That look will forever be etched in my brain. I had never felt like a failure until that night. I blamed myself for so long because of the mistake I had made.

It didn't matter that my father had constantly drilled into my head that the accident wasn't my fault. It didn't matter how often he told me. I believed it was.

Rome believed it was.

My phone buzzing in my lap pulled me from my thoughts. I heaved a sigh, expecting Ashton's name to pop across my screen. When I saw Tierra's name, I smiled and slid my finger across the screen.

We hadn't spoken since I was about to board my flight at the airport. "Hey, girly," I greeted.

"I'm sure glad you're not in some ditch in Sageport," she replied. "What happened to keeping me updated?"

I sighed. "I have been helping my father out at his restaurant, so I haven't had much time to sit and update anyone."

"How is your father doing?"

"Better. He had a slight mishap yesterday when he fell out of bed. The doctor said he just bruised his tailbone."

"Sheesh, how are you handling all of this?"

"I'm good, surprisingly. His fiancée has been a big help too, so I don't have to worry too much about him."

"Whoa, wait a minute. Your father is *engaged*? You never told me this small juicy piece of information."

Marie and my father had gone out to dinner tonight. It was just me enjoying the breeze on the porch swing. "That's because I just found out myself . . . She's sweet, though."

"Can you imagine had she not been? That would have added more stress to an already stressful situation."

"Tell me about it . . . What's new with you?"

"I'm in Phoenix with family. You know I'm already ready to go." I envisioned her rolling her eyes. "So, have things changed there?"

"In town, absolutely. In my father's house . . . Hell no. He still has things from my mother."

"That's normal. What did you want him to do? Toss all memories of her out the window?"

"T, he has her house slippers still at the front door . . . hasn't touched her side of the sin—"

"Oh hell, you sure he's all right? It's normal to keep a favorite blanket, maybe even some sweatshirts, but her sink is the same? That's *not* normal."

"Who are you telling? I had to have a conversation with him about it. I nearly had a panic attack walking into this house."

I smiled and waved at Mrs. Browning, who was heading to her car. "Take it easy, Faith. As much as you're there to help and check in on your dad, make sure you are checking in with yourself too."

"He asked me to stay for the holidays," I whispered.

"Um, what's wrong with that? It sure beats the empty house that's waiting for you in Georgia. The girls will be in New York with their dad. It's good for you to be around family."

"I didn't even pack enough clothes to stay through the holidays."

"That's why they make these stores with clothes, Faith. Buy whatever you need and spend time with your family. You've had a tough year with the divorce."

"I wish you would stop reminding me."

"Somebody has to. Ashton will be with the girls and his family. You'll be alone if you go back home . . . Think of this as something you're doing for me."

"For you?"

"If you return home, I will be forced to worry about my friend. So stressed that it will take away from me enjoying the holidays with *my* family."

"Is this blackmail?"

"It can be whatever you want it to be . . . I just need you to stay your butt there in Sageport."

"Fine, whatever . . . I hear you," I agreed, although I had already made plans to stay.

Marie was so excited about the plans to freshen up the house, so I couldn't let her down. Between focusing on her own baking clients and being there for my dad, she didn't have the energy or time to take on the restaurant.

I could tell Trixie wasn't the biggest fan of me taking over. However, she still respected that I was in charge and my father owned the restaurant.

"This is the perfect time to bond with your father. Faith, you only get two parents, and since he's your last parent, you should make those memories."

"When have you become so sentimental? Weren't you the one screaming in celebration when I signed my divorce papers?"

"That was because I knew you deserved better . . . I *do* want you to be happy, Faith. Out of anybody, you deserve to be happy."

Although Tierra and I were close, I had left out a few parts of my past. Rome was one of them. It hurt to think about him, so it was better if I didn't talk about him or the past that we shared together.

Plus, there was nothing to tell her about.

Rome was probably visiting his parents for the holiday with his wife and kids. Had my marriage survived, I would have been heading to New York to do the same.

We spoke and were pleasant with each other. That encounter would probably be the last I saw of Rome Atkins. We were madly in love as teenagers, and that ended years ago.

Life moved on, and he had probably done the same. Mrs. Atkins hated my guts, so she probably found him a cute, wholesome girl who came from money. Either way, Rome Atkins wasn't my problem anymore.

❄

"Of course, baby. Santa is going to come to our house too," I told Madison.

"Santa isn't real, Maddy." I heard Mayven scream in the background.

Mayven was always guaranteed to give me problems. While her sister wanted to hold onto every tiny piece of being young, it seemed like Mayven wanted nothing to do with it.

She didn't want to believe in the Easter Bunny, Santa, or the tooth fairy. I wanted to keep them babies for as long as I could.

I never got to keep my innocence.

There was never anyone putting money under my pillow or hiding Easter eggs around the yard. My father never dressed in a bunny costume while handing out Easter baskets.

I promised myself when I had my daughters that I would do all the things I wanted as a child—the holidays, parties, and everything that came with being that mom.

I wanted it all.

The girls have always had a birthday party filled with all their friends and their favorite characters. I always stayed up late to decorate and make sure their party was everything they would have wanted.

I never had that.

I wanted my girls to grow up and smile at how much their mom loved them. As a kid, I wanted my mother to show me how much I meant to her.

She never did.

"Can you put your sister on the phone, baby?"

"Mayvennnnn!" Madison screamed into the phone.

I giggled and pulled the phone away from my ear. "Yes, Mom."
That "mom" word always causes me to cringe.

When did I become just "Mom" to her? I wanted to be her
mommy for as long as I could. I thought I had until middle school
for her to switch from Mommy to Mom.

"Stop telling your sister that Santa isn't real."

"Becca Henderson told me that Santa isn't real. She said her
father puts the gifts under the tree when she's asleep."

I cleared my throat. "Well, how would Becca know if she's
asleep?"

She grew quiet for a second.

"Her big brother Bradly told her."

"Hmm, well, Becca should know that big brothers are liars."
I didn't mean to call poor Bradly a liar. However, I needed to keep
my girls believing in Santa for as long as possible.

Mayven gasped. "They are?"

"Yup. You wouldn't know because you don't have a big brother
. . . but they are liars."

"Do you have a big brother, Mom?"

"No, I have something even worse."

She gasped again. "What?"

"A big cousin."

I wanted to laugh so bad, but I knew I had to keep a straight
face for them.

"Big cousins are liars too?"

"Uh-huh. Make sure you don't believe a word they say."

The girls had older cousins on their father's side, and they
usually picked on the girls, so adding the "big cousin lie" was to
help them more than me. Whenever her older cousins visited,

I spent most of the time consoling my daughters because they either played too rough with the girls or teased them.

"I sure will, Mom."

"All right. Have a safe flight, baby . . . Make sure to listen to your nana too, all right?"

Ashton was going to fly to New York and meet them there. I knew his quick work trip wasn't going to be so quick.

"All right. We will listen to Francis too."

"Francis?"

"Daddy's girlfriend."

I tried to keep my tone the same. "Oh, is she going too?"

"Uh-huh. Nana is excited too."

Of course, she would be.

"All right, babies . . . I love you and will talk to you soon, okay?"

"Okay, Mommy!" Madison hollered into the phone.

I ended the call feeling sad. This wasn't just some girlfriend who would be gone in a few months. She was a serious girlfriend who he was taking to spend the holidays with his family.

She was even traveling with his mother and the girls without him. Clara must have already met and approved her for him to feel comfortable bringing her around.

When Ashton and I were dating, he didn't bring me around his family until we had been together for a year. Even then, he tried to make excuses about why he wanted to keep me to himself.

I used to think it was cute.

Now, I knew it was a ploy to cover up the fact that he didn't want me to meet his family.

The flags were in my face, and I always ignored them.

"Big brothers are liars, huh?"

I nearly jumped out of my seat. "R . . . Rome, hey." I tried to quickly recover from being scared.

"I didn't mean to scare you," he chuckled with his hands in his pants pockets.

He was wearing a dress shirt and slacks.

"You're fine . . . I see the food keeps you coming back . . . Picking up another to-go order?"

"Actually, no. I came to see you."

I choked midsip of my coffee. "Me?"

"Yes. I'm on my lunch break and wanted to see if you had a few minutes to spare."

"Lunch break?" I replied, confused.

"Uh-huh." He nodded, exposing that dimple on his left cheek.

The lunch rush was pretty slow today, so I couldn't use that as an excuse. I took a peek at my watch and nodded toward the patio seating. Since it was slightly cool today, no one was sitting out there.

"Sure . . . I have a few minutes to spare." I made sure to let him know that I had a limited time.

I was scared.

What could he possibly want to talk to me about? Everything that happened between us was in the past, and we both needed to leave it there. I was only here through the holidays, and then I would be back in Georgia, piecing my life together.

Rome pulled out my seat, and I gently sat down, crossing my legs. Underneath the table, I secretly played with my hands, anticipating what this conversation would entail.

"It was so good seeing you yesterday," he started.

"You sure were a sight for sore eyes," I smiled, wishing I hadn't said that.

That was something my father would have said. Rome must have thought the same thing because he stared at me in a funny way. "Ever since we ran into each other, I haven't been able to get you out of my head."

My heart stopped, and my breathing shallowed.

"Oh?"

What else was I supposed to say? The fact that he admitted that he couldn't stop thinking about me scared me. Mostly because I felt the same way. All I had been thinking about was Rome and wondering what I had missed out on in the last fifteen years.

What we could have been over fifteen years.

He put his keys on the table and stared me in the eyes. "When I saw you . . ." His voice trailed off, and he looked away. "All those good memories came rushing back. I felt good and haven't felt that in a long time."

"The same happened to me. I couldn't help but smile at some of the stupid things we used to bicker about or how you used to judge me for getting extra pancakes down at the diner."

He laughed. "Five pancakes are crazy, Fay. Even now, I don't know how you fit all that in your tiny body."

"Those pancakes at McCray's were amazing . . . I saw that he sold it."

He nodded. "After he got sick, he couldn't afford to keep it open . . . His son ended up selling it and moving him to Miami with him."

"Mr. McCray loved Sageport. He used to brag about being buried right over on the beach near his favorite spot."

I couldn't believe that McCray's had closed down. If you wanted the best pancakes for cheap, you went to McCray's. He always had a booth waiting for me or my father.

"His hands were tied. You know his wife passed when we were in high school, so it wasn't like he had anything tying him here once his son sold the diner."

"Wow, that used to be our favorite spot."

"Remember when I kissed you there . . . You got syrup right on my top lip . . . I can still taste that natural maple syrup."

I blushed, looking away.

I remembered that day as if it happened yesterday. Rome took me to get a stack of pancakes because I failed my final. It was my first failing grade in a long time, and I didn't take it well. He looked into my eyes as he poured that maple syrup all over my pancakes until I smiled.

Once I smiled, he switched spots and cut into the pancakes to feed me. He pushed the fork into my mouth and got syrup on my lips. Instead of wiping them off, he reached in and kissed me on the lips.

"You could have used the napkins that were on the table."

"What's the fun in that?" he winked, exposing that award-winning smile that I loved.

"I truly can't believe that McCray's is closed . . . I had those pancakes on my list of things I wanted to enjoy before I left."

I turned my head right in time to catch him staring at me.

"Fay, can I take you out? You've been away for a long time. Let me show you the new Sageport."

I was stunned.

Unsure of what to say or how to act.

I didn't know what this conversation would be about, and I didn't expect him to ask me out on a date. I hadn't been on a date in a very long time. How does one act when going on a date these days? I didn't even pack anything date-worthy.

It was clear that Rome either moved away and then eventually returned, or he never left town. Judging from how he knew information about McCray's, I would assume he had never left, which made me sad.

"I don't know, Rome. Do you think this is a good idea?"

I was scared.

There was so much turmoil from our past that I hated to relive it. We both had moved on with our lives, and I didn't want to bring up old things that could cause old resentments to flare up.

Rome reached his hand across the table. I surveyed the Rolex that sat perfectly on his wrist, then moved to his ring finger. He wasn't wearing a wedding ring, just a gold and onyx ring on his middle finger.

"I'm not asking for much . . . just one night to catch up. I think we owe it to ourselves."

I promised to go shopping with Marie today, and I didn't want to cancel on her. "How about Friday? I promised my father's fiancée shopping today."

He nodded his head in agreement. "Even better. Gives me time to perfect our itinerary."

"Goodness . . . Do you still plan out your days?"

He smirked. "How else will I be on time?"

"God, Rome . . . You need to let that planner go," I teased.

As a teen, I thought it was ridiculous that he planned out every moment of his day. Rome knew what he was doing from the moment he woke up to the moment he lay his head on his pillow. His football practices, gym runs, and academics were all planned accordingly.

I think the reason my father allowed us to date was because he was so organized. If he were taking me to the movies, we would make it back before curfew and before Rome's alarm went on to remind him of his night run.

"Never."

Now that I was an adult and had planned the girls' day out down to the hour, I could appreciate how organized and plan-oriented he was. Ashton was the complete opposite. He couldn't be on time or stick to a schedule to save his life. Even when he had an assistant, he could never get it right.

"I hate to admit that I follow a planner these days too," I snorted.

"Not Ms. Stone . . . You hated my planner with a passion. Didn't you try to throw it in the fireplace that year?"

"Rome Atkins!" I squealed. "You *know* that was an accident . . . You *tickled* me."

"Hmm, that's debatable. I remember you balling her up while trying to toss her into the fireplace."

"You are a storyteller," I accused.

We both shared a laugh. "I missed you, Fay."

"I missed you too, Rome," I admitted.

This conversation felt good because we were discussing the good times. What happens when we revisit some of the not-so-happy memories? I didn't want to leave Sageport more traumatized than before.

Rome quickly looked at his watch. "Give me your phone to program my number into it."

I handed him my phone and watched as he entered his number. When he handed it back to me, we stood and hugged.

I melted into his arms as he wrapped them around me. We hugged for a few seconds longer than expected before we broke our embrace. "I'll walk you up to the front."

He held the door open for me as we walked through the restaurant. More people had filed in for lunch. I smiled and greeted some on my way to the front.

"I probably should have gotten some lunch too," Rome laughed. "See you Friday, Fay."

"Friday," I confirmed, excited and nervous, all in the same breath.

"Have a good day, Fay."

"You too."

Trixie stood at the hostess booth on her phone. My father made sure I knew that he hated phones while working. All the employees knew how he felt about them, so I didn't understand why she would pull out her phone.

I wasn't as strict as my father regarding the staff using their phones. If you need to check your messages or calls, duck off to the side and do it. Trixie was right at the front on her phone while customers were walking in.

She had finally looked up from her phone, and that was when she noticed that both Rome and I were standing there. I watched as she quickly put her phone into the pocket of her apron and smiled at the party of three waiting on her.

"Welcome to Carl's ... How many are with your party today?"

The woman looked fed up. Rome noticed the interaction and saw his way out while I decided to step in. "Welcome to Carl's ... I'll get you seated. Right this way, please," I smiled and led the lady to one of the best seats in the house.

It was a round table near the kitchen. Your food came out quicker, and if you weren't on your phone, you caught a glimpse of the chef cooking your food. I could tell my father had put a lot of work into the renovations of this place.

It still kept that homey charm with a modern twist. "Thank you ... Rodney loves this seat," the woman smiled.

Her mood had improved.

When I used to waitress, I learned a long time ago that a happy customer was an easy customer. The woman was already irritated that she had to wait while Trixie sat on her phone.

"Isn't that perfect ... Today must be your lucky day," I gently pinched the little boy's cheek. "My name is Faith, so if you need anything, please let me know."

"Faith ... as in Faith's Shepherd's Pie?"

I smiled.

Since coming back, I hadn't browsed the menu. Marie usually had dinner prepared when I returned to the house, so other than a quick salad between the lunch and dinner rushes, I hadn't had time to try anything new.

Faith's Shepherd's Pie wasn't anything new. My father had this shepherd's pie on his menu since he opened the place. It was one of his most popular dishes, next to the meat loaf and candied yams.

"Yes, ma'am," I beamed with pride.

"It's Laila's favorite meal. It's the only time I can get her to eat something other than McDonald's." She teased her daughter, who was too occupied with her tablet.

That was why I had a no-screens policy during dinner for the twins. I had tried allowing them to use their screens when we went out to eat so we could keep the peace. While they were quiet during dinner and didn't cause a scene, they never ate and were so stimulated by their tablets that they had no clue what was happening around them.

"I'm glad that she loves it. When I was her age, it was my favorite too . . . Enjoy your meal."

I quickly excused myself and went to the front, where Trixie assisted another party. I took over the hostess booth while she showed them to their table.

"Faith, I'm sorry for being—"

"I'm nice . . . Maybe even too nice. My father has his rules, and while I may disagree with them, I respect them. I cut you guys slack to check your phones in the back. To sit up here with your phone out was a slap in the face, Trixie."

"You're right, and I apologize for that."

"Thank you." I took a breath.

I didn't want to come off as a bitch who acted like the boss's daughter. However, I didn't want her to think she could get over on me. She already showed up late twice this week, and I let it slide.

First, it was car problems; then her dog had gotten sick. I didn't want Trixie to think I would keep allowing her to slide with all the excuses she made.

"So, Fay . . . You and Rome Atkins must go back deep—nicknames," she smirked, causing me to blush.

Trixie was that employee you wanted to fire every week, then decided against it because you would be bored without her around. I knew that was probably the reason my father kept her around. More than anything, she kept him young with her shenanigans.

"Get back to work." I walked back toward the bar where I had been sitting before Rome walked up on me.

"Actually, I'm on lunch . . . so you can just spill the tea while I eat this sandwich." She skipped over and took a seat beside mine.

Trixie was twenty-eight, single, and lost on what she wanted to do with her life. I knew this because she and the cook seemed to be cool with each other.

I think he liked her, but that was beside the point. At her age, I was already a mother and wife with a host of responsibilities. I would never say I regret my daughters. Nonetheless, I probably would have killed to be carefree and kid-free like Trixie was at twenty-eight.

I never truly got to live my life for myself. Before the girls, I lived for my husband and did what I thought he needed.

Making his life easier.

Then when we got pregnant with the girls, my life transferred to being their mama. It wasn't a job I took lightly, and I loved being their mama. Some days, I thought about my life and questioned if I had been living my life for me.

"We dated back in high school. I moved away, and I guess he stayed back."

"You guess? You didn't keep in touch with him?"

"Did you keep in touch with your ex-boyfriends from high school?"

She paused and pondered the question. "Well, I would, except he's locked up. Attempted murder on his roommate . . . but he was the best fuck of my life, so I would have kept in touch if he didn't get arrested."

I stared at Trixie for a few seconds before I shook my head.

"Girl, you sound crazy. Why did you even move to Sageport . . . Nobody *ever* moves here. We all move away."

"I love the beach and needed to escape the big city."

"What big city?"

"Charlotte. I wanted someplace new and small . . . a place where the people smile when they greet you."

"And you felt Sageport was the place to go?"

"Not exactly. My plan was Tampa or Miami, but I saw the sign while driving here and decided to stop for a night."

"And never left."

"Nope. This place gave me a good feeling, so I rented a room and walked over here to apply. Your father hired me right on the spot . . . old man saved my life."

"If he hears you calling him an old man . . ." I giggled.

"I tease him with it all the time," she said, taking a bite out of her sandwich. "I know I'm not his favorite person, and I constantly get on his nerves, but I think he keeps me around because I remind him of you."

"I can see that," I lied.

Trixie and I were nothing alike. While I was quiet and timid sometimes, she was the complete opposite. Trixie was the type who said what she was thinking.

"Anyway, I guess you should know that Rome and I went out on a few dates."

I raised my eyebrows. "Really?"

"Yeah, but I decided we were better off just being friends. He has a lot going on, and I'm not sure I'm the kind of woman he needs."

Everything inside of me wanted to pry. What did she mean he "had a lot going on"? Did he have children? Had he gone through a divorce too? I played it cool and continued to look over my father's social media pages for the restaurant. The last time anybody had posted on them was over three years ago.

Social media was a big part of a restaurant's success. With people like Keith Lee, you wanted to have social media so that people knew where to find you. While looking through my father's pages, I could tell it had been neglected. Sageport was a small coastal town that generated a lot of tourists because of the beaches and our white sand.

With the foot traffic the city center got, my father's restaurant should have been blowing up on TikTok for the portion sizes alone.

"Do you know who was running the social media for the restaurant?"

Trixie shook her head as she chewed. "Your father swears by word of mouth. I told him people barely even speak anymore . . . Everyone is always on their phones."

And she was right.

My father was used to doing things the old-school way. Since I have been here, this place hasn't been empty. The lunch rush may have slowed down some, but there were still butts in each of those seats.

"He's so old school," I mumbled.

"It took all of us to convince him to add to-go orders. Some people don't have the time to sit and have a meal. If they're like me, they want their food so they can go and be greedy in peace."

"I feel you," I snickered.

If I could grab my food and eat at home, it would be a win for me. As much as I enjoyed getting cute, going out to dinner, and experiencing the restaurant's ambiance, I enjoyed sitting in my house watching my favorite shows while eating too.

Ashton and I got creative when we had the twins. Our fancy dinners had stopped, but we still wanted to have that time for ourselves. We would order from our favorite restaurant and set the dining table after we put the girls down.

That was when we both equally tried.

I missed the way we would talk and laugh about everything. Most of our conversations revolved around the girls and the silly things they had done during the day while he was at work.

I would scoot next to him and show him what I had recorded, happy that I could keep him updated on our girls.

Those home dates stopped shortly after. Neither of us tried to set one up because we were both tired.

"So, what's Friday?"

"You weren't that consumed with your phone."

She smiled. "Don't try to deflect from the date you have planned with Rome Atkins."

"I'm not deflecting. He asked me to hang out on Friday . . . It's not a date," I tried to convince myself, although Rome had used the word numerous times.

I was trying not to get myself excited. My nerves were already bad, and Friday was two days away. "Sure, sounds like it . . . Rome loves Carl's, but he doesn't come in twice in the same week."

"Stop making this more than what it is. We're two friends reconnecting and catching up . . . nothing more."

"Yeah, you can say that all you want. I know a match made in heaven when I see it." She checked her phone, cleaned up her trash, and strutted off.

"Work the tables for the dinner rush," I called behind her.

"Sure thing, boss." She winked and went toward the back.

I shook my head and continued my deep dive down on social media. Before I left, I was determined to get some buzz on the internet about Carl's.

Chapter Eleven

ROME

"**O**NE BEER ALWAYS turns into six with you, Pat. I got an early morning tomorrow, and I'm not trying to stay out late," I told my best friend, Patrick.

Whenever he wanted to meet at the bar for a drink after work, I ended up nursing a hangover the following day. It never stopped at one beer when it came to Pat.

"When was the last time we got a beer together? It's been months, Ro . . . Come on," he tried to convince me.

"*One* beer," I reminded him.

"Yeah, one beer . . . I heard you."

Patrick and I played on the football team together. In high school, we weren't the best of friends. We were cordial and hung out anytime the whole team was hanging out. It wasn't until my brother passed away that he reached out to me.

He started by bringing me my missing work. Then that turned into bringing over video games to help get my mind off everything happening. Pat didn't know how much I needed that and a friend.

I had not only lost my brother but also my girlfriend too. My parents were fighting and going through their own grieving process, so I was lonely. Pat would come over after school and chill. Some days, we never said anything. Just his presence alone was comforting.

Since then, he has been there for every major change I have gone through. Like when we were teens, he would just show up with my favorite food and a shoulder. No words ever had to be exchanged. His presence was just needed.

"Anyway, now that we got *that* out of the way . . ." He held open the door to our favorite bar.

Mizzy's was the only original bar that was around. We used to sneak in here to grab beers when we were in high school. Mizzy never cared about the legal age limit, which is why his liquor license had been revoked several times throughout the year.

He always got it back, no matter how often it was taken. With all the fancier bars in Sageport, we needed a down-and-dirty dive bar where we could talk our shit and shoot pool in.

"It doesn't make no sense that I always have to give you this pep talk before we come."

"Yeah, whatever. I had a stressful day at the shop."

Pat went on to open his own mechanic shop. The dealerships frequently utilized his shop whenever we had a car come in that needed to be fixed.

"It's been hectic at the dealerships too. I had to fight my way out to take lunch . . . and I didn't even *eat* lunch."

"Then what the hell did you do?"

"Went to Carl's."

"Oh yeah? How is Mr. Stone? I heard he wasn't well not too long ago." Pat accepted the beer from the bartender.

"Why did everyone else know except me?"

Pat guzzled half of his beer. "Because you work and go home . . . I damn near have to force you to come out of the house." He polished off the rest of his beer. "Why did you go to Carl's and not get any food?"

"Faith was there."

Pat's eyes widened as he signaled for his second beer—after he told me we would have *one*. I hadn't even had my first beer, and here he was, signaling for his second.

"Faith Stone is back in town? How did that fly under my radar?"

"I'm surprised your nosy ass didn't know before me."

"So, damn, she's really back?"

"For the holidays, at least."

"How does that make you feel? I remember when you broke up with her and were going through it."

"I didn't break up with her," I defended.

"Then what would you call it? You allowed her to leave town without a goodbye, and you haven't checked in on her in years . . . You *broke up* with her."

I didn't consider Faith and I breaking up. We never shared those words, only the emotions. I was so angry with her and had no reason to be. Faith didn't get behind that wheel and kill my brother. We missed out on a life together because I let my anger take over.

When the dust had settled, I thought I had time to fix things between us. But by that time, she had already moved out of town, and I was too hurt to look for her. If she didn't feel the need to stay behind for me, then maybe things weren't worth fixing between us.

Now that she was back, I felt like this was a second chance at something we both missed out on. I wanted to know what the past years have been like for her. She obviously had kids since I overheard her talking to them earlier.

I wanted to know more, though.

I wanted to get to know the Fay I had let slip through my fingers fifteen years ago. Time had hopefully healed some of our wounds, and maybe we could fix things between us.

I was harsh to her that night.

She didn't deserve the way I acted toward her, and it had been on replay in my head since I had run into her at her father's restaurant the other night. As much as I was in pain that night, I was still a selfish asshole to her, and she never deserved that from me.

"Either way, you have a second chance . . . What are the odds that she came back to celebrate Christmas with her father? I thought she died because of the way Mr. Stone acted. He never speaks about her."

"Yeah, I know. I figured she was married or something."

"How are you not sure she's not married? Maybe hubby is driving up here after work gets out."

"Then why was she wishing her kids a safe flight?"

"Shit, you heard all that?"

"Yeah. I don't know the situation yet, but we're going out on Friday."

"My man!" Pat dapped me up.

I tried to talk myself out of asking her on a date, even brushed it off as something I needed to leave in the past.

But I couldn't.

I couldn't brush Faith off like she was just an old high school friend. She meant more to me than that. Faith was the only woman who had ever meant something to me. I wanted to marry her and have a future with her. We would lie in her bed and talk about our future. Some nights, when I lay awake in bed, I thought about the future that I almost had.

It was right in my hands, and I could feel it.

Nothing was worse than having the future you always envisioned ripped out of your hands in a flash. Neither of us knew that night would alter our lives and rip us away from each other.

Our futures were altered.

Our relationship was ruined while both of us suffering losses. My biggest regret would always be not being there for her the way she wanted to be for me. Had I not been so deep in grief and hurt, we could have healed each other with time and patience.

"I just clocked in, so if you need anything, let me know." Yasmine winked as she tied the apron around her waist.

I watched as she walked toward other patrons who needed her help. Pat bit the back of his hand while watching her swish away.

"Damn, she knows she fire as hell," he continued to gawk at her ass—an ass I had hit more times than a few.

I polished off the rest of my beer. "You say that every time she works."

"You're wild for breaking things off with her."

Whenever Yasmine worked, he gave me the same half speech about ending things with her. "Drop it. We're cordial, and that's all I care about."

"Cordial? There's a lot of things I want to be with her, but being cordial isn't one of them," he snickered.

I shook my head. "Yas is good people . . . I didn't want to waste her time. She was ready for something that I wasn't ready for."

Yasmine was ready and willing to accept all the baggage that I came with. I never had to question if things were too much for her. She knew about my family and all we had gone through.

I wanted to love her how she was trying to love me. Everything inside of me wanted to make something work with Yasmine. My mother loved to sit and talk to her, although she always asked who she was. Everything about her was good, even the pussy.

It was a few months after I buried my father, and I had a lot of stress. I went from being the eldest son to the man of our family in a matter of months. Everyone was relying on me to step into my father's shoes and fill them.

They wanted me to make everything all right like he used to do. In good faith, I couldn't string Yasmine along because I wasn't mentally ready. Our conversations were great, and the sex was even better, but I wasn't ready for what she wanted.

She was ready for marriage, children, and everything that came after you committed yourself to each other. How could I be prepared to be a father when I was practically raising my mother?

I knew I couldn't stop living my life because of my mother, but I felt like she needed me more. I had to dedicate all my remaining energy and time to her. That wasn't fair to Yasmine, so I broke it off with her.

It was hard.

Hard ending something that you wanted to work out yourself. Marrying Yasmine would have been taking the easy way out. Even with our great chemistry, I knew she wasn't the one for me. I didn't know what I had been looking for at the time, but now, I know it was Faith.

In some weird way, I feel God brought her back to Sageport for me. I hadn't found the one because he was bringing her back to give us a second chance that many didn't receive, and I couldn't let it pass me by.

For years, I had allowed life to pass me by because I was too afraid to live. I was more concerned with making sure that my mother's care came first. Although my mother wasn't Faith's biggest fan, I knew she would have wanted me to be happy.

"At least you're honest about it. Many men would have wasted her time just to keep getting more of her."

I chuckled. "A lot of men . . . or you?"

"I'm a man, right?"

Pat was a certified man-whore. If you asked him who he was dating, you would receive six different answers and even more names. Settling down was never his style, and I never judged him for it.

All of us couldn't be so lucky to find the one straight out of high school. Most of the guys on the team moved away and played college football. A few stayed back in town and were either married, divorced, or had children.

Pat and I were the only two not married or had kids. While that was perfectly fine with Pat, I often thought about it. At the time, I wasn't ready or prepared for what Yasmine wanted. As I've grown older, I often thought about a life with a wife and some children.

When my mother was first diagnosed with dementia, I read so many medical journals and articles about the disease. A few articles suggested spending time with children was great for those suffering from the disease.

"Shit!" Pat looked at his phone.

"Everything good?"

"Got to pick up Reese from work. Forgot I was using her car this week." He kissed his teeth and tossed money on the bar. "This round was on me."

"Round? I had only one beer, to begin with. How did you forget you were using . . . never mind. Hit me whenever." We dapped hands, and he quickly exited the bar.

Yasmine sauntered over and grabbed the loose bills that Pat had tossed onto the bar.

"Pat left a pretty decent tip this go-round," she smiled.

"How you been?"

Yasmine did hair at the hair salon in town. We remained cordial over the years because she came to the house and washed Mama's hair for free. She adored my mother and would never take out any ill feelings she felt toward me on her.

"Tired . . ." She hit the button on the cash register and stuffed the money inside. "How about you? I feel like I haven't seen you here in forever."

"Been busy with work and Mama."

She smiled. "How is Mrs. Atkins? I haven't been by the house in a while to wash her hair . . . Please tell me you're not using dishwasher soap."

"Quit playing like I don't know how to wash hair," I laughed. "If you must know, her aide handles her hair pretty well."

"That's good. Guess you wanted to just cut me out of your life completely," she gently pinched me.

"Stop. Don't be like that."

"I'm kidding." She tucked her hair behind her ear. I peeped the engagement ring on her finger, and she knew I saw it. "Are you going to ask?"

"Are you going to answer?"

"Maybe."

I licked my lips. "Are you happy?"

That was the only thing that I truly cared about. Even though Yasmine and I didn't work out, I still cared about her. I wanted to make sure that she was well taken care of.

"We have our moments. He does make me happy and loves me," she replied.

"That's all I care about."

She offered me a weak smile. "I'm going to miss you . . . miss Sageport."

I half-expected her fiancé to be someone from here. "You're moving?"

"After the holidays. He owns a home in Denver, so I'm going to move to be with him."

"Denver? What's up in Denver? . . . You really going to leave the best weather for the snow?"

She pinched my cheek. "We all have to leave Sageport one day, Rome. I've been here my entire life . . . It's time for something new."

I felt her.

Except I didn't have that option. My entire life was here, and I was stuck in this town like a rat in a sticky trap. It didn't matter how much they changed or how many fast-food places they placed here. There was no escaping this town.

"You deserve that, Yas."

"Thank you. I'm just working at the bar to save more money. When I move there, I won't be working for a while, so I want to have my own money saved."

"Smart. Don't hesitate to call me if you ever need something from me." I grabbed her hand.

"Thank you, Rome . . . I do appreciate that."

She smiled before going to refill someone's drink. "I heard Faith Stone has returned. Walked into Carl's, and she was running things like she never left," one man said.

"Carl did right by getting her out of this town. No kid should have to live with the consequences of her drunken mother," the other one replied.

I went into my wallet and took out a few bills to leave on the bar top. Even though Pat had just paid for our beer, I added a little something extra for her. Yasmine was a good woman, and her fiancé was a lucky man. I wished her the best and was happy she was leaving this town for love.

If only I had been that brave.

Chapter Twelve

FAITH

MAYBE THIS WAS too much.

I shouldn't have accepted this invitation because I was nervous. I had been running around all day like a chicken with its head cut off. The staff was excited that my father came today to poke his head in. Nothing could keep this man away from his restaurant, not even a mild stroke.

He would have tried to stay until closing, except Marie reminded him of his doctor's appointment a few doors down. The only reason he was able to convince her to come inside was because they had to walk past the restaurant. He had spent so many years building this restaurant along with its reputation.

Nothing could keep him away from here.

I was satisfied to know that he approved of the job I was doing. Everyone was easy to work with and respected me. I felt weird having to come in here and take control.

To them, I was a ghost that my father never really spoke about.

As much as I felt weird, I also felt a sense of empowerment. I had been a stay-at-home mom and wife for years, so it felt nice to be needed. Every morning when I woke up to head to the restaurant, I felt like I had a purpose.

It reminded me of the time before I became someone's wife or mama. I had a job and needed to earn a paycheck, although I refused to accept any money from my father.

Ashton's alimony checks were doing just fine. He had to pay alimony and all the bills for the next three years. Now, I understood why he wanted to work all the time.

It still didn't excuse him.

My phone chimed, alerting me of a text message.

Found myself thinking about you, Fay. Hope you're having a good day so far.

I smiled when I read Rome's text message. He hadn't been into Carl's since he popped up on me during lunch.

I am now. Thank you for putting a smile on my face.

It's been so long . . . I need to know if seafood is still your favorite food.

Can't believe you remember that.

I watched you put away a pound of crawfish and shrimp. I don't think anyone can forget that.

I giggled until Ashton's name popped across my screen. As nice as it was to text and feel those butterflies I had for Rome, Ashton's call reminded me that my life wasn't the same as it was all those years ago.

"Hey," I dryly answered.

The girls had called me from their iPads earlier this morning. Mayven was homesick and wanted to be with me.

I knew the girls loved spending time with their dad. It was a change of scenery for them. They didn't visit their grandparents' house often, and with all their family flying in, I knew it was overwhelming for them.

"How's it going out there?"

"Great. I'm helping Dad out as much as I can."

"How is Carl doing?"

"Better."

"Oh, okay."

The conversation was forced. He was trying to figure out what to say next. I sat with the phone to my ear, wanting the conversation to end.

"Ash, everything all right?"

"Y . . . Yeah. We're good over here. I figured I should tell you that Francis is spending Christmas with us."

This is what I hated about Ashton. His lack of communication had always been a problem for me. I thought as our marriage matured, or even us, that he would grow into being more open and able to communicate openly with me.

First, he didn't think telling me about his girlfriend was important. Then he introduced his girlfriend to our girls without so much as a conversation with me. Now, he was taking her to spend the holidays with his family. Not once did he call or even ask me if I was OK with that.

If I had a boyfriend, I would have at least cared about his feelings. This was the first Christmas we were spending separately, so I would have taken that into consideration. I hated to even play the bad guy because he would just assume that I was jealous or wanted him back, which was far from the truth. I didn't want to be the jaded, jealous ex-wife. All I wanted was some open communication from him.

Yes, I was hurt when he revealed that he had a girlfriend. I was hurt because it took a hell of a lot more energy to date someone new than to work on your marriage.

It was typical of Ashton to take the easy way out, and this new girlfriend was the easy way out. "Thank you for telling me."

"The girls already told you, huh?"

"They did. Wish it would have come from you instead."

He drew a breath. "I figured that it would send you over the edge."

I laughed to myself. "The edge? I don't care about your girlfriend, Ashton. I care about you parading this woman around our kids without talking to me about it."

"You're right. I fucked up," he admitted.

I was shocked that the words even left his mouth. Usually, he accused me of overreacting. "You did."

"Faith . . ." he paused.

My stomach became queasy. I didn't like the way the tone of his voice had changed. "Ashton, is everything all right?"

"I got a job offer."

"Okay . . ."

"It's in New York. I would have to move to New York for this new position. It's a great position, Faith. More money for you and the girls."

"Please don't add me into the mix."

"How could I not? I pay you alimony and all your expenses," he reminded me like he always did when he brought up selling the house.

"Please don't act like I'm running around here spending all your money. I do it for the girls."

"I'm not saying that," he sighed.

"You're barely around for the girls as is . . . What does this mean now? Even more broken promises? I . . . I can't keep cleaning up your mess, Ashton."

"I'm not asking you to. I'm just doing this for my girls. That's two college tuitions we have to afford, Faith."

"They're eight years old, Ash. Who knows if they even want to attend college? I think they would rather their father be around than a fat college tuition."

I know my girls well enough to know they would be heartbroken. They wanted their father around more than he was now. When he moved out of our home, that was hard for them. I can only imagine how they would feel with him moving to a new state.

"I can't let this opportunity slide past me, Faith."

It was always a promotion, opportunity, or something bigger he was always chasing. I loved how ambitious and driven he was when we first met. It was one of the qualities I admired about him. But when was it ever enough?

When would he finally realize that his girls were all he needed? If he had a great career and his daughters, that was all that should have mattered to him.

"What do you want me to say? Make it better for you . . . Do your dirty work by talking to the girls about it? There's a reason you called."

Trixie walked into the office, and I shooed her out the door.

"I want you to be okay with it too."

"I'm never going to be okay with you wanting to split our family further apart."

"You already did that, Faith. Don't put that on me."

My mouth dropped as I looked at my phone in disbelief. "Wow, Ashton . . . That's low."

"I'm sorry—"

"You already know what you want to do. We're not married anymore, so you don't need to run it by me."

"We share children together."

"How about you make this decision without me? You know . . . like when you introduced that woman to our daughters without discussing it with me. Kiss my babies for me." I ended the call.

Ashton wanted me to make him feel better about the decision he had already made. My ex-husband didn't just learn about this new New York job opportunity.

He had already known about it for months. I knew this man better than he knew himself, which is why he wanted to call me to talk about it. Ashton was either seconds or days away from accepting a proposal from the company, and he wanted to see how I felt about it.

I was already a divorced, single mother doing my best to make sure the girls didn't feel like they were missing out on anything. In a perfect world, things would have been like they used to be.

Except this wasn't a perfect world.

We were now divorced, and he was accepting a job in a new state. I didn't even want to know if the girlfriend was moving to be with him. It all made sense why Ashton wanted to spend the holidays in New York. More than likely, he would be handling work and trying to secure a new place. The girlfriend was definitely going to move with him.

"Hey, the lunch you ordered was dropped off." Trixie held a paper bag in her hand.

I guess that was why she had come into the office before I shooed her away. "I didn't order any lunch today."

"Well, someone must have bought you some . . . I need to get back to the front." She quickly placed the paper bag onto the desk and headed back out.

I opened the bag, and the aroma from the garlic made my mouth water. I snatched the receipt and read the handwriting on the back.

Wanted to make sure you kept that smile on your face. This has become a favorite of mine.—Rome

I opened the tin container and smiled at the charbroiled Parmesan garlic oysters. On the side were some cocktail sauce, horseradish, crackers, and lemons.

Oysters were my favorite food. You couldn't live in a coastal town without seafood being your favorite food. My father used to bring home oysters every Friday. We would sit at the kitchen table and shuck them open before popping our favorite condiments on them and gobbling them up.

Those were some of my favorite memories with him. It felt like the longer I was here, the more I could remember the good memories I shared with my father. I couldn't, in good faith, shoot him a text message, so I pressed his number in my phone.

"I take it that you received your lunch."

"I did . . . I didn't know that I needed lunch dropped off for me," I blushed, taking a seat.

"Figured you were busy and didn't have time to feed yourself."

"Well, that was sweet of you, Rome. Oysters are my favorite."

"I'm glad to hear that they still are."

I pictured his perfect smile, cute dimple, and the twinkle in his eyes. "What are you doing right now?"

"Are you sure you want to know?"

"Yes. I do."

"Heading to the Pinewoods Farm to cut down a tree for one of the dealerships."

"Well, I didn't know you were that kind of person who decorated at work," I teased.

His boisterous laugh warmed me. "Linda in HR has been on me about putting some holiday cheer around the office."

"Maybe I should get a tree for my dad's house."

"I could use the company."

I had been at the restaurant since this morning and was due to leave soon. "If it's not too much, you can swing by and pick me up. Let me give Trixie the rundown."

"See you in a bit."

I packaged my food back up and brought it to the front with me. "Leaving?"

"Yes. Do you think that you can handle everything?"

"Faith, I know everything there is to know about this place," she said, waving me off.

I shouldn't be as worried about leaving Trixie in charge. She had been working here before I even came into town, so she knew how to run things. I think she tolerated me out of respect because I was the owner's daughter.

"Please let me know if things become too overwhelming."

She smiled. "Faith, go and enjoy the rest of your day. I know you probably have some Christmas shopping you have to do."

I hadn't thought about Christmas until today when Rome mentioned going to get a tree. Without my girls, I just wasn't in the Christmas spirit. But even with me not being in the Christmas spirit, I wanted to do something nice for my father.

It had been so long since we spent any holiday together, so I wanted to show him that I was excited to be here and spending it with him. This holiday would be hard without my girls, but it was something I needed to get used to. There would be many more holidays that would have to be split, and I had to get used to our new normal.

When the door chimed, Trixie and I both turned to look. Rome had stepped in from the outside with his hands inside his denim jacket.

"Hey, you ready?"

"Yep. Trixie, call me if you need anything," I reminded her.

Trixie was like your teenage daughter, blocking everything you said until they needed that useful information.

"See you tomorrow!" she called behind us.

Rome held open the passenger door to his Range Rover for me. I nodded in approval. This was the same model that I had begged Ashton to get me when the girls turned five.

He didn't think I needed a car that expensive to chauffeur the girls back and forth to school. Meanwhile, he drove the newest Mercedes and upgraded every year.

It wasn't like I drove around in a lemon or anything. I was a mom, so there wasn't much for me anymore. That car would have made me feel normal again, as if I was appreciated for giving birth to his girls and raising them to be respectable young women.

"I see you brought your food with you for the ride," he smirked while getting into the car.

"I forgot to ask . . . Just how long is this ride?"

"It's an hour's drive."

"Well, if you don't mind eating in your car . . . I can just eat my meal on the way."

He looked over at me briefly before pulling out of the parking space. "Do you . . . only if you're going to share."

"How does that work? You bought me the food to mooch off my plate?"

We shared a laugh.

It felt nice to laugh again and mean it. For the past year, I felt like I had been on autopilot, laughing, smiling, and existing on cue. Whenever I saw a neighbor, I pretended all was well in my world. All the PTA moms knew about the divorce and whispered behind me. Despite knowing that they were whispering, I was expected to show up and act like everything was picture-perfect.

It was never perfect.

They didn't see the nights I drank myself to sleep or cried in the shower. I had a routinely scheduled cry session in the shower these days. I wanted to be strong for my girls. It didn't matter that I asked for a divorce. I had to be the one who was strong for myself and the girls. I couldn't appear weak to the outside, although I was breaking with every day that passed.

Meanwhile, Ashton was off dating, breaking promises, and living his life. He didn't have to sit and have a million conversations about divorce. I didn't see him browsing Barnes & Noble to find children's books on divorce. He never had to worry about any of those things. All he was responsible for was packing his things and sending movers to take them to his new place.

Divorce sucked.

"I gotta eat too . . . I'm doing all the driving while you're playing passenger princess."

"Passenger princess is my favorite role to play." I messed around with the knobs. "Especially when it comes with heated seats."

"You seem very familiar with the knobs and fobs over there," he mentioned.

"This car was on my vision board for three years straight."

"Never made the jump?"

"My husban . . ." I coughed. "My *ex*-husband said it was an unnecessary purchase."

"Fresh in the divorce process?"

I snapped my head in his direction. "How'd you know?"

"You said 'husband' and quickly corrected yourself. Only a freshly divorced person would make that mistake."

"We're coming up on a year divorced," I revealed.

I felt like a failure, admitting that I was divorced. Why did I feel like damaged goods?

"Sorry about that."

"I asked for the divorce." I felt the need to add.

He raised his eyebrow with an impressed expression. "It's not every day you hear the wife wanting the divorce."

I opened the container up and started spreading my condiments on the oysters. My mouth was watering from the aroma coming from them. They were still nice and hot when I used my little fork and popped one into my mouth.

"I couldn't continue to lie to myself anymore. Neither of us was happy, and we were doing it for the kids more than anything."

"Faith Stone is a whole mother out here. I didn't think I would live to see the day," he joshed.

"Oh, please. I always said I wanted to be a mother."

"Yeah, after you became a Supreme Court judge, an astronaut, and a lawyer," he laughed.

Being with Rome reminded me of everything I wanted to accomplish in my life. I had such big dreams for myself. We planned to leave Sageport and become something. We would be long distance for a while and then eventually move into our condo overlooking Central Park.

Yeah. Our dreams were massive and a little unrealistic—but they were still ours.

"You'll be happy to know that I didn't accomplish any of those things. You're looking at a regular, suburban, stay-at-home mama."

"Can't nothing be regular about you, Fay."

I blushed, looking out the window while balancing the tray on my lap. "I'm spilling all my business . . . What about you? I know you made your mom a grandmama already."

The smile slowly disappeared from his face. "No kids."

I was cautious about how I approached the subject of his family. "Okay . . . What about a girlfriend or wife?"

"You think I would send you lunch if I had somebody I was remotely interested in?"

The silence between us was comfortable. It wasn't tense or weird like I expected it to be.

"My mother has early onset dementia."

I immediately stopped chewing my food. "Rome, God, I'm so sorry." I reached out and touched his arm.

"Thank you. We found out shortly after my father passed."

Now, I didn't want to finish my food. I started wrapping it up. "You don't have to stop eating," he said with a soft chuckle.

"I don't have an appetite anymore." I paused. "I'm sorry, Rome. I had no clue . . . My father never updated me about the comings and goings of Sageport."

"That was what was best for you. You needed to get out of here and live your life."

"I didn't live much of a life," I chuckled.

"You had love, fell out of love, made children, raising them . . . I would say that's a hell of a life to have lived so far."

While I was complaining about being a newly divorced single mother, I should have been grateful. Grateful that I had been able to escape our town and have those things.

I offered a weak smile while I continued to rub his arm. "How have you been? I mean, *really*."

Rome was always used to hiding how he felt. He was the oldest, so he was always used to putting that brave front on for Allen. Allen thought his older brother was the strongest man alive. You couldn't tell him any different when it came to Rome.

He shrugged. "I have been pushing on to push on . . . This is my life and the cards that life dealt me."

"Yeah."

I didn't have a response because I felt guilty. Guilty that I had left here and never looked back. I was so hurt that I didn't want to face him anymore. After the way his mother told me off, I knew that I had to move on. Just because I moved on didn't mean I loved Rome any less. My heart hurt every day when I thought of him. As time went on, my heart hurt less, and I didn't think about him that often.

We finally arrived at the tree farm, and Rome opened the door for me. I stepped out and watched him grab the equipment to cut down a tree. As a kid, I remember watching different families drive through town with their freshly cut trees on top of their cars. The smell of pine brought back the memories of my father trying to give me a Christmas.

He always tried.

I put my bag around me. "So, what kind of tree are we looking for?"

"Something small . . . I'm not trying to be picking up pines for months after Christmas."

"Okay, Scrooge."

He gently shoved me. "Says the person who wasn't thinking about a tree until I mentioned it."

"Touché."

We slowly walked while surveying the trees. "I'm sure your father was surprised you came into town."

"He was. I hate it had to be under these circumstances . . . He's happy, though."

"What do you think about Marie?"

"She's amazing. I love how she cares about my father." I smiled, thinking of the two of them.

Every night, they sat on the porch while listening to old-school music. Seeing my father being loved the way he loved others was comforting. Marie truly cared about him, which is why I wanted to help redecorate the house for her. She deserved to live in a home that represented her—not living in another woman's shadow.

"Her cakes be hitting too."

"Whew, I think I'm going to gain weight with how she bakes."

Rome looked down at me. "It's going to go to all the right places." I watched as he licked his lips.

"Oh, please. I remember when you swore that you loved my little booty." Rome would go on long debates about how he loved my butt.

"I did . . . I just didn't know Fay-Fay could grow something like *this*." He looked me in the eyes and swiped my booty.

"Rome!" I squealed, secretly wanting him to grab a handful of it.

It had been so long since I'd had sex and had a real man take control of my body. My toys and countless memories of the good days shared between Ashton and me kept me pleased.

"What? I wanted to see if it's as soft as it looks."

I cut my eyes at him and walked ahead. "You're going to get into trouble."

"Shit, I hope it's the good kind."

Rome's thick brown lips sent chills down my spine. I wanted to feel those lips on mine again. However, instead of being nasty, I focused on the trees.

"I think this small, cute tree will work for my dad's house."

"Damn, Fay. This one is worse than Charlie Brown's tree."

I giggled. "No, it's not . . . It's cute and has potential."

"The potential to die on our way back to Sageport."

I shoved Rome and walked over to the tree next to it. "What about this one?"

"I mean, it doesn't look like it's on his last leg . . . Guess that's an improvement."

"When did you become a tree critic?"

"I just know a good one." He walked over toward a tree that was nearby. "This's a good tree. Not too tall, full, and look." He started shaking the tree, and a minimum of pine needles fell.

"Doesn't shed too much."

"Exactly. I think this one would be nice for your dad's house. Does he know you're getting a tree?"

"Nope," I said with the biggest smile.

My father was a big fan of plastic, reusable trees. I was sure he probably stored our old tree in the attic as if it wasn't nearly twenty years old. I planned to remove those curtains and open up that window to let some air into the house.

"Why do you have that devilish-ass smirk on your face?"

"I plan on going full HGTV on my father's home. Do you know he has never changed anything? My mom's house slippers are still by the door."

"Stop lying."

"I'm serious."

"Poor Marie."

This was why Rome and I always got along. Our thoughts were the same when it came to certain things. "Exactly."

"I'm off on the weekends and Monday, so if you need a hand, let me know."

I eyed him down. "Rome Atkins, I remember you failed your workshop exit project . . . Just how can you help me out?"

"Damn, Fay. Why you gotta go there with it?"

I laughed. "I *will* need some muscle, and you have plenty of that," I batted my eyelashes.

"Why you treating me like some jock?"

"Go ahead and cut down my tree . . . Let's get going." I snapped my fingers and laughed at him.

After Rome cut down the trees, we paid for them, and the farm owner secured them on top of his truck. Like the gentleman he was, Rome opened my door for me again.

"Ready for the ride back?"

"Yes," I smiled.

Rome pulled out of the farm and headed to the expressway. I was excited that we had spent some time together. This was exactly what I needed to feel more comfortable about being in Sageport for the holidays.

The sun had already set when we pulled into my father's driveway. I spotted Marie and my father sitting on the porch in the swing.

"Why do I feel like we're teenagers again, and you're dropping me off after a date?"

"Don't feel like that yet . . . We still have Friday." He touched my cheek and then got out of the car. "How are you doing, Mr. Stone? Hi, Marie."

"Doing much better than I look. I hope my daughter has told you all the ways she and my fiancée are forcing me to rest."

"Dad, you need to rest your body. Marie and I have things handled," I assured him as I put my purse onto my shoulder.

Rome started to untie the tree from his roof.

"Faith, please don't tell me you got us a tree?" my father groaned.

It wasn't that my father disliked Christmas. He never had a reason to celebrate it with me living out of state. He called in the morning to wish us a happy holiday and then headed into the restaurant to ensure everything was in order for Christmas lunch and dinner.

Marie stood up and started to clap her hands. "A tree! I wanted to get one myself but knew how Clyde felt about them."

"We have a perfectly brand-new one up in the attic."

"Daddy, that tree is almost twenty years old . . . We're going to enjoy this new and fresh pine tree . . . You smell that?" I sniffed the air.

He couldn't help but laugh. "Faithy." All he could do was shake his head and allow my shenanigans.

"Let me go and clear out some space for it." Marie quickly went inside the house as Rome lowered the tree down.

My father slowly stood up. "I guess I need to blame you, Rome," he winked.

"I'm innocent in all of this, Mr. Stone." Rome pled the Fifth.

It took him less than ten minutes to carry the tree into the house and place it in the stand. Marie was all too giddy about having a real tree in the house.

"I'm going to walk him to his car," I called over my shoulder to Marie and my father.

"Have a good night, Rome," they both called back.

Rome shoved his hands into his pocket as we slowly walked back to his car.

"Thank you for today."

"I should be thanking you . . . That hour-long trip would have been boring without you riding shotgun in the car."

"Awe, you're sweet."

"I'll let you get back to decorating your tree. Your father has some decorations," he teased, knowing I shut my father down about the withering Christmas decorations he was trying to get me to dig out.

"Oh, be quiet—"

My words were cut short when Rome covered my lips with his. My hands stayed stiff, unsure where to put them or what to do with them. He slowly broke our kiss, then pecked me on the lips once more.

"I've been wanting to do that since I first saw you ... Have a good night, Fay." He walked backward to his car.

"Um ... By ... Bye, Rome," I stammered.

My heart had been jolted back to life with the feel of his lips on mine. I stood at the curb while he pulled out of the driveway and headed down the street.

"Hmm."

I jumped when I heard Marie's voice from behind me.

"It was nothing." I tried to brush it off like it was an innocent kiss. I sat on the swing because I truly needed to process this before going in.

Marie took a seat beside me. "Clyde told me about you guys' history with each other."

"So, you know why this is a terrible idea. We shouldn't even try to revisit or explore our old feelings."

"That's even *more* a reason for you both to revisit what was lost. You both were very young when this happened."

"So much pain has occurred, Marie. Neither of us can start something without revisiting what happened. Our relationship wouldn't last if we did that."

"So, revisit them."

I shook my head. "That's the problem. I don't want to go back there."

"You can move forward without fixing the past. Rome is a good man, and I can tell you know that."

"He told me about his mother and father. Why do I feel responsible?"

It was such a sick feeling being the daughter of an addict. Kimba had been gone for over fifteen years, and I still felt responsible for her wrongs. You couldn't tell me that I wasn't to blame myself for Allen's death.

"You couldn't have caused the cancer in his father's body or his mother's dementia. People age, and life happens."

"I'm responsible for Allen's death."

"Would he have kissed you if he believed that?"

Marie was making perfect sense, which is what scared me. I needed to live in my delusion for a bit. Have a pity party and feel sorry for myself like I always did.

I knew it wasn't healthy to do.

It had always been my coping strategy.

"We're going out on a date Friday."

Marie placed her hand on my thigh. "I don't know the situation behind your divorce, but I do know you deserve to love and be loved again."

I watched as she stood up and headed toward the door.

"Thanks, Marie."

"Anytime, doll." She winked and closed the door behind her.

I leaned back on the swing and looked up at the stars. It had been so long since I had been kissed with such passion. Rome stared at me like I was the moon, sun, and stars. While driving back, I caught him out of the side of my eye, staring at me.

He was all too happy and excited to have me back in his life, even if that meant just for the holidays. The feeling was mutual as well, even if this was something just for the holidays.

Chapter Thirteen

ROME

I WALKED INTO THE office humming "When Will I See You Smile Again?" by Bell Biv DeVoe.

Before I came home the other night, I stopped by the dealership to set up the tree. I knew Linda would be thrilled when she arrived the following day. I stopped decorating or even caring about Christmas shortly after my father passed.

We tried to keep the holiday spirit going after Allen died, but it just never felt the same. Even though we all knew it didn't feel right, we continued to try. My father wanted to spend his last Christmas in the house surrounded by his family, so I made that happen.

My mother and I cooked and did everything we used to do as a family of four. Allen wasn't here to steal the Hershey's Kisses that went on top of the Snickerdoodle cookies. Mom and I tried to make it as familiar as we remembered.

After my father passed, I knew I didn't want to pretend anymore. Pretending hurt more than not doing anything. My mom barely got out of bed after losing my father, so it wasn't like she was looking forward to anything. I usually ordered our favorite Chinese takeout and watched whatever game happened to be on.

Had Linda asked to decorate the office last year, I probably would have turned her down.

This year felt different.

Faith Stone had a lot to do with that. Did I secretly smile when she revealed that she was divorced?

Hell yeah.

I felt like things were lining up perfectly for a reason. We were supposed to give this a second chance and make things right with each other. Enough time had passed, and we both had grown a lot.

We had both experienced life; now it was time to do what our hearts wanted. I could tell she was nervous when she stiffened up during our kiss. Still, she wanted this as much as I did. I wanted to show Faith I could be the man she needed, and she wouldn't have to worry about getting a second divorce.

"You seem pretty joyful, Rome," Linda noted and handed me a cup of coffee. "I stopped by Carl's Joe coffee shop and got the office some coffee."

Carl could give Starbucks a run for their money with the beans he used. His coffee always got me up and ready in the morning. The coffee shop was never empty and had a line anytime during the day. I was shocked that Linda could grab as many coffees as she did.

"You just made it more joyful," I said, sipping my coffee.

"Two creams and four packets of sugar . . . with a dash of honey."

"Perfect, Linda." I gave her a thumbs-up and headed into my office.

Linda worked in HR when my father was alive. He always bragged about her never missing a day of work. She was the hardest worker that we had. It didn't matter what kind of day Linda had; she always came into this office with a smile on her face.

I put my coffee and bag on the desk and plopped in my chair. While my computer started, I checked my phone for any messages I had missed during the night.

I stopped scrolling on my phone at night and refused to answer any messages during the morning. My mornings were for me, so I used them to shower, meditate, and spend time with Mama if she was awake. This morning, she was in a good mood and happened to be sitting at the counter while Pia made her breakfast.

Pia wouldn't let me leave unless I ate, so I put my keys down and had breakfast with Mama. It had been so long since we could sit and laugh together during breakfast.

Pia was even surprised by how upbeat my mom had been this morning. It usually took her an hour to get her out of bed. By the time I was leaving in the morning, she was just getting Mama in the shower.

Good morning, handsome. Have the best day.

I smiled at the text message that Faith had sent me.

I was glad to see that kiss didn't scare her away.

Morning, Fay. Man, am I excited to see you tonight.

Was that tonight? Omg.

Jk.

She quickly followed up with a "just kidding" text message. I had been looking forward to this date all week.

Since Faith loved seafood, I booked us the best table at Pier 3. The ocean and fishermen's boats were our view.

Pier 3 had the best ocean-to-table seafood I had ever tasted. I knew she would enjoy almost everything on the menu.

I was excited to sit across from her with our undivided attention. We had so much to talk about, and I wanted to make sure we were on the same page about everything.

I was excited to sit across from her and catch up. We talked on the ride to the tree farm, but things got quiet when I brought up my parents. It felt like she pulled back some.

Faith acted like her father usually acted, as if they didn't know how to handle being around me. I didn't want her to feel guilty for anything that had occurred in my life. Shit happens, and she wasn't to blame for any of it.

Not even Allen.

For so long, I would sit in anger, thinking of how reckless she had been about those keys. How could she have left them in the house with her mother? It was . . . until I sat with that thought and realized that it was selfish of me. Selfish to place that blame on Faith when she was a teenager looking to have fun.

Her mother was the adult, not her. We missed so much because we were too hurt to fix what happened. I didn't want any more time to pass us by.

I wanted Faith to know I didn't blame her.

I wanted her to forgive me.

Faith didn't stay away from Sageport because of her mother. It wasn't because of Kimba and all the horrible memories she had with her. She stayed away because of me. Faith avoided visiting her father because she didn't want to see me or run into my parents.

The memories were too painful for her to come back and visit. I wondered what changed besides her father getting sick.

On my way to work, I would drive past the restaurant and see her running it like she never left. I would catch her smiling or laughing with the customers.

Sageport needed Faith back.

I needed Faith back.

My life hadn't been the same since I left her in that hospital waiting room. I wanted to make it right with her. Show her that I could love her how she needed to be loved.

When I looked into her eyes, I could see the pain that she endured. She had been hurt, her heart neglected, and I wanted to fix all that.

I should have been there so she didn't have to go through that heartbreak. We would have probably been married and happy.

I wanted to make Faith happy.

I could tell she had been pretending to be happy for so long that she didn't know the difference. If sending her lunch put a smile on her face, then I would do it until her cheeks hurt.

"Hello?" she answered on the first ring.

"Got a quick question."

She grew quiet. "What's that?"

"When did you become a comedian."

"Rome!" I could see her face, and we weren't even on FaceTime. "You are so corny."

"I could say the same about you forgetting about our date."

"Speaking of the date . . ." She allowed her voice to trail off. "Should I dress up or down? This date is already costing me money . . . I had to buy more clothes for it."

"Spending a little bit of money to have forever isn't that bad."

"Is that right?"

"Yes, beautiful." I eyed Linda making a beeline to my office with files in her hands. "We're going to a fancy restaurant. I have to get back to work, but have a good day and keep that smile on your face."

"Fancy. Noted. I will sure try to keep it."

I hung up the phone and prepared for the mountain of files Linda had for me to sign. For the past week, I had been avoiding her and trying to get out of having to sign my name repeatedly.

I knew there had to be a specific reason she brought my coffee to me. I sipped some coffee, got my favorite pen, and prepared for her to tap on my door.

Like I guessed, she tapped on the door a few times, entered, and then closed it behind her.

"Have you thought more about if you're going to sell the dealerships?"

I knew that was the first thing that would come out of her mouth, which is why I had been avoiding Linda for the past week.

"I've given some thought," I lied.

The sale of the dealerships had been the last thing on my mind since running into Faith. I knew I had to decide soon and couldn't afford to sit here and play games.

"I could always tell when your father was fibbing." She sat down in the seat in front of the desk. "I've been working with you so long that I can tell the same."

"I have given it some thought."

"Not enough to decide on it, though."

I sighed. "I don't know . . . Just don't feel right. My father worked hard to build this, and I feel like I'm betraying him."

My father started Atkins Family Dealerships before I was born. This had always been his dream, something to leave his future kids when he left this earth. As a kid, I watched him bust his ass to make these dealerships into what they were. Everyone in Sageport respected my father and loved the dealerships. They knew when they drove one off our lots that they would get a good car and excellent service.

They also knew that Dale Atkins would be on the other end of that line if they ever needed anything involving the car. My father loved our town and made sure he donated any and every little bit of time he had to it.

I wasn't built the same.

The dealerships were *his* dreams. For so long, I had put my own dreams on the back burner because that was what was expected of me. I was supposed to hold our family down and be the perfect son for my parents. I was their only son left, so I couldn't leave them.

I didn't even know what my dreams were any more. I just knew that waking up and coming to the dealerships every morning felt like hell. I didn't wake up to chase my own dream. I was prolonging my father's dream. The dealerships were successful.

You couldn't drive down the Florida Turnpike and not see an Atkins Family Dealership sign. I was grateful that I didn't have to sit with my father's financial advisor and hear how much debt my father had accumulated.

It was the complete opposite.

The dealerships were doing so well that my mother and I never had to worry about money. His will was iron-clad with instructions he wanted me to follow.

He had so many plans for the dealerships, and I felt guilty because none of them excited me. I wanted to sell all of this to dedicate more time to living my life and enjoying the time my mother had left.

"This was Dale's dream. We all knew how much he loved this place and how his face lit up every morning he stepped through the door."

"He was such a morning person . . . Allen and I hated it."

"I think we all felt the same. While he was all chipper and happy, we were chugging our fourth cup of coffee to keep up." She let out a little laugh.

"Sounds like him."

"You don't need to make this decision overnight. I just need you to put some thought behind it. Maybe hire someone to run things so you don't have to be here daily."

"Then it wouldn't feel like AFD, Linda."

"Well, you have some paperwork to get signed so I can fax them off . . . Maybe that will help make your decision for you." She smiled and neatly stacked the files on my desk.

"Thanks."

"Your father would be proud of you no matter what. How you stepped up for your mom would make him so proud." She smiled and closed the door behind her.

Faith was all smiles as we headed toward the coast. Everyone in Sageport lived more inland and traveled the twenty minutes to the coast to get away. My family used to own a home right on the beach. I made the difficult decision to sell it when my father passed away. It was too much upkeep, and we never visited anymore.

With all the memories of Allen, my mother refused even to go. When I suggested it when my father was alive, he refused. The house was a tomb of our memories that we would never get to remake again. Our real estate agent tried to convince me to rent it out and make income from it.

I wanted to get rid of it.

It was already hard enough going in there to pack everything from our favorite beach football to our tricycles that my mother could never let go. It made sense why she refused to come to the beach house. There were too many painful memories for her. The beach house used to be her place of peace. She would pack up the car, and we'd drive down to spend our summer. Mama would yell out to us when dinner was ready and beg us to toss on sunscreen.

The last time she packed up her car and stayed there, she had two sons and a husband. I never made her visit it before I put it on the market. I don't even think she knows that we sold it. That was how out of the loop she was with things.

"I haven't been to the coast yet." Faith broke our silence.

The cool breeze entered the car while she touched up her makeup.

"It's not the same coast as it used to be. A bunch of restaurants and mega-beach houses. I usually avoid over here."

"You don't even come to your beach house anymore?"

"I sold it a few years back," I revealed.

"Oh, wow."

I have never regretted selling the beach house until now. Dinner at Pier 3, followed by holding Faith around the waist while I stood on the balcony before entering one of the bedrooms . . .

Shit.

"Ever since the accident, my mother refused to go back. Pops tried to keep it for as long as he could, but I sold it after he passed."

"I get it. Too many painful memories."

"Something like that," I replied.

Faith was like a dog with its head out the window when we turned onto the coast. "A *Dairy Queen*? Are you *kidding* me?"

"Yep. That been there for two years now."

"Liquor store and bars? Do you know how much we probably would have enjoyed this when we were younger?"

"Not your lame ass . . . You never liked to have a drink."

"When you witness your mother drink as much as mine did, you kind of steer away from alcohol."

Damn.

"What about now?"

"I have a glass of wine to help me sleep . . . side effect of a divorce," she giggled, trying to make light of what could have turned into a dark moment.

I pulled into the restaurant and waited for the valet to collect my keys. Once they did, I made my way over and opened the door for Faith. When her gold heels stepped onto the pavement, I wanted to get down on the floor and kiss them.

Her white toes were perfectly placed on the gold, six-inch heels she wore. I watched as the heels of her feet turned a beet red from the pressure of her weight on her feet. The powder-blue asymmetrical dress she wore exposed her right thigh. It glistened under the lights in the lobby of the restaurant.

Her curly hair was pushed up into a tight topknot, exposing her best features. Faith had aged like good wine, and I desperately wanted to sample it.

"You are staring at me like you want to eat me up," she whispered when we entered the restaurant.

I leaned closer to her ear. "That's because I do."

She gave an inward giggle and grabbed hold of my hand.

"Welcome to Pier 3 . . . Do you have a reservation with us tonight?"

"Yes, under Atkins."

She touched her little iPad a few times before she welcomed us with a brighter smile. "Welcome, Mr. and Mrs. Atkins. We have the best seats in the house ready for you."

"Oh, um, we—"

"Thank you." I cut off Faith and pulled her in front of me. I held her waist as we followed behind the hostess to our seats.

The enormous floor-to-ceiling windows looked like a screensaver. The sun was setting perfectly as the fishermen unloaded their boats. The purple and blue clouds reminded me of cotton candy at the state fair when I was a child.

"This is breathtaking." Faith was so amazed that I had to remind her to take a seat.

Our backs were turned from the rest of the restaurant while the water was our only view. It was like watching the National Geographic channel with a delicious meal. We sat next to each other as she continued to fawn over the view of tonight's sunset.

"I knew you would enjoy this." I smiled.

"Welcome to Pier 3. I can see the night is already starting out well . . . You have the best seats in the house."

"Really?"

The waitress turned and pointed to the view. "Do you even have to ask?" We all shared a laugh. "My name is Amanda, and I will be your waitress tonight. Tonight's special is roasted duck and lobster with a peanut and garlic glaze."

She handed both of us their electronic menus. "That sounds delicious. I don't think I ever had lobster and duck together."

"It's our version of a surf and turf . . . It's divine." Amanda continued to big up the special of the night.

"Sounds amazing." Faith continued to scan the menu.

"We'll take a bottle of your best pinot noir," I ordered.

Tonight wasn't the night to drink anything harder than wine. I wanted tonight to be memorable for both of us. Whenever I had anything stronger than wine, I became impatient and irritable.

Tonight wasn't the night for that.

"Of course. Do you have a preference for the year?" she asked.

"1973," I replied.

"Of course. I will give you a minute to review the menu while I get your bottle from the cellar."

I loved that she didn't remind me that it was a thousand-dollar bottle of wine. Nothing pissed me off more than someone reminding me the price of something.

If I knew the wine down to the year, of course, I would know how much the bottle cost. Faith was worth the pricy bottle of delicious wine.

"When did you become a sommelier?" she joked.

"I enjoy a good glass of wine occasionally. Do you remember Joe from the football team?"

"Fat Joe?"

"He's not so fat anymore," I smirked. "He got married in Napa Valley two years ago. I spent so much time tasting and learning about wine that I decided to take it on as a little hobby."

"Don't tell me you make your own wine."

"Not yet. I enjoy going to wine-tasting events out of town. I don't do it often because I can't be away from Mama too much, but I enjoy attending them."

"There's this amazing venue in Georgia . . . It's called Vinewood Wine—"

"Winery," I finished her sentence.

"You've been?"

"A few times. I haven't been in over a year, but I love to drive up and stay for a few days."

"I went for my birthday last year. Spent the entire weekend alone with my divorce papers."

"I'm sorry." I touched the small of her back.

She smiled at me. "It's all right. I think that weekend was the first time I realized I would spend a lot more time alone."

"Damn, Fay . . . You making me feel bad."

"Don't feel bad, Rome. I've had nothing but time to heal from this divorce."

"Are you, though?"

It was a serious question. I wanted to know if she had truly healed from her divorce. "Honestly, I'm not sure. Some days, I wonder if I made a mistake by ending my marriage. Then others, I'm happy I did it. More than anything, I will always regret it because of my girls."

"Why?"

She removed the stubborn strand of hair that the wind from the car made loose. "Guess I wanted to give them something I never experienced. Having two parents that were truly in love . . . just having that two-parent household."

"Fay, you used to say you wished your father divorced your mother and put you both first so that you and your dad could live happy lives."

"I remember."

"You did for your girls what you wanted your father to do for you. I don't know the situation between you and your ex, but I know you chose your girls' happiness and yours."

"It was nothing like my mom," she sniffled, trying to look up to avoid a tear from falling. "I grew tired of feeling like I was putting my all into something that never seemed enough for him. We were both unhappy, and I had the balls to call it finally. I just wanted more from my partner."

I moved closer to her. "Tell me what more you want from your *next* husband."

She turned to face me, placing her hand on my face. "I want him to love me . . . *all* of me. I want us always to put each other first, even when it hurts. I don't want him to run away or cower when things become too real." She leaned closer. "I want him to pin my hands behind my back, bend me over and spank my ass with his dick before he slams it inside of me."

My dick didn't even wait for her to finish her sentence before he stood at attention. I wanted her more than I wanted this expensive-ass bottle of wine. The way her perfectly painted brown lips moved when she told me what she wanted from me . . .

'Cause what she didn't know was that she was already telling her next husband exactly what she wanted from him.

"You want to order to go?"

"Rome," she squealed. "You looked forward all week to this date. We're *not* going to leave early."

"Shit, I'm looking forward more to everything you just told me."

She rubbed my face. "You asked what I wanted from my next husband . . . Who says that's you?"

I nodded and looked at Amanda as she brought over the wine. She carefully popped the cork and poured us a glass before setting it inside the ice bucket.

"All right, lovebirds . . . Do we know what we want tonight?"

"I'm going to do the crab cake risotto with a side of broccolini." Amanda used her tablet and typed in my order.

"I think I'm going to try the special tonight," Faith decided.

"Charbroiled oysters as well. You can bring those out first," I added.

"Sounds good. I just put those in . . . Please let me know if you need anything else," she replied before going to the next table.

"How do you know I *won't* be your next husband?" I continued the conversation we were having before Amanda returned.

"I'm only in town for Christmas, and then it's back to my regular life." She took a sip of her wine. From her facial expression, I could tell she enjoyed it. "Rome, I don't want to hurt you again," she whispered.

"You never hurt me the first time, Fay."

"I have memories that can prove you wrong," she nervously laughed.

Bringing this up made her nervous. It was something we both had been tiptoeing around since we ran into each other. Neither of us wanted to talk about the demise of our relationship.

The altercation that caused us to go without the other for the past fifteen years.

I knew it was something that we needed to discuss for us to move forward. As hurtful as it was, we couldn't keep sweeping it under the rug.

"I was wrong, Fay."

"You weren't. I should have been smarter and beat myself up for years about this. I should have just put the keys in my clutch that night." Tears spilled from her eyes as she stared straight ahead. "I should have been smarter, and I wasn't that night."

I reached over and wiped her tears. "That isn't your burden to carry. I was wrong that night, angry, and just fucking hurt from everything ... I shouldn't have put that on you, but ..." my voice weakened. "You were there ... the only person that I could blame at that moment."

"You were right to blame me."

Because I had never been able to make things right between us, she had lived every day thinking this was her mistake. "No, I wasn't. You lost your mother that night like I lost Allen ... I should have been there for you too. You didn't deserve to be treated that way."

"You shut me out," she whimpered.

"I know, baby ... I know. I swear I regret that shit every day. I should have been there ... your rock, like you were trying to be for me at that moment. I failed you."

"Your mom told me that you didn't want anything to do with me," she told me.

"Wait, what?"

Faith explained how my mother came to her house and told her to stop contacting me. "I called your phone, and it was disconnected."

"Fay, it was disconnected because I threw it at the wall in the hospital. I didn't give a damn about that phone after hearing about Allen."

"God, you were so angry. I couldn't eat or sleep for weeks after the accident. I wanted to come over; I wanted to force you to talk to me, but your mother told me she would press charges if I did."

This was the first time I heard that my mother went to Faith's house. During that time, my mother barely left the house. If she did leave, she would end up stopping at the driveway because her anxiety refused to let her leave.

I came up from the basement to try to put something on my stomach. It had been three days since I had eaten anything other than a cookie from the downstairs kitchen. I knew I had to eat. Allen would be so pissed if I didn't put something in my stomach.

When I came up, I saw my mother putting her car keys on the quartz countertop.

"You can try again another day," I encouraged her, knowing she didn't make it further than the mailbox.

She jumped, turning to face me quickly. "T . . . Thank you, Rome," she stammered nervously.

I watched as she took the keys and set them on the hook. "Everything all right with you, Mama?"

She seemed nervous and jittery. After what our family had been through, I didn't know what normal was anymore. I watched as she touched the counter and took a deep breath.

"I'm not all right, Rome. My son has been in the ground for the past two weeks . . . Nothing will ever be all right," she snapped at me.

My problem was that I always wanted to make things right for people. Even in the middle of the hurt, I wanted to fix things for them. When it came to me, I couldn't care less if things were fixed. I knew my mother was hurting. I heard her sobbing in Allen's room nearly every night. She could barely mention his name without her voice going in and out.

I desperately wanted to take that pain away from her. If I had to carry it all so my mother could get back to normal, it was a feat that I would gladly take over.

"Sorry," I mumbled.

She quickly spun around to face me. "You know they had her funeral today. She's lying in a casket in the same space my son was weeks before. The goddamn nerve of them!" she hollered.

Spit flew on the counter as she slammed her hand down once more.

"Carl is a member of that church too." I defended, although I was just as angry as she was.

It didn't matter how we felt. He was a part of Sageport just like we were. As much as I thought she should have been burned as a send-off, she was someone's mother and wife.

Someone I cared about very much.

"Fuck Carl Stone and that little fast tail you love chasing behind," she responded, disgusted that their names were even mentioned under our roof.

"Mama—"

"The one thing that came out of this is that you two are not together . . . She's cancer, and you'll be better off without her." Mama left the kitchen before I could respond.

"Rome?" Fay's voice brought me back to reality as I looked around the restaurant and realized where we were. "You're crying, love." She reached out and wiped the tears that had fallen from my eyes.

I had been so paralyzed by that memory that I didn't realize that I had been crying. "Yeah, shit was fucked up for us, Fay. We could have avoided all the pain we put each other through. Especially me . . . I played the biggest part in us ending things."

"We both played our par—"

"Stop trying to make it a shared thing, Fay. I said some mean shit to you, pushed you away, and blamed you for the death of my brother." I took a breath. "You loved Allen just like I did . . . You would have never done something to cause him harm."

She took hold of my hand and kissed the back of it. "I've missed you every day since then, Rome. Every 'first' I experienced, I wished it was with you. I shouldn't have left."

"Leaving here was the best thing you could have done. Look at me . . . I'm stuck in an episode of *Groundhog Day*. You left to live and experience the world outside this small town."

Amanda and another gentleman came and placed our oysters down. I could tell she wanted to ask if we were all right, then decided against it. "Enjoy your oysters," she gently said and headed off.

"Leaving this town was our dream. Yeah, I got out of this town, but look at me . . . I'm a divorced, single mother with no career. I didn't accomplish anything that I wanted for myself."

I took an oyster, prepared it how she liked it, and fed it to her. "I'm gonna feed you to keep you quiet. That divorce doesn't define you . . . Your role as a woman and a mother does. Fay, I don't even have to know your kids to know that you'd give your all to see them happy and at peace."

"I would," she softly replied, accepting another oyster into her mouth. "That doesn't take away the fact that I couldn't keep a husband."

"That husband wasn't meant for you to keep. I look at it like this . . . God brought us back to this place for a reason. We could either ignore what he wants or give this a second chance."

I held onto her chin and pulled her face close to mine. We shared a kiss with our tongues dancing in and out of each other's mouths. When we broke our kiss, she took a sip of wine while holding tightly onto my hand.

"You're spending the night with me."

"Rome, I can—"

"I said what I said," I confirmed and kissed her lips once more. I was determined not to let Fay get away from me again.

Chapter Fourteen

FAITH

THE SOUND OF pans crashing around in the kitchen caused me to lift my head. The sounds, sun, and body aches from last night made me collapse back down onto the foreign king-size bed.

After dinner, we decided that we wanted to spend the night together. Well, Rome decided and drove us to his house. I was so nervous about coming to his home and facing Mrs. Atkins. I didn't want my face to bring up any memories that her dementia caused her to forget about.

Luckily, she was already in bed when we arrived. Rome introduced me to Pia, Mrs. Atkin's aide, and then walked her out to the car. His townhome was beautiful and a sure sign that Sageport didn't stay the same. You could tell he had handpicked every piece of artwork and paint color—even his bedroom.

The earth tones blended perfectly with the carved stone headboard that was the showstopper. I smiled at the pictures of him and his brother on the dresser next to his bottles of cologne and jewelry. I wanted to climb out of this bed and freshen up, but those heels I wore last night didn't allow my feet to.

I never dressed up anymore, and it had been almost a year since I slid my feet into heels. When Marie suggested those heels, I wanted to laugh in her face. Sneakers, Uggs, or Birkenstocks were my usual choice of shoes. With two active girls, I had to be comfortable at all times.

I took a deep breath and tiptoed into the bathroom. Everything was so perfect and put together. There were no toothpaste stains on the sink or the mirror, and the toilet seat was even down.

I quickly peed, did a speedy finger brush, and fixed my hair. Although nothing happened last night, we both wanted it to. But I had too much to drink, and all I wanted to do was lie down. It had been so long since I had a warm body to lie next to.

Let me rephrase that. It had been so long since I had a warm body that *wanted* to lie next to me. It was the way Rome rubbed my booty while giving me soft kisses on my forehead until I fell asleep that sent shocks to wake up those butterflies. The affection was what I needed; it was what I craved.

I wanted someone to *want* me.

To feel like they wouldn't be able to breathe unless I were near them. Rome made me feel like that, and it was a feeling that I never wanted to lose. It made me scared for the day that I would be climbing into my rental car and driving back to the airport.

When I left the bathroom, he was already in the room with breakfast. "Please don't tell me it was you banging up those pots."

I watched as he started laughing. "I never said I was a cook or nothing. Pia usually hooks me up with breakfast or dinner."

"It was so nice to meet her. You could tell she truly cares for your mother." Pia was like a breath of fresh air.

Those were the kind of caretakers many children wanted for their aging or sick parents. "Yeah, she said the same about you. She took Mama to the farmer's market to get some air."

"Awe, how nice." He set a tray in front of me, and I looked at the runny eggs and toast. "This looks good."

"Stop lying to me."

"No, I'm serious . . . This has potential." I picked out a piece of eggshell and put it on the paper towel.

"Damn, you became a food critic?"

"My father does own one of the best restaurants in town . . . I would say I know a thing or two about food."

"Okay, you got me there," he smirked.

"Rome . . . I want to avoid your mother if that's possible."

He looked confused. "Why?"

"I don't want to bring up any memories she may have forgotten."

He sat down beside me and took my hand into his. "Mama thinks Allen is still alive and well, and we play along with it. She already has night tremors, so we avoid doing anything to upset her."

"How does that make you feel . . . You know he's not alive, so it must be hard for you."

"It is. I try to switch the subject from him when she tries to get deep. I have to do what is best for me and Mama. If this makes her happy, I'll deal with my own issues on my own."

"Awe, babe," I kissed the back of his hand.

It hurt my heart that he had to live daily pretending that his brother was alive. Rome was such a good person and son; he was always about his family. When Allen was alive, Rome always put him first. Allen could call him at the last minute, and Rome would drop everything to be there for his brother. Rome was the kind of person you knew you could depend on and wouldn't do you wrong.

"I'm good, I promise," he assured me.

"As much as I love this breakfast . . . Can I please go downstairs and show you how to throw down?"

He stood and extended his arm. "Please, I beg of you."

I grabbed his robe from the back of the door and headed downstairs into the kitchen to make us a proper breakfast.

After breakfast, Rome drove me back to my father's house. I needed a hot shower and a hair wash to start the day. When we arrived, Marie was in the yard with a few paintings.

"Hey, you two . . . I take it the date went very well," she winked at me.

Rome stepped right in to help her. "Let me take those."

"Such a gentleman," Marie nudged my shoulder as Rome took the paintings into the house.

"Where's Dad?"

"He's taking his afternoon nap on the back patio . . . He loves that chair I got him out there. Plus, the sun does him good." We walked up the steps and into the house.

The house was much brighter after we got rid of those old maroon curtains and dust-filled blinds. Marie oversaw ordering the window treatments. As much as I wanted to do this for her, I wanted her to make this home her own. What I would pick wasn't necessarily something that she would pick herself.

"Let me get you both a slice of cake and some coffee," she said, rushing into the kitchen.

Marie's love language was feeding others. She lived to feed people and loved to see the expression on their faces when they moaned out in pleasure from her scrumptious desserts.

"I sure could eat."

"We just had breakfast," I called him out.

"Breakfast ain't this pecan cake that she's cutting." He sat down at the table and rubbed his stomach in anticipation.

My phone buzzed in my purse. Fishing it out, I quickly answered when I saw it was Mayven's tablet. "Hey, baby . . . I was just thinking about you and your sister."

"Mommy, I want to come with you. I don't like it here at Nana's house," Mayven cried into the phone.

Whenever my girls cried, I was always there to console them. I felt helpless sitting at this table because I couldn't pull her into my arms, swipe her hair out of her face, or kiss the pain away.

"Oh, baby. I'm sorry . . . This is your father's holiday. You were so excited to spend it with him. What happened?"

"Francis happened," I heard Madison in the background.

It was like they both had switched roles. Mayven was usually the least emotional, and she never called me "Mommy." Madison didn't seem as upset as her sister did.

"What did Francis do to you, May?"

I would book a flight to New York right now if I needed to. "Daddy doesn't spend any time with us. He's so busy showing Francis around—"

"And looking at condos . . . Why does he even need a condo? We live in Georgia," Madison cut her sister off.

I hated that he didn't speak to the girls about this. "Have you tried using your words? Remember what you learned in therapy."

Rome didn't touch his cake because he was concerned. "Mommy, he's not here . . . He and Francis went off to look at homes in New Jersey. Mom, what's 'commute'?"

I shook my head. Ashton was looking at homes in Jersey and had planned to commute to work if he took the job.

When he took the job.

Clearly, he had already taken the job if he was now looking for places. I really hated this for our girls. They went to New York to spend much-needed time with their dad, and he was too consumed to give them any time.

"Baby, where is your nana?"

"Talking with everyone in the dining room. It's too crowded here," she complained.

"Mommy, can we please come with you?"

Ashton would never agree to the girls coming to Sageport with me. He was the one who insisted on having them for Christmas this year. I would have gladly given Thanksgiving up.

"I don't think so, babies. How about I talk to your dad . . . How does that sound?"

"Like a waste of time," Mayven muttered.

I smiled. "There's my sarcastic princess. I will talk to your father, all right?"

"Okay," they both said in unison.

I wanted desperately to get my babies, but I knew I had to do things correctly. Despite how I felt about the situation, I couldn't just show up in New York to scoop them up.

The girls sounded so excited to meet Ashton's girlfriend, but that changed quickly. I feared that things would change even more if they became more serious.

What would happen when they had kids together? Were our girls going to be put on the back burner because his kids with her would come first? I hated even thinking like that, but you couldn't be sure with Ashton.

It seemed like overnight, he told me about this new job, and now, he was house hunting with another woman in New York and New Jersey. The part that sucked was that he should have been bringing the girls along to get them excited. That would have been a good way to break the news to them.

Instead, he left them with his mother while he probably showed this woman all over New York and New Jersey.

I ended the call with the girls, and Rome touched my hand. "Everything all right?"

"No," I sighed.

Marie set our coffee on the table and sat across from us. "What's going on?"

"My ex-husband has accepted a new job position in New York. He says it's a better opportunity for him and, of course, more money."

"Except he didn't tell your daughters about it." Rome read my mind like he always did.

"They don't know, and I don't want to do his dirty work for him. I'm always doing his dirty work, and I can't do it anymore."

"Honey, you shouldn't have to. If he made this decision, then he needs to be the one to tell the girls." Marie sipped her coffee.

It was a tough situation to be in. I didn't ever see myself having to share custody of my girls with my now ex-husband. When we got married, I wanted this to be a forever kind of thing. I didn't want to split weekends or holidays with our girls.

It wasn't fair to them.

Why should their life be split in two because we couldn't work things out? I've watched our girls solve problems independently at eight, and we couldn't figure out our marriage as grown-ass adults.

It always made me feel sick.

"The girls want to come here with me."

Marie grew excited. I had shown her pictures of the girls, and she had even been in the room when they were on FaceTime with me. "We have a tree and everything. The spare bedroom is cleared out so they can sleep there." Her mind was moving a million miles per second.

"I have to talk to their father about it. I'm sure he's going to give me a hard time . . . So don't get your hopes up."

Rome rubbed my hand. "What do you need from me?"

I loved a man who wanted to help solve my problems. Rome was sitting there waiting for me to tell him what I needed him to do for me.

"Can you convince my stubborn ex-husband?" I joked.

The look in Rome's eyes told me he would try if I weren't joking. "Baby, if you need me to do it . . . Give me the man's number."

Marie and I chuckled. "He's a good man," she smiled.

"Enjoy your cake, love . . . I'll talk to Ashton about it later. I need a second to breathe before calling. I hate hearing my babies sound that way."

Rome started to rub my back while he enjoyed his cake. Whenever my girls were distressed, I wanted to fix the problem immediately. What do I do when the person who's causing them distress happens to be their father? I had grown tired of Ash's selfishness when it came to skipping out on their recitals and games. But to bring them to another state and completely ignore them was another thing.

I took tiny breaths while rehearsing what I would say when I called the man I had vowed to love forever.

Vows didn't mean shit.

Chapter Fifteen

ASHTON

"*S*HIT . . . What does she want? Turn that down, baby," I told Francis as I slid my finger across my phone's screen. "What's up, Faith?"

"Just checking in on the girls . . . What are you guys doing today?" She was pleasant, almost too pleasant.

"They're hanging with their cousins. Francis and I snuck away to have some lunch. Want me to have them call you when I'm back?"

She was quiet.

Whenever Faith was quiet, I knew something was brewing.

"We're not married anymore, Ashton. I didn't think you would still be lying to me."

More than likely, the girls had already called her, so that was why she was calling me. Faith never called me unless she had to, so I knew that had to be the reason.

"What's up, Faith? Why are you really calling me?"

"The girls called me sobbing, Ash . . . fucking sobbing because you're too busy with your new girlfriend."

Francis looked at me and shook her head.

"Not true."

"Wow. You're calling our girls liars now? Unbelievable," she callously laughed.

"I'm not saying that. They wanted to follow us everywhere, and I was busy looking at some real estate. I didn't want to bring them because I still haven't spoken to them about it."

"Wouldn't this have made the perfect time to bring it up? Showing them future homes or bedrooms they may have?"

Fuck. I hated it whenever she was right.

"You're right."

Francis looked at me with disbelief because I was agreeing with her. I watched as she rolled her eyes and crossed her arms.

"Look, the girls want to come be with me. They're miserable there . . . Mayven even called me 'Mommy,' Ash."

"Shit, she must really be miserable."

Even I knew how much it irked Faith that Mayven called her mom instead of mommy. Secretly, it always brought me a little joy to see her bothered by it. People always said there weren't any perfect moms, but they never met Faith. She was the perfect parent and would do any and everything for our girls. Because of work, I often missed things, and I always became jealous that she was able to attend.

"Uh-huh. My point wasn't to call and argue with you. Lord knows we've done enough of that during our marriage. We promised always to do what was right for the girls."

As much as I looked forward to spending Christmas with the girls and our family, I couldn't deprive them of being with their mother. This was the longest they had gone without her.

We had a little over two and a half weeks until Christmas. As much as I wanted to do all the New York Christmas things I had grown up doing with the girls, I knew I had to do right by the girls. I could tell they weren't having a good time.

Lord knows Mayven wouldn't let me forget it. I thought if I just shoved their tablets in their faces, they would forget about wanting to leave.

"I get it. Can I at least talk to them first, and I'll fly them down there next week?"

"Fly them to Orlando, and I can drive to pick them up," she replied.

I knew she was secretly dancing while trying to keep her cool. "Sounds good. I'll reach out when I book our flights."

"Perfect."

As much as I wanted to be petty and keep the girls, I knew my kids would end up paying the price. Although this was my holiday time with them, I was willing to allow the girls to spend it with their mother.

We ended the call, and I turned up the music again. Francis aggressively turned it all the way down. "What the fuck, Ash?"

"What now, babe?"

"Agreeing with her? The way she spoke to you, and you just going to agree with her? What the fuck?"

Francis didn't understand the peace I had with my ex-wife. My colleagues told me horror stories about their exes, and I considered myself lucky. Faith never bothered unless she had to, and more than likely, I was in the wrong.

This time, I knew I was in the wrong and would take full responsibility for it. Since we arrived in New York, I haven't spent any one-on-one time with my daughters. I was either helping my mom out with something, catching up with my family, or making sure Francis felt comfortable. It wasn't until my realtor started sending me listings I would be interested in that I started going with Francis to look at places.

"Babe, I haven't spent any time with the girls. No wonder they called their mother crying."

I expected her to agree with me, but she folded her arms together even tighter. "We've watched movies with them every night since we arrived."

The girls always fell asleep before the movie could ever fully play out. I didn't consider that spending time with them. By morning, they were already up and out of the house with Mom and cousins.

Francis and I had it made here. My mom took over and allowed us just to relax and do as we pleased. I think that was what Francis loved the most. The part where I acted like I didn't have kids to be responsible for. I loved my girls and tried hard to get it right for them. Some of those times, I fell short, and I hated that.

"You knew I had kids before we got serious. My girls come first, Francis . . . If they're not happy, then it's my job to fix it."

She groaned. "I'm not saying that you shouldn't. It feels like whatever your ex-wife wants, she will always get."

When you didn't nag me the way Faith didn't, she could always get what she wanted. Except for that expensive-ass Range Rover she begged me for. I was able to continue to earn a living for our family while knowing my kids were well taken care of. I couldn't thank Faith enough for the sacrifices she had made. Faith had always cheered me on while I followed my dreams, but I never did the same for her. She had dreams of her own, and I selfishly asked her to stay home and raise our kids.

I didn't support her like she had always supported me throughout the years. Faith was so good because she never threw that in my face. There were a few arguments when she could have tossed that back into my face.

She would never, though.

Raising our girls was her biggest blessing, and she would tell anybody that. Although she was tired and not appreciated as much as she should have been, she never took a day off or complained. Whatever the girls needed, she was there to provide that for them.

"When it comes to knowing what our girls need, I trust her judgment." I pulled into my mother's driveway and killed the engine.

"So, I'm supposed to play the second forever."

I turned to face Francis. "When have I ever made you feel like you're second? You wanted me to tell her about us, and I did what you wanted. All I'm asking is that you don't get involved when it comes to us discussing our kids."

If the shoe were on the other foot, she would want the same as well. Faith deserved respect, and I refused to have them both bickering. Not when there was no need for it. The girls were already trying to get used to our new normal, and I didn't need them witnessing their mother and Francis arguing.

"Fine." Francis opened the door and slammed it behind her.

"Fuck," I muttered.

I sat in the car for a minute before I joined her in the house. My mother was in the kitchen cooking dinner as usual. I think I gained five pounds with all the food she's been cooking.

My mother lived for this, though.

She enjoyed having her family around and cooking massive meals for us all. I watched her light up while watching the kids play in the snow out back. If it were up to her, she would sit and watch them all day and never grow tired of it.

When all my cousins and siblings got together, we already knew we had a built-in babysitter. My mother took care of everything without any complaints.

"Hey, baby . . . I hope you're hungry," Mom said as she stirred the big, worn pot that was simmering on the stove.

"Always. Where's everybody?"

"The kids are up in the loft area, and your brothers and cousins are in the basement."

"Ma, the girls are going with their mother next week."

She looked so crushed. "What? I thought we got them for Christmas, Ash."

"They miss their mom." I spared her the other details about why they wanted to go with Faith.

She kissed her teeth. "She has them too spoiled, Ash. They rely on their mother for everything."

"They're eight, Ma. I relied on you for everything at that age too."

She side-eyed me. "You're their father...Tell them no. They need to spend time with their family. We're baking cookies tomorrow."

"I'm not going to do that."

Although my mother babied the shit out of me, she was also firm too. She didn't believe children had a say in things as they grew up. Once a decision was made, then that was the final word about it.

Faith and I were raising our girls differently. They were being raised to be respectful, but they also have a voice. "Ash, this is going to ruin my Christmas."

"I mean, I can choose to fly to Jamaica after dropping them off with their mom," I added.

The reason I chose to come to New York was so the girls could see their family. When I originally made the decision, I truly wanted to hurt Faith. I was so angry with her for calling for the divorce, although I knew it was needed. I was madder because she had the balls to do what I had kept putting off.

"Are you serious?"

I shrugged and headed to find the girls. They were sitting in the corner together on one tablet. They brought both tablets, but they were together, which was rare. The girls hated to be up under each other, so this was a sign that they wanted to leave.

I should have noticed that early on. Even miles away, Faith was so in tune with our girls.

"May and Maddie ... Want to go grab some ice cream?"

"It's cold," Mayven snapped.

"Hot chocolate?"

"From Starbucks?" Maddie negotiated.

"Sure."

They put down their tablets and followed behind me.

After we got our coats on, I helped them into the car. Mayven quickly strapped herself in, and I climbed into the driver's seat. Francis was more than likely up in our room on the phone.

"Francis isn't coming?" Madison asked.

"Just us, kiddos," I smiled in the rearview mirror.

While we drove to Starbucks, the girls sang along with the radio. This was what I should have been doing once we arrived. The only reason I asked Francis to spend the holidays with my family was because she kept pushing.

Pushing me to reveal our relationship to Faith.

Pushing to meet more of my family.

I thought meeting my mother would have shut her up. Instead, it lit a fire under her to meet my entire family during Christmas. As much as we were in love, I needed her to be more patient regarding my kids. While the kids tolerated her, I could always tell when she was irritated with them. I wanted us to work.

I *needed* us to work.

However, I would always put my daughters first if it came to it. Francis had to learn that my girls came before anyone. We had only been dating for six months, and she was making unnecessary demands. Faith wasn't a problem in our relationship, and here she was, making her one.

Whenever Faith called, we only spoke about the girls. She never held any side conversations other than what was going on with the girls. It wasn't like she called at weird hours, either. She usually called when I was at work or sent a text message. Since we've been divorced, she preferred texting anyway.

She didn't take the news of me having a girlfriend well, but that was my fault. Faith was more bothered by me not talking to her about it first, and I had to admit she was right. I would have been livid had she introduced a boyfriend to our daughters without talking to me about it first.

I helped the girls get out of the car as we walked into Starbucks. They ordered what they wanted, and I scanned my phone to pay. We took a seat toward the back while they made our drinks. Mayven was playing around with a straw while Madison sat staring at me.

Madison was just like her mother.

All curious and knew when something was up. "Thanks for taking us for hot chocolate, Daddy," she said.

"You're welcome, baby. I owe you both an apology."

"For what?" Mayven chimed in.

"I haven't been around much or spending time with you two. Francis and I have been in our own world, and I'm sorry for that." I reached across the table and grabbed their hands. "Mommy called and told me you guys want to be with her."

"We do," Mayven confirmed.

I have to admit, but that shit stung a little bit.

My daughters were confident in who they were because of their mother. While Mayven's response hurt a bit, I knew she was being honest.

"Well, Mommy and I had a conversation, and we both agreed you should go to Sageport . . . you know, so you can see where Mommy grew up."

"And see Pop-Pop's restaurant," they both cheered while happily staring into each other's eyes.

"Yup, you get to do that too. I need you both to make me a promise, though."

"What?" Madison answered.

"Call me on Christmas morning . . . I want to see both of your beautiful faces first thing in the morning."

Mayven smiled. "We can do that."

They were so excited that they couldn't even sit still. I grabbed our hot chocolates and brought them back to the table. "How would you feel if Daddy moved away?"

"From Georgia?" Madison quizzed.

"Uh-huh."

"Sad," Mayven answered.

"Would you?"

"Yes. We don't get to see you a lot now," she added.

She had a point. Work took me away from the girls too often. I always tried to make myself feel better about it because I was providing for them.

"You both know that Daddy has to work, right? I would never purposely avoid spending time with you girls." I took a sip of my hot chocolate. "Daddy got offered a new job here in New York."

"So, you would have to move?"

"Yes."

Mayven's tears welled up in her eyes.

"Don't cry, May," her sister consoled her.

"I would be able to spend much more time with you guys then, and you can come visit me here all the time." I tried to make it sound better because seeing my baby girl becoming emotional had me fucked up.

I hadn't taken the job yet. We were in the final stages of negotiating, and I had them put in that I could take off two weeks every other month. I wanted to use those two weeks to spend time with the girls in Georgia or if they came here. I also had lined their school holidays up with times that I would be able to work remotely.

I was serious about wanting to be there for the girls more. Faith already did so much, so moving here meant she would have to do more. I wanted to make the transition as smooth as possible.

"Is Francis moving with you?"

"She is."

The plan was for us to both move here and get separate places. But the more we discussed it, the more we decided to move together. We both had spoken about our future and knew what we wanted.

She wanted kids and marriage.

I knew this, so I was prepared to have more children and get remarried. These were things in the future, though. Nothing would happen in the next year.

"How fun," Mayven sniffled, wiping away the tears that dropped down her cheek.

"Girls, you know I love you both so much. I won't do this if you don't want me to."

Madison was quiet.

Too quiet.

"Can we please go back to Nana's house?"

I knew not to push them. "Madison, are you all right?"

"Francis is stealing you away from us," she blurted, breaking out into a loud wait.

I abandoned my chair quickly and grabbed my baby. I held her in my arms and kissed her face. "Baby, nobody can take you from me. I love you girls so much . . . I'm always going to be here for you."

We sat on the floor of Starbucks, holding one another. I hated hearing how my girls felt about Francis. It was my fault because everything had been about her since we arrived here. It wasn't fair for them, and I understood why they now wanted to spend time with their mother.

Parenting was hard.

Chapter Sixteen

ROME

"A SURPRISE VISIT...What do I owe this visit?" I held my office door open for Fay.

She was wearing a pair of baggy jeans, sneakers, and a cropped top. Her curly tresses were pulled up into a big curly ponytail. "I figured it was my turn to bring you lunch at work . . . plus, I stopped by the coffee shop to check in there."

"Hmm . . . You know the way to a man's heart."

"Or stomach," she snickered and took a seat. "Dad says you always order the Faith's Shepherd's Pie."

"I do . . . Damn." I licked my fingers while tasting the food. "How is it possible that it gets better each time I have it?"

"You know I've never tried the one dish named after me."

I stabbed my fork into the pie and held it up. "Taste."

She took a bite and nodded her head. "Okay, yeah, that's amazing."

"Told you. I get it every time I'm in the mood for some good home cooking." I smiled at her.

"So, with the girls coming to town, I'm going to be pretty busy," she started.

"I respect that. Whenever you can make time for me, I'll take it."

She smiled. "You're so sweet."

"I'm not trying to be when I . . ." I allowed my voice to trail off as she swatted me.

"I want you to meet the girls."

Out of all the things I thought she would say, I didn't expect her to say that. I expected she would be more protective of who her children meet, which I respected. I never wanted to push her to do something she wasn't ready to do.

"Seriously?"

"Yes. Madison and Mayven are my pride and joys, and I want you to meet them so you can understand why I chose to be their mama instead of a career."

I stood up. "Baby, I don't need to understand that. My mom was a stay-at-home mother my entire life, and I watched her sacrifice and do more than my father, who worked at the dealerships. I know how important being a stay-at-home mom is. I just need you to understand it too." I kissed her on the lips.

She stood on her toes and kissed me again. "Rome, I'm so scared of this."

"Of what?"

"Us," she replied.

I wasn't scared.

Far from it.

I knew I wanted Faith since I saw she was back in town. In my heart, I believed God answered my prayers. I always sent up a prayer for a woman who was accepting of my situation and who wasn't scared to be loved.

Faith came back for Christmas at the right time. I knew I wanted this with her, and I wanted to accept her children too. I just needed her to accept that my mother didn't hate her.

"You know what scares me?"

"What?"

"My situation with my mom being too much."

She kissed her teeth. "Rome, I know your situation, and it could never be too much. Your mom is a part of you, so I love her just like I love you."

"You still love me?" I smirked.

"Never stopped, baby."

We shared another kiss, and I broke our kiss by staring into her eyes. "I love you, Fay."

"I love you too."

"The long-distance thing . . . Is this even us?"

We never spoke about what would happen when the holidays were over. When she returned to her life, and I was still living mine, would our relationship survive?

"Let's cross that bridge when we come to it. Right now, I'm enjoying being back in Sageport."

I couldn't believe she had said that out of her mouth. "Damn, any chance you moving back?"

"Don't push it." She shoved me. "So, the girls get in this week . . . Want to take a ride to Orlando to pick them up?"

"You only wanna use me to drive."

"Well, is that so wrong?"

"On so many levels."

"I can't help it if you're a better driver than me." She batted her eyelashes at me, trying to butter me up.

"You know exactly what to say to get me to do what you want." I kissed her once more, then went back to my food. "Is your ex-husband cool with this?"

She shrugged. "Honestly, I didn't even talk to him about it. It's not like he talks to me about the things he's doing."

"I don't want to be a pawn in your battle with him, Fay."

"You're not. I don't have a battle with him . . . He knows I'm right when it comes to the girls. We've known each other for years . . . This new girl he just met not too long ago. Ash will survive."

She brushed off the subject as not being important. I had no problem driving to Orlando to pick up the girls and meet her ex-husband.

That wasn't my problem.

I didn't want my attendance to cause problems between them. Since being a teen, I have always been protective of Fay. I couldn't sit back and let him come sideways out of his mouth to her.

I didn't care if he was her ex-husband or the kids were around. I wanted to avoid the drama as best as I could while being there for Fay.

She walked around the desk and rubbed my back as I ate. "Seriously, I would never use you to make Ashton jealous. Our marriage is over, and it was over long before we got divorced."

"Are the girls excited to come to Sageport?"

Her smile lit up the room whenever she mentioned her girls. I could tell she was an amazing mother. "They are so excited. I told them bits and pieces about Sageport. They're mostly excited to visit their Pop-Pop's restaurant."

"In that case, I can definitely recommend the shepherd's pie."

She moved the loose strand of hair from her face. "You've probably had enough to consider yourself a professional critic of it."

"Can't critique it because it only gets better with time."

I finished the last of my food before discarding the container in the trash.

"I'm free for the day . . . Do you want to go down to the coast?"

"Didn't I tell you I didn't go out there too often?"

She pouted. "I thought we could grab some blankets and sit on the beach . . . maybe even have lunch."

"What was this that you brought? Prelunch?"

She giggled. "Well, dinner . . . Nothing fancy. Maybe we can grab some burgers for the ride back home."

I stared at the stack of files that Linda had been on me to sign and decided to throw caution to the wind. It was a crisp, sunny day, and I didn't want to be stuck behind a desk signing a bunch of papers all day.

Spending the afternoon at the coast with Fay seemed like a dream. It was something I had been envisioning for years, and now I had the chance to do it.

"Am I the one driving?"

She held up her car keys. "Nope. I have the keys to my rental. Now, you can sit back and rate my driving."

"I remember your driver's ed course . . . Remember? I was in the backseat," I clowned her.

Fay couldn't drive worth a damn when we were in high school. She always used the excuse that she wouldn't need to drive in New York City. It made me wonder who taught her to drive.

"Shut up, jerk," she snorted.

I checked in with everyone before leaving for the day. Luckily, today was Linda's off day, so I didn't have to worry about her on my ass about those files. While we were in the car, I called Pia to check in on my mother. She informed me that she was taking a nap and she could stay late today.

"Everything cool with your mom?"

"Yeah, she's taking her midday nap." I yawned, reclining the seat back some.

Fay drove while singing along with the radio, and I watched Sageport through the passenger window for once. Usually, I drove and focused on the road, so it felt nice to be driven around for a change.

Since Fay had arrived back in Sageport, everything seemed to change. The resentment that I held for this town was starting to fade. Being back with Fay showed me that there were such things as second chances.

"I was thinking about throwing Marie and my dad a small engagement party at the restaurant. Marie told me she never did those things with her ex-husband."

"I think they would both enjoy that."

"It would be special too . . . We can celebrate my father with the girls and me in town," she smiled.

I could tell being away from Sageport and her father was needed. However, just because it was needed didn't mean she didn't miss both. Her aura just seemed different these days.

"Even if you had it in a public bathroom, it would still be special. You and your daughters mean a lot to your father."

"I know."

When we arrived at the coast, she parked near the beach and hopped out. I watched as she grabbed blankets and a picnic basket.

"Hmm, sounds like someone's been plotting all along."

She blushed. "The plan was to bring the shepherd's pie, but you would have smelled it as soon as you got into the car."

"What's all of this?" I asked, helping her and taking the basket from her.

"Fruit, chocolates, wine, and cucumber sandwiches."

"Cucumber sandwiches?"

"Don't ask. I got invited to a brunch with some moms back home, and I've been hooked on them ever since."

While she held the blankets and I carried the basket, we held hands and walked onto the beach. We found a perfect spot that wasn't too close to the water but wasn't that far, either. The cool breeze whipped around us as Fay put on her Sageport high hoodie.

"You still have that?"

"I told you, my father kept everything." She wrestled her ponytail out of the back of the hoodie.

We settled onto the blankets. Fay sat between my legs as I rubbed the side of her thighs while we looked out at the water. The waves crashed against the beach and the rocks off to the side of us.

"I hate to admit it, but I've missed this," she said, rubbing her hands together and leaning back further into me.

Fay was like the missing puzzle piece I could never find. She fit perfectly in my life. While we sat together in our own world, it didn't feel like any time had passed.

As if this was always meant to be and had always been.

"It has missed you . . . I know I did."

She kissed the back of my hand. "I don't want this feeling to go away, Rome."

"It doesn't have to go away."

She was scared.

Shit, so was I.

Neither of us knew how this would work. We lived in different states and had different responsibilities. It wasn't like I could just up and move with an ill mother and a business. Even if I sold the dealerships, that still left my mother. I wasn't ready or willing to put her into a facility yet. My mother was used to seeing my face daily and being around familiarity. I couldn't take that away from her.

Not even for true love.

"It's been so long since I've felt like this . . . felt taken care of . . . You know, mentally." I didn't want to know the ins and outs of her marriage, but I wondered how a man married a woman he wasn't ready for.

Every time Fay spoke about her ex-husband, she let small pieces slip, giving me a deeper insight into their marriage.

It was sad that she sat on this beach with me and could admit that it had been a while since she felt mentally cared for. "I want to take care of you physically too."

She turned her head and kissed me on the lips. While we shared a kiss, I slipped my hand into the top of her jeans, sliding it deeper into her satin panties until I felt her cat.

The blanket on her shielded anyone from knowing what was happening under it. Fay's eyes grew wide as she stared at me and let a soft moan escape. Since it was during the cooler months, the beach was practically empty, other than a few joggers running by.

Fay opened her legs wider as I slipped my fingers inside of her opening. She gave me soft pecks as I refrained from flipping her onto her back, snatching off those jeans, and sucking on her pussy until I heard her scream my name.

For now, this would do. I watched as her mouth curved. She tossed her head back while grinding on my fingers. I flicked my finger across her pearl, which sent her into a frenzy. She wanted to rip off her clothes and have me take her now, but neither of us wanted to sit in jail for indecent exposure.

"R . . . Rome, I'm about to c . . . come, baby," she squealed out while holding onto the side of my face.

I bent my head down and sucked on her lips as my hands moved like a guitarist under the blanket. "Fuck, Fay . . . Give me some tongue," I demanded.

She shoved her entire tongue into my mouth while I continued to get her off. Her body moved every which way because it felt so pleasurable. And it wasn't like we were discreet with what we were doing. We were lucky there wasn't any traffic on the beach. Fay's soft moans had turned into loud wails until her body went limp.

I took my hands out from her pants and sucked every finger before kissing her. She lay between my legs, too spent to say anything, so I kissed her lips.

"Looks like I'm the one that's driving back," I smirked.

Her mind, body, and soul hadn't been taken care of, and I planned to do all that. "Yes, please," she begged.

"Think you can handle round two?"

She nodded. "Guess I should text Marie and tell her I'm staying out again."

"Yeah, do that." I kissed her lips.

Fay lay in my bed, her legs wide open and ready for me. I slapped my dick against her thigh a few times before I slowly inserted it into her. She held onto my shoulders while staring into my eyes.

This wasn't the first time we had been at it. Since we stepped into the house last night, we had been at it all night. Pia already knew what was going on, so she made sure she gave Mama melatonin so she could sleep peacefully throughout the night. The minute we made it through the door, I tossed Fay onto the bed and ripped off her clothes.

I ate her pussy in so many positions that we should have broken a record. Fay surprised me when she shoved all of me into her mouth. The way she stared into my eyes while she gobbled me down made me growl. After sexing each other until the early-morning hours, we found our way downstairs to make something to eat.

Well, Fay made us something to eat.

We had gotten so damn heated in the kitchen that we went back upstairs, ready for more. It wasn't until five that we both decided to get some sleep. This bed was expensive, and so was the mattress. However, it never felt comfortable until I lay in it with Faith.

She held onto me as if she never wanted to let me go while I kissed her lips. When my morning alarm woke up, it woke someone else up too. So now, we were in this bed about to indulge in some more grown folk business.

I stared her in the eyes and leaned down to kiss her lips. "Fuck, Fay . . . Why you been keeping this away from me?" I groaned into her ear as I pulled out and pushed my way back in.

She wrapped her legs around me while she held my face, kissing me each time. "Better late than never, right?" She gave me another peck on my lips.

"I don't think I can let you out of this room . . . I need this every morning now." I continued to deliver slow yet steady strokes to her.

"You're trying to have me walking around like a cowboy, baby . . . I'm so sore." She kissed me again.

It was my turn to kiss her. "We gonna have to start the day soon . . . I'm gonna mis—"

"Rome Atkins! What in the world are you doing with a girl in your father's and my bedroom?!"

I jumped off Faith and grabbed the blanket to wrap around my body. Fay fought for the sheets and covered the rest of her body. "Mama!"

Since she moved in, my mother had never come upstairs. I considered upstairs my sanctuary because she never came up here. "Get that little fast tail out of my damn bed and out of this house! A fast one like your mama, ain't you?" She pointed at Faith.

Faith looked mortified as I gently pushed my mother out of the bedroom while having a blanket wrapped around my body like I was going to a toga party.

"Mama, enough," I scolded her as I led her back downstairs. "Where is Pia?" I asked as if she was going to answer me.

With the way she was scratching and fighting me to get down the steps, I could tell today would be one of those days. "Your brother would never do something like this . . . Let go of me!" she hollered as I sat her down in the recliner.

"Why were you upstairs? Why?" I hollered, irritated and guilty for how she spoke to Faith.

"Don't you go trying to influence Allen with any of this. Your father and I will deal with you when he comes home tonight," she continued, further infuriating me.

"Allen and Dad are fucking *dead*!" I screamed.

It was wrong, and the moment I yelled it out, I felt guilty. Everything was happening so fast that I didn't know what to say or do as I stood in front of her dressed in my comforter.

"D . . . Dead? Not Allen and Dale." Her hands started to shake as she touched her face. "I have to go to the hospital." She tried to stand, and I blocked her to sit back down.

"Mama, relax . . . Please, relax." I relaxed my tone to try to calm her. "Allen is at school. Dad is at work too," I continued to lie.

She took a deep breath. "Rome, what has gotten into you? Why did you say something so horrible like that about your brother and father?"

I spotted Fay standing near the stairs from the corner of my eye. She stood there with one of my shirts on while holding my phone. If the situation hadn't been so damn fucked up, I probably would have taken her right on the steps.

"Tea, Rome . . . The caffeine bothers me," she informed me.

It was always decaf whenever Pia gave her coffee, but she didn't know that. "Tea, I got it."

I pulled Faith into the kitchen with me.

"Rome, before you start apologizing, don't," she stopped me. "You warned me ahead of time what I was getting into."

"Why the fuck you so perfect?" I took her face into my hands and kissed her lips, holding onto her body.

"You need to utilize those locks on the door so this doesn't happen again," she warned me.

I started pulling out the stuff to make Mama's tea. "That's the thing . . . She never comes up the fucking stairs. Since she's been like this, she hasn't been up there once. Pia is usually here by now."

Fay snapped her fingers. "Your phone . . . She called you a few times. We were occupied, so you probably didn't hear it."

She handed me my phone, and I saw six missed calls from Pia. My heart started to race as I called her back. It rang a few times before she answered.

"Pia? Are you all right?"

"Yes, I'm fine . . . I got into a car accident this morning on my way over there. The EMTs are on the scene. They said I blacked out a few times, so they want to keep me for observation."

"Fuck. I'm so sorry for not answering the phone."

Pia let out a hoarse chuckle. "Rome, don't apologize for finally enjoying your life. The doctor wants to keep me overnight, but I should be out by morning. I can come aft—"

"You crazy? I will make sure you get picked up and taken home to rest. I can handle Mama for now."

"No, Ro—"

"Pia, you're like family. I can't have you out here dying on me. Please, just rest."

She kissed her teeth. "How about I have the agency send someone over . . . someone just as good as me? I can't rest knowing you don't have the help that you need."

"Long as it isn't you . . . I'll accept the help."

"Okay. I'll make some calls while waiting for them to give me a room." Pia sighed.

"Feel better . . . Let me know if you need anything."

"I will. Thanks, Rome."

I ended the call and continued to make my mother's tea.

"Is everything all right?"

"She got into an accident this morning. It explains why Mama came looking for me."

"How about I bring Pia some stuff up there to make her comfortable? You stay here with your mom, and we can check in with each other after I leave the hospital."

It was usually up to me to make decisions and plans on what would happen next. Had Fay not been here, I would have been trying to figure out what to do with Mama while trying to be there for Pia too.

"Yo, I don't know how I can even thank you, Fay."

She walked over to me, wrapped her arms around me, and pushed her head onto my chest. "You don't have to thank me, Rome. Take a minute and breathe . . . You can't do it all, and you don't have to at this moment."

She stood on her toes and kissed me on the lips.

"Fay, I love you . . . never stopped."

I never stopped loving Faith Stone. Even when I was angry with her, the love in my heart for her never left. With her being back in my life, that love amplified ten times more.

"Love you too." She kissed me.

I handed Mama her tea while she was enjoying *The Price Is Right*. It was her favorite thing to watch in the morning. Her doctor encouraged it because it kept her mind sharp.

I really didn't know how true that was.

After making sure Mama was settled, I headed back upstairs to find Fay pulling on her jeans. She offered a warm smile as she buttoned up the pants. Her frizzy hair was all over her head.

"What's on your mind?"

"You."

She blew me a kiss. "Babe, have you considered a facility for your mom? I know she means the world to you, but you're stressed."

I sat down on the bench in front of my bed. Faith slowly walked over to me and started rubbing my shoulders. "Out of the question, Fay. I'm not locking my mother away in one of those places."

"Stop thinking about it like it's a prison."

"Is it not? She won't have any of the comforts she has here with me."

She placed soft kisses on my neck. "There are some nice places that can care for your mother. You can have your relationship back with her again without the burden of a caretaker."

I jumped up from the bench. "Burden? My mama is *not* a burden," I snapped.

She held her hands up in surrender. "I never said that, Rome. I just thought that maybe it would be less stress—"

"Stressful for you or me? I'm good at taking care of her needs. Did I want her busting up in my room while I was fucking? No, but we're good."

Fay took a deep breath. "You're taking my words out of context. All I'm saying is that maybe it would take some stress off your back. I'm going to go up to Target and then head to the hospital for Pia." She slipped on her sneakers and grabbed her purse.

Fuck.

I grabbed her arm on her way out. "I'm sorry, Fay. I didn't mean to snap at you the way that I just did."

She looked up into my eyes with tears welled in hers. "I just want to help. All I've ever wanted to do was help, Rome."

I stepped back and stared at her, feeling like this was déjà vu.

"I'm sorry, baby . . . I know that . . . I know." I hugged her tightly while kissing the top of her head.

Whenever I was stressed or angry, I tended to lash out. All she was trying to do was help me with solutions, and I scolded her and got defensive. That wasn't fair to her, and I needed to do better.

I couldn't push Fay away again.

I wouldn't let myself do her the same way.

Chapter Seventeen

FAITH

I COULDN'T, IN GOOD faith, head up to the hospital without washing off all that sex on my body. As much as I wanted to run errands and head to the hospital, I needed a hot shower to rinse off all this goodness from my body. With how Rome worked me last night and this morning, this shower was very much needed.

My father and Marie were out when I returned home. The tree looked so beautiful in the living room. It brought life to a dreary and dead house. After a quick shower and change of clothes, I headed back out the door.

When I met Pia, she was so sweet to me that I wanted to do something nice for her. I grabbed a few things from Target to make her hospital stay more comfortable. While in Target, I called the restaurant and ordered her some food.

I discovered I hated hospital food when I gave birth to the girls. A fresh, hot meal from my father's restaurant would brighten anyone's day. It seemed like I was a chicken running with its head cut off with everything I had been doing lately. I had been moving around so quickly that I didn't have a moment to digest the things Mrs. Atkins had said to me.

It was easy to brush it off and blame her dementia. However, she would have said those same exact things to me had she been in her right mind. She was never a fan of mine or of Rome's and my relationship when we were teens. What mother liked their first son's girlfriend? As an adult, it caused me to worry. I never wanted Rome to feel like he had to pick between his mother and me.

With how upset she got when she noticed it was me in bed, I didn't want that to be a daily occurrence in their lives. What if seeing me caused her to become upset every time? That wasn't fair to Mrs. Atkins, Pia, or Rome. I watched as Rome had to calm his mother down and how stressed he got. He was embarrassed, and I didn't want him to feel like that. Nobody spoke about how stressful it was to care for aging parents.

It was a full-time job and could be stressful for him. His guilt wouldn't allow him to put his mama into a facility that was better equipped to handle her condition.

I was never suggesting that she was a burden for him or me. When Rome told me about his mother, I had to decide whether to accept it or tell him it was too much. The moment we kissed, I knew I would accept it because Mrs. Atkins was a part of him.

Flights are booked. See you tomorrow. I read Ash's text message as I killed the engine in the hospital parking lot.

This parking lot made my stomach queasy. It was the same parking lot I sat in with Rome before life as we knew it changed. I still remember the section where he parked his mom's car before we climbed out to chase behind Mrs. Atkins.

Great, I replied and took a deep breath.

Checking my reflection in the mirror, I climbed out of the car and headed into the emergency room entrance. Pia still hadn't been brought up to a room, so I, unfortunately, had to go into the dreaded emergency room that held so many memories I wished I could have forgotten.

I spotted Patient Information and slowly walked over toward the desk. "Hi, I'm looking for Pia Greene."

She smiled. "Sure thing, hon . . . P . . . I . . . A, correct?"

"Yes, ma'am."

While smacking her gum, she typed in the same and then looked up. "She's right down that hall to the left. Triage room three."

"Thanks so much," I smiled and headed down the hall.

It didn't matter what hospital it was. I hated hospitals. This particular one was at the top of my list of most hated. This hospital had taken so much from me.

I turned the hall while wishing I had a piece of gum to chomp on aggressively. An older woman walked past me and then backed up. "Faith Stone?"

I turned to face her to get a good look in her eyes. "Dr. Thompson? Oh, wow."

I hadn't seen Dr. Thompson since the day I stayed at her house until my father got back into town.

"Oh, my goodness. Faith, it's been so long . . . Look at you." She gave me that older Black lady look-over. "Jesus, time has been amazing to you."

"You too, Dr. Thompson. It's been so long."

"How have you been? What has life been like for you?"

I didn't want to get into my life story in the middle of a hospital hallway. But Dr. Thompson didn't look like she would move until I did.

"I moved to Georgia, and I have twin girls . . . They're eight."

"Jesus, twin girls . . . What a blessing. Your mother would have been so proud."

I wanted to tell her that my mother wouldn't have been proud. She probably wouldn't have cared if she was still alive, which is why my girls knew nothing about her.

"She would be," I said through my teeth.

I was so thankful that I stopped wearing my wedding ring. Her beeper started to beep again. "Look, we need to catch up . . . How about we do lunch at your father's restaurant this week?"

"Sounds good," I lied.

Dr. Thompson was a good woman, and I was glad she was still doing God's work as a doctor, but I didn't want to sit down and discuss my mother. Since I've been here, I have been hell-bent on not giving her any more energy than she deserved.

"Here, take my card and shoot me a text or a call on what day works for you. I'm on Thursdays."

"Sounds good . . . It was great seeing you again."

"Likewise," she smiled and quickly walked down the hallway to the code that had just been yelled over the loudspeaker.

I found Pia's room and knocked before opening the door. She wasn't there.

"Ms. Greene went down for testing a little while ago. She should be back in a few," the nurse passing by informed me.

"Oh, thanks," I replied, setting down the flowers and small makeshift basket I made for her.

I sat in one of the empty chairs and stared blankly at the TV screen. It made me wonder if this was how things would have gone had my mother lived. Would I have been sitting in this small room with her while she told me all the ways the accident wasn't her fault?

Would Rome come to find me to tell me that Allen had broken his leg, but he was going to make a full recovery once it was healed? Mrs. Atkins would still give me and my mom the stink eye because she just hated my mom, and because she hated my mom, that trickled down to me.

Except . . . That was how it could have gone in a perfect world. We all know the *real* way that it went, and it didn't go well for any of the parties involved.

"Here, cover yourself up . . . It's cold tonight." Dr. Thompson gave me her lab coat as she started her car.

I watched as she quickly pulled out of her assigned parking spot and drove down the darkened Sageport streets. I covered my body while staring blankly out the window. My heart hurt, and my soul felt shattered seeing Rome get into his father's car.

I screamed for him, but he refused to look back at me. I would have probably still been on the floor looking at the car drive away had it not been for Dr. Thompson. She was the one who pulled me up and helped me to her car. Raindrops started falling onto the car, making an irritating sound I never enjoyed.

"Finally, some rain. We were due for some," Dr. Thompson muttered.

How was she able to keep it all under control? My mother wasn't just some patient to her. She was her friend.

Well, she used to be.

Either way, how was she able to keep so calm like she hadn't just called the time of death on one of the deaths tonight? One being her good friend.

"Rain?" I scoffed. "You care about the rain and not the fact that Allen Atkins or Mom just passed away?"

Her facial expression remained the same. She didn't screw up her face or scold me for being disrespectful. "You're allowed to grieve your way, and I'm allowed to do the same." It was all she said.

Those simple words left me stunned.

I couldn't speak or think of anything else to say, so I leaned my head onto the window while I silently sobbed. It didn't matter how I felt at this moment. I should have died with Allen and my mother because that's how I felt. Rome didn't want anything to do with me, and now my family would be on the front page of the paper tomorrow morning, detailing the horrific events of the accident.

We arrived at Dr. Thompson's four-bedroom, three-bathroom home she shared with her husband. I never knew much about Dr. Thompson's life because she never offered anything. The only reason we knew she had a husband was because he attended charity events at the hospital with her.

"This is the guest bedroom, and the bathroom is right across the hall." She went inside a small linen closet. "These are my workout

clothes, but you can wear them so you can get out of that gown. Rest tonight, Faith. We can figure out everything in the morning."

I nodded and accepted the folded gym clothes she put into my arms. Locking the bathroom door behind me, I stared at my smeared makeup in the mirror.

I was so proud of my makeup today. This wasn't the way I thought it would have been smeared. Heaving a sigh, I dropped the dress onto the ground and stepped into the shower, hoping I could wash the night away.

"Faith, what are you doing here?" Pia asked when she was wheeled back into the room. "Did Rome force you up here? That man doesn't know how to take no for an answer," she smiled.

"No, he's home with his mom. I wanted to bring you a few things to make your stay here a little more comfortable." I pointed to the basket.

I put a pair of pajamas, slippers, and chocolates inside the basket. Pia was petite, so I got her a medium size so it would be comfortable for her.

"Hon, you did *not* have to do that . . . but I really appreciate it."

I grabbed the food from the restaurant and set it next to the basket. "I also got you some food. Oxtail stew."

"Oh God, I think my mouth just watered."

"Good."

I sat down, and she stared at me briefly before she spoke. "Rome is different with you around."

"Awe."

"No, I'm serious. I see him much happier and more excited about life. I even caught him humming last week," she cracked up laughing.

"He makes me happy too. I enjoy spending time with him." Rome brought out a happiness that I hadn't experienced in a while.

The happiness I got from my girls was different from this one. Everything he did fed my soul, my thoughts were clearer, and I knew what I wanted. Rome was what I wanted, and I could say that a thousand times in front of the entire town.

"I'm not one to get into your business, but I do hope you both find a way to make it work long distance."

We never discussed how this would go when I returned to Georgia. We weren't that far from each other, and a quick weekend road trip or flight could cure our thirst for each other.

However, we could only do that for so long before we became tired and wanted more. Long-distance relationships weren't easy and often didn't last. We both had responsibilities. I had the girls, and he had his mother. Neither of us could just pick up and leave without putting enough thought into it.

"I'm sure we'll figure something out," I assured her.

I stayed with Pia for a bit before she was moved to her room. We said our goodbyes, and I nearly ran out of the hospital to get to my car. The minute I touched the outside, I realized just how much I was suffocating inside of there.

Sorry about earlier, Fay. Come over? I read the text message from Rome. He had been apologizing since we shared that hug in his room.

I wasn't angry with him about the argument. It was a high-stress situation, and he lashed out because of that. Maybe it wasn't my place to sit there and suggest things. Rome knew what worked best for him and his mother. Why did I think I knew better?

I promised Marie that I would help her clear some boxes out of the spare room, I replied.

Okay.

As much as I wanted to head back over there, maybe some space would do us good. We still have the two-hour drive to pick up the girls tomorrow. I didn't want things to be tense or weird tomorrow.

Marie was sitting on the porch when I pulled into the driveway. She had a cup of coffee and was swinging peacefully.

"How did everything go?"

"Good. Pia was admitted overnight."

"Poor woman. These young kids around here speed without any care in the world."

"Where's Dad?"

"Back porch nap," she smiled.

Like Pia noticed a change in Rome, I noticed a change in my father. Had Marie not been around, keeping him from working would have been nearly impossible. I watched as they went on small dates and did things they enjoyed.

I loved that for them.

"Makes sense."

"How do you feel about the girls coming?"

"Excited and nervous."

"Why nervous?"

"I want them to like Rome."

She gently nudged my shoulder. "If they see what your father and I see, they will have no problem liking him. They want to see their mama happy, and he does that for you."

"He does." I leaned back, allowing the wind to push the swing for us both. "We kind of got into it earlier."

"About?"

"His mom. She walked in on us . . ." I hinted.

"Oh, Jesus."

"Exactly. She has never liked me, even before the dementia, so you can imagine she had some unkind words to say."

"I'm sorry, Faith."

"It's fine . . . I'm used to it."

"Just because you're used to it doesn't make it fine."

There was nothing that I could do about it. Mrs. Atkins had never liked me, and that would probably never change. I could spend time trying to get a woman with dementia to understand I wasn't the enemy or deal with it.

I chose to deal with the situation.

Brushing off Marie's statement, I continued. "I suggested he put her into a home . . . You know, somewhere she can be taken care of, so he wouldn't have to stress about her care."

"And I gather he didn't take it well."

"At all. He got so upset and defensive."

"It's a tough situation. That's his mother, the last piece of his family that he has left. Imagine having to put your last living relative in a home."

I couldn't imagine it. My father had always been independent and able to care for himself. He was my only relative besides his side of the family. Rome had other family as well. I remember they would come down to hang out at their family's beach house years ago.

I wasn't sure how close they were anymore. or if he even kept in contact, but I understood what Marie meant.

His brother died, and then his father passed not too long after. Signing his mother into a home would make him feel the same as if she had passed away too.

"I feel like crap now."

"Don't feel like that. You just wanted to help him the best way you knew. It's not something that can throw you both off course. Make it right with each other."

"We will," I assured her. "Ready to tackle this spare room?"

"Yes. Your father said pretty much everything can go. He did say that you can keep anything that you want . . . you know, things of your mother."

I didn't want to keep anything from that woman. Everything could go in the trash or to charity. I didn't say that to Marie, though. "Okay."

While I pulled the boxes from the closet, Marie stripped the beds and went to wash the linen. I sat on the bed and went through each box, looking at old pictures of my parents. Most of the pictures were of my mother in her cheerleading uniform.

She was so happy and full of life.

Her smile could light up an entire room. I never noticed how much we resembled each other until looking at her older pictures. As I grew up, she was so unkempt that I could never picture how she used to look. It was clear that I got my curly hair from her.

I grabbed another bunch of pictures and flipped through them. "Wait, is that Mrs. Atkins?"

I flipped the picture over and read my mother's handwriting describing each picture and the year.

Cheerleading and football camp, 1989. Kimba Cassidy, Keisha Wilson, Debra Brentwood, and Richard Blake.

No wonder Mrs. Atkins walked around like her shit didn't stink. She was stunning with her perfectly curled brown hair. Mr. Atkins locked her down before anyone else could.

Rome looked so much like his mother. It was surreal seeing this picture. I could never imagine my mother laughing, smiling, or doing anything that brought joy to someone. I had always known she was a cheerleader, and that was because my father let it slip one time.

That was the reason I ended up joining the cheerleading squad. I thought it would bring us closer if I took an interest in something that she used to love. She never came to one game or even acknowledged that I was on the team. I ended up quitting the team a few months later.

I continued to go through the pictures while battling with myself if I wanted to keep them. My girls knew nothing about their grandmother, so who would I be saving them for? Undecided, I put the stack of pictures to the side and grabbed the papers all balled together under the box. I straightened out the papers while fixing them.

There were a bunch of old apartment rent receipts and pediatrician papers from when I was a baby. I started to toss them out . . . until I came across a birth certificate.

My father had given me all my documents before I left Sageport. He told me to guard those papers with my life, so I did. Why was this another birth certificate that seemed like the original?

I always assumed I had the original copy.

My eyes widened when I looked at the line for the father's signature.

"*Richard Blake*," I whispered.

This birth certificate had to be mine. It had my name, birthday, and the hospital I was born in. Why the hell was this man's name on my birth certificate?

I rummaged through all the photos for the one with my mom, Mrs. Atkins, Dr. Thompson, and the infamous Richard Blake. Who was this man, and why was *his* name on my birth certificate?

Clyde Stone was my father. He was all I had ever known. This other man couldn't possibly be my father.

"Faith, what's going on? You're shaking, sweetie." Marie came and sat beside me.

I couldn't form any words, so I shoved the birth certificate and the picture into her hands. She quietly studied the birth certificate and then the picture. I could tell when it clicked because her eyes grew as wide as mine.

"Is my father *not* my father?" I whimpered, confused.

Marie didn't know what to say. "I . . . I don't know, love."

What could she tell me? She didn't know my parents' past or why this man was on my birth certificate. I was sickened by the thought of not knowing who I was.

I wanted to run and interrupt my father's nap with all the questions racing through my head. I needed to know what all of this meant, and only he could tell me. While I wanted to demand answers to these questions, I didn't want to disrupt him or cause any of his health issues to flare up. I took a deep breath and folded the picture and birth certificate.

"Here," Marie replied, pulling out a small cloth black journal with roses on it.

Why did this journal feel familiar to me? It felt like I had seen and even held it a few times. It was thick with tattered corners and covered pages. Every page was covered from front to back.

"I feel like I've seen this before."

"It may give you the answers you're looking for . . . I don't know if Clyde is strong enough to deal with this right now."

"You're right," I agreed.

We were just getting back to this good place, and I didn't want to ruin it. Especially not before the girls could get here. I put the folded-up picture and birth certificate in the book and took it to my room. I slid it under my pillow and then returned to help clean the spare room. Marie and I were both silent while we worked to finish clearing everything out. Neither of us knew what to say.

The quiet was welcomed.

It allowed me to figure out my thoughts and think of what was next. If I couldn't get answers from my father, I needed to get them from someone. This could give me a look into my mother's life and why alcohol was her prized possession.

I spent the night reading over my mother's journal. It wasn't until Rome texted me, reminding me that he was coming early in the morning, that I finally put it down.

The journal highlighted everything that happened during her high school year. She detailed how her mother forced her on the cheerleading squad and how she and Dr. Thompson had bigger dreams. They wanted to move away from this town and had already started saving money. She told how they worked at the A&W in town to save for their first apartment together.

Debra Atkins was clearly one of the fast-tailed girls she accused me of being. She got around with most of the guys on the football team until Dale came to their school. My mother detailed every person in her life at that time except my father. I searched the book from front to back to see if I could find something about my dad.

Richard Blake was all throughout the journal. At first, she didn't like him and thought he was a jerk. He grew on her over time and throughout the pages, but she still considered him a jerk. Their relationship seemed strange. She didn't seem to love him like he had professed to love her. She seemed stalled, as if she didn't know what to do when it came to being with him. Despite feeling confused, she continued to be with him—even going to prom with him.

Before Mom and Richard became a thing, he and Debra were a bigger thing. Mom even suggested that he started dating her to make Debra jealous. Even with her knowing that, she continued to date him. He teased her for being a virgin and for not wanting to take things to the next level.

Such a loser.

My mother battled a lot with her inner thoughts. She knew what was right and what she wanted, but she always went against it. At Debra's birthday party, she didn't want to drink spiked punch, but he made her feel like a child because she turned it down.

Rome's horn forced me to pull my head up from Mom's journal. I smiled and grabbed my purse and a bag filled with snacks for the girl before heading to the car. He stepped out dressed in jeans, a white T-shirt, and sneakers. Rome could dress so basic, but it always suited him.

"Hey, you." I smiled and hugged him.

"Missed you, Fay." I looked up at him, and he kissed my lips. "Even if it was for one night."

"Missed you too," I said as he walked me to the passenger side. "Can we agree not to argue ever again?"

"There's going to be arguments . . . Can we agree that we will always work them out, no matter how difficult they are?"

"I like that." I kissed his lips, and he closed the door.

I put the snacks in the backseat and quickly put on my seat belt. Rome climbed into the car and then pulled out of the driveway. "Ready for this drive?" he asked.

"So ready. We should arrive as soon as the kids land."

"Let's hope traffic is decent."

"Uh-huh," I replied, not really paying attention because I opened the journal again and was going over the details of Debra's party.

Rome was talking, and I had no clue what he was talking about.

"Fay, what are you reading? I asked if you wanted to stop and get some coffee before getting on the road."

I snapped my head up. "Sorry. I found an old journal from my mom . . . I learned a lot of information yesterday while cleaning out her stuff."

"What do you mean?"

I told Rome everything about what I had discovered yesterday. He was so tuned in that he nearly went through a light. "You mean to tell me that my mama and yours were *friends*?"

"Apparently so. It seems like they let a guy get in between them . . . Richard Blake."

"Richie? My father had a picture of him in his office when he was younger."

"So, they were friends?"

"Seem to be."

"Does he still live in Sageport?"

"Fay, he passed away when they were younger. Car accident."

I found it funny that Dale and Richard were friends when he and Debra dated. "Wow."

"Yeah, he died while my father was away at college."

"Shit."

"So, Clyde isn't your real father. How do you feel about that?"

I shrugged. "Confused. I feel like I've also been living a lie. Why did they decide to cover it up?"

"Did you try asking your father?"

"I figured that this wasn't the time to ask him . . . or ever."

Rome rubbed my thigh. "I agree. Right now isn't the time with the girls coming, but you can't avoid it forever, Fay."

I shrugged. "Why does shit like this happen to me? It was already bad that my own mother never loved me . . . Now this."

"She loved you in her own way."

"I would never love my daughters in the way that she loved me. Her love did more damage than good for me."

"Sorry."

"It's not your fault."

"I know. I just feel bad. Everybody deserves to feel that motherly love. The shit is the best . . . speaking from experience."

Rome got to experience what it was like to feel love from the person who gave him life. Mrs. Atkins loved her boys with all her body and soul. There wasn't anything she wouldn't do for them.

This was why I loved on my girls the way that I did. I knew how it felt not to have love from your mom, and I never wanted them to experience that. It didn't matter how wrong they were or if they made a mistake. I would always have their back.

I may not always agree with them, but they never had to worry about my love fading for them. Everything that my mother did wrong, I made sure to fix it when it came to having children of my own. Being the kind of mother that I was to my girls healed the inner child inside me. Allowing them to have a voice and know that no matter what, they were loved brought tears to my eyes.

When we arrived at the airport, we parked and went inside to wait for Ash and the girls to deplane. He had shot me a text when their plane landed, which happened to be the same time we were exiting the highway.

I was so giddy that I had trouble staying still. Rome stood behind me with his arms wrapped around my shoulders.

"Why am I so nervous to meet two eight-year-olds?"

"Don't be nervous. My girls are sweet."

"If they're anything like you, then I have everything to worry about."

I snorted. "I'm sweet . . . I'm the nicest person you probably ever met."

"Yeah, whatever . . . I've seen the mean side of you."

"Once before, when Fat Joe stepped on my foot. In my defense, you would be upset too."

"Fair," he agreed.

My foot hurt for an entire week after that incident. Did I call him every name under the sun?

Yes.

Did I have a reason to?

Absolutely.

He stomped on my toes, being stupid, and that was typical of Joe. He was a clown, and everyone put up with his antics.

Not me.

I happened to be up late the night before, arguing with my mother about her liquor. She accused me of giving it to my friends or drinking it myself when she was the one who had drunk the entire thing alone. By the time I did fall asleep, I had to get back up for school, not even three hours later.

"You cussed his ass out into next week," Rome laughed, remembering how angry I was after that.

I couldn't focus on my classes because of my throbbing toes. Joe was sweet, apologized, and even offered to buy my lunch that day. I was too angry to accept his apology or the free lunch. Whenever I held a grudge, it was hard for me to let it go.

"Mommmmmmmmmm!" Mayven screamed as they came down the escalator.

"May and Maddie!" I squealed while waiting for the escalator to bring them down.

I noticed Ashton's face as he looked Rome up and down. He was trying to figure out what was going on.

"Mommy!" Maddie was the first to run into my arms.

"God, I missed you, princess." I kissed her face and ruffled her curls.

Mayven flew into my arms as soon as I released her sister. "Baby doll, I missed you too." I kissed her on the cheeks.

On cue, both girls looked up at Rome, who stood there looking down at them. I stood up and took Rome's hand. "Girls, this is Mr. Rome." I introduced them.

"Fay, come on . . . not Mr.," he begged.

"Fay?" Ashton raised his eyebrows.

Rome cleared his throat. "Rome . . . Nice to meet you," he extended his hand and shook Ashton's hand.

"Ashton . . . Nice to meet you. How do you and Fay know each other?" Ashton had no right to ask questions I never asked him.

"Not your concern," I quickly shut it down with a smile. "Did you check any bags?"

He stared at me briefly before he responded. "Yeah. I checked their bags . . . Um, can I talk to you privately?"

"Sure."

The girls were already asking Rome a bunch of questions. They wanted to know why he was so tall and how he grew his beard the way he did. I laughed and walked over toward the baggage carousel with Ashton.

"New boyfriend? Weren't you just on my case about Francis, but you bring yours to the airport?"

"Why do you care?"

"I come down the escalator to see the mother of my children hugged up with some random man. What the fuck, Faith?"

"It shouldn't matter what I do with my personal life. I only asked you to communicate openly, and you failed to do that each time. You set the tone for how things will be, Ash."

"So, this is what it is?" He laughed. "Tit for tat . . . Is that what we're doing now?"

I folded my arms, tired of this conversation already. "What did you need to talk about?" I spotted the girls' bags and went to grab them.

"This. Who *is* that man?"

"He's my high school boyfriend, Ashton. We reconnected . . . Why are you so concerned?"

"Baby, let me take those from you." Rome grabbed the girls' suitcases as they trailed behind him.

"Mr. Rome, you can carry both at the same time?" Madison asked as they walked toward the exit, giving Ashton and me privacy.

"*Baby?*"

"What's wrong with that? You're happy in your relationship, so it shouldn't matter what's going on in mine."

"You admit that this is a relationship."

Neither Rome nor I sat down and put a title on what we were to each other. I didn't think we needed to because it felt so right between us.

Ashton didn't need to know all of that. "It doesn't matter. When I feel you need to know something, I'll update you. Thank you for bringing the girls," I said.

"We have a six-hour layover before heading to Jamaica," he informed me as if I cared what was happening with him and his girlfriend.

"Cool."

"Goddammit, Faith . . . Drop this nonchalant act you've been having for months."

It wasn't an act.

When I divorced Ashton, I could either sit around and care way too much, or I could move on with my life. I chose to move on with my life while feeling the aftermath of becoming divorced. Did I have those days when I wanted to call and tell him I wanted to make this work? Of course. I think every divorced woman has regrets about her divorce.

The more he showed how irrelevant the girls were, the less I cared to call him, and the less I regretted my decision. He wanted me to care so much, and I didn't have it in me to give a shit about what he had going on and who he was doing it with.

"Bye, Ashton . . . Have fun in Jamaica," I replied and headed over toward the girls.

They both grabbed my hand while Rome carried their suitcases. "Mommy, is this your boyfriend?" Madison just had to know.

"I'm your mommy's future husband," Rome winked.

The girls all squealed. "Mommy, you're getting married? Can we be the flower girls?" Madison was all too excited about this imaginary wedding that wasn't happening.

"Baby, we're not getting married. If—"

"*When*," Rome corrected me.

"When we do, you girls will be the first to know," I assured them, and they were satisfied.

Chapter Eighteen

ROME

I DROPPED FAY AND the girls back at her father's house and headed home. I wanted to give her time to relax and settle with the kids. It was different seeing this side of Fay. She was a mom and a good one at that. I knew she was a mother and heard her speak to the girls whenever I was around. It was something else witnessing it for the first time, seeing how soft, caring, and attentive she was to her girls' needs. It was my favorite part about watching her.

The new aide, Agnes, was just as good as Pia. The difference between her and Pia was that she could work nights. While Pia wanted to return to work upon leaving the hospital, I forced her to take time off with pay. I knew this was how she provided for her family, and I never wanted to take that money away from her.

I also didn't want her to return to work quicker than she was healed. When her doctor cleared her to return, she and Agnes would work together. Agnes would work nights while Pia handled Mama during the day. After snapping on Fay the other day, I realized that I needed to delegate more when it came to Mama's needs.

Having her all riled up over catching Fay and me together was a lot. The next day, it was like it had never happened. She didn't even bring it up or mention anything close to it. With her wanting to roam the house more, I needed more care to ensure she was safe and secure. I had ordered a child gate for the bottom stairs so she never walked upstairs unsupervised again.

There would be more mornings where I held Fay down as we kissed and talked in between giving her soft and gentle strokes. I wanted to make this work as much as I could without having to decide to put Mama in a home.

I couldn't do it.

Hiring around-the-clock care seemed like the best alternative. She could be in our home, where she was truly loved and cared for. I've heard horror stories about places like some of the facilities, and I didn't want my mother to experience anything like that—ever.

When I returned home, I sat at the kitchen table and observed Agnes and my mother watch *Jeopardy* together. Agnes didn't cook like Pia. She made Mama a frozen dinner, which she enjoyed.

How did I know?

She insisted on saving the box to show it to me. My mother's appetite was always up and down. Some days, she could eat me out of a house, and then others, we could barely get her to eat a slice of toast. The fact that she loved this Boston Market TV Dinner spoke volumes, so I took a picture and made a mental note to grab a few more of them.

I tried to give her home-cooked meals daily, even if they were leftovers. Before Pia, I was grabbing food from different small businesses in town to give her that home-cooked feeling. I didn't want her to get hooked on that processed junk.

It seemed that she enjoyed it more than the meals that Pia busted her ass to cook. I sat downstairs for a bit before Agnes told me she would help Mama bathe before bed. There was a spare bedroom right across from Mama's room, and we even put a baby gate at the end of the hallway so she wouldn't be able to get into the living room or kitchen.

As soon as I plopped down in my chair, my phone rang. I sighed when I saw it was Linda's name. It was no secret I had been taking more time off from work, and I hadn't gotten to those files she had requested.

"Hey, Linda, everything good?"

"No. I went into your office earlier, and those files were in the same place where I had put them. Not even one signed, Rome," she scolded.

Linda was the only person who could get away with scolding me like a child. She had basically watched me grow up, so I extended that right to her.

"Yeah, I was going to come in tomorrow and handle those for you."

"You were supposed to handle them last week," she reminded me like I didn't already know.

"I know. Stuff was tough this week with Mama. She's all good now, so I'll be in tomorrow."

I didn't have any plans to go to work tomorrow. In fact, I made plans to pick up some donuts from Dinky Dooughynuts and bring them over for the girls.

Santa Claus was going to be at Sageport Square, and I was going to see if Faith wanted to take them.

"You know," she heaved a sigh, "if this is all too much, just consider the offer. I know you saw the offer letter come through the fax. It's a very generous deal."

It was a generous deal.

The day that Fay came and surprised me with lunch was when I first saw it. I was deep in thought when she popped up. Instead of focusing on that, I welcomed the distraction.

At that moment, I didn't want to think about any of that. The thought of signing my name on the dotted line and giving up everything my father had worked hard for felt so wrong.

Then I thought of having a life outside the dealerships and got this sense of excitement. My father had made very smart investments that my mother and I still lived off of. Money wasn't a problem when it came to us. I could afford to provide for my mother and pay for her care without ever touching the money if I decided to sell the dealerships.

"Need more time, Linda."

"Okay. In the meantime, put on your boss hat and get those papers signed for me tomorrow."

"Will do." I ended the call.

I knew I wouldn't be able to sleep tonight, so I put my sneakers back on and headed to the dealership. All I wanted was to spend time with Fay and her girls, so knocking out these documents tonight would keep Linda off my back and avoid my having to come into the office tomorrow. I didn't know what I wanted to do with the dealerships or if I even wanted to sell them. This had been my father's dream, not mine. Still, I felt wrong giving up the last piece of him. Were the dealerships even the same without the Atkins family owning it? Until I made my decision, I had to operate as the head man in charge, as usual, and that meant getting shit done that I didn't want to.

When I arrived at Carl's house, the girls, Marie, and Carl were gone. They were heading to the coast to show the girls around, and then they planned to meet back at the restaurant to have lunch.

I found Fay sitting on the porch with her mother's journal and a laptop. She was so focused on what she was doing that she didn't notice me walking up the steps and standing in front of her.

The wild stuff she found out about her dad not being her biological father was crazy. I couldn't even express how I would feel if I found out something like that.

"Hey, baby." She kissed me on the lips. "Donuts? You must have wanted to make a good impression on the girls. Too bad they're off to the coast."

"They'll have a snack for later." I set the box down and sat beside her. "What's all of this?"

"I've been going down the rabbit hole of all the friends my mom mentioned in this book to try to contact. Somebody has to know something . . . It's not like I can ask your mom." She realized what she had said. "I'm sorry, Rome. I didn't mean it like that."

"You're good, Fay. I'm not easily offended because it's the truth. Some days, Mama knows more than others . . . but you know where you can get the truth from?"

"Where?"

It was right under her nose.

"Dr. Thompson."

She sighed. "I was hoping to avoid her."

"Why?"

"Because I can't help but be reminded of that horrible night every time I look at her face. It's not her fault, but she's a reminder of everything we lost." She touched my face.

"She didn't cause it, Fay. Dr. Thompson had nothing to do with what happened to your mom or Allen."

"Yeah."

I gently grabbed the journal and closed her laptop. "How about we get out of the house too? The tree lighting is taking place in town . . . Let's grab some hot chocolate and do some Christmas shopping."

"I haven't even thought about that. Now that the girls are here . . . I really need to get on that."

"That's the spirit."

We went back into the house so she could take her stuff into the bedroom. I put the donuts on the kitchen table and followed behind Fay. She quickly changed out of the sweats to a cute sweater dress with thigh-high boots.

"Can I see the boots without the dress?"

"Last time we got caught by your mom. I don't want to get caught by my father and daughters." She kissed my lips, but that wasn't enough for me.

"I can be quick."

"You are many things, Rome Atkins, but quick *isn't* one of them."

"Wanna bet?"

Fay was competitive as shit. Seeing that sly grin across her face told me she still was.

She pulled up her dress, slid down her panties, and climbed up on her bed, showing me how perfect that arch was.

I closed the door behind me and wrestled with my pants. My dick helped me get it out of my boxers. "Fuck," I groaned before I even touched her.

Grabbing her waist, I pulled her closer to me as my dick found its way inside of her. She was so warm and tight that I wanted to stay in here all day. But we were on a timer, and I wanted to prove to her that I could finish quickly.

Without warning, she threw that ass back at me, and I wasn't prepared. Holding tighter, I beat it from the back as hard as I could. Luckily, nobody was home because the sound of my balls slapping her ass filled the room.

"Aweee . . . mmm," she moaned out while she continued to toss it back at me. I slapped her ass and watched as it jiggled like jelly on a dining room table.

The boots and the sight of her bare ass bent over this bed were making me even more erect than I already was. I bit down on my bottom lip as I held her in place and rammed my shit into her harder and harder.

"Say my name, Fay . . . Tell me how much you want this."

"Da . . . daddy, I want this . . . I want this dick," she squealed as I continued. "Rom . . . Rome, I looveee you," she screamed out.

Hearing her profess her love for me caused me to empty myself inside of her. "Fuck . . . Shit, Fay," I grunted as I pulled out of her.

She collapsed onto the bed. "Fine. You win."

I helped her up and kissed her lips. "I told you I can handle business quickly."

While she went to clean herself up, I went to grab a donut from the box. Sex was always off the chain when it came to us. We could get it on anywhere, and both end up satisfied.

Faith Stone brought that out of me. She made me feel like a teenager again. One look into those beautiful, brown, doe eyes could get my dick hard in a second.

It was the way she stared at me . . . as if I were the most important thing to her. Faith could get any and everything from me without ever speaking a word.

"You ready?" She came out wearing a different dress and sneakers. "I wasn't going to last long in those heels."

"I like it when you dress down more," I said, grabbing her and spinning her around. "I'm always ready when it comes to you."

We shared one more kiss before we piled into my car to head into town. Christmas was always a sour holiday for me. I avoided the town center because of all the decorations and cheery people waiting for Christmas. If it weren't for Linda, I probably wouldn't have gone to get a tree.

When we were younger, my mother would pile us into the car to head to the town center. We would watch the tree light up, get hot chocolate, and then my father would meet us in time to grab dinner at McCray's. Those memories were something that I tightly held onto.

I would never get those memories back with my parents and brother. Christmas was my mother's favorite holiday. Everyone who lived on our block looked forward to when she put up the decorations. She would spend weeks preparing the menu for Christmas dinner and baking cookies for our school. My teachers always loved the goodie bags she would prepare for them at Christmas.

Now, I tried to avoid mentioning certain things for fear of how she would react. It was better to live in the past if it made her happy. I would give anything to see my mother in her prime, celebrating Christmas like the old days.

"What's on your mind?" Faith asked as we walked through the town center. We stopped in her father's coffee shop and got hot chocolate as we strolled.

The weather was perfect.

That was the thing about Christmastime in Florida. It was cooler than usual, although still warmer than the other states. I wore a thin button-down shirt and a pair of cargo shorts, and I was warm.

"My mama."

She squeezed my arm a bit and leaned her head on it. "I'm sorry."

"It's my turn to ask why you're apologizing."

"I don't know. I feel guilty, I guess," she shrugged.

"You didn't cause this," I reminded her.

"Okay."

We stopped walking. "I need you to understand that, Fay. None of this was your fault, so I want you to stop feeling guilty."

She gave me that look. "Okay, Rome."

We continued walking. "Do you know what you're getting the girls yet?"

"Not yet. Being here in Sageport seems more than enough for them."

"Kids are so simple. Spending quality time with their Pop-Pop seems to be enough for them."

"I know, right? Had we been home, they would have asked for the world. I love seeing Dad with them, though," she admitted.

"Means you need to come visit back home more . . . Let the girls get to know their grandfather and Marie."

"Or do you want me to visit more because you're here?"

"That too."

"What are we going to do about us?"

It was a question I often asked myself. This felt so right that I never wanted Christmas to come. If I could hold us in this time forever, I would have. Everything seemed perfect, although things were far from it.

"You can't move here, and I can't move to Georgia."

"Who says you can't?"

"Mama isn't going to do well with change. She threw a fit when the TV went out last year because of the new remote. I don't even want to imagine how she would be in a new house or state."

"Yeah, I get it," she sighed.

"Aye, look, we will make it work with us no matter what," I promised her. It didn't matter if I had to make more trips to visit her or we had to assign weekends. We would find a way to make this work.

"Okay." She looked into my eyes with such promise that I would do everything I could to make our relationship work.

We didn't go through all this not to figure out a way. If this meant as much to us as we both said it did, then we would work it out. Faith was a priority for me, and it was one that I took seriously.

We entered a few stores where she found some items for her father and Marie. I watched as she got so excited about giving to others. Faith's love language was gifts; I could tell from how she bought everything she thought Marie or her father would enjoy.

By the time we finished going from shop to shop, we walked over to the tree lighting. They had a DJ playing "If Only You Knew" by Patti LaBelle. The older crowd was dancing while waiting for the lights to come on.

I took the bags from Faith and placed them on a table nearby. Grabbing her hand, we danced to the middle with the other couples who were years older than us. Everyone was enjoying themselves, even the people who weren't dancing. The vibes out here were unmatched, and I didn't know why I expected anything else.

"*If you only you knew, how much I do, do need you,*" Fay sang to me while staring into my eyes.

I kissed her neck. "I need you more, Fay."

It was true.

This woman didn't know how much I needed her. How much she changed my life in the short time that she's been here. This song spoke to my soul as I held her around her waist, and we slowly danced. All the feelings I felt in high school were real.

I remember my mother telling me I didn't know anything about love. I used to question if that was true. Did I know what true love was back then?

It took me fifteen years to realize that even as a pimply-faced teen, I knew exactly what true love was because I felt it with Faith every time I looked her in the eyes. As we stood here, those same feelings were swirling inside me. They were stronger and more intense than before.

I never felt like we had much to lose back then.

Now, I knew that if I lost Fay again, I couldn't move on. Having love and losing it twice didn't sit right with my spirit. Faith was everything I wanted.

"I need you too, Rome." She held the side of my face and stared into my eyes. "I've always needed you."

The song ended, and we still stared into each other's eyes. It was like nobody else existed around us. Faith and I were in our own world.

Exactly how I liked it.

Chapter Nineteen

FAITH

"**M**OM, WE'RE GOING with Ms. Marie to the restaurant today. She's going to show us how to bake pies." Mayven leaned on my bedroom door.

Seeing my baby leaning on my old bedroom door felt surreal. The girls were having way too much fun spending time with their Pop-Pop and Marie. I enjoyed seeing how my father lit up whenever they called him for something. Since I had got them from the airport, I hadn't had to step in and do anything. The girls wanted to spend all their time with their grandfather, and I wouldn't deny that.

They had spent many years not really associating with him, and I didn't want that pattern to continue. "Sounds fun, May. Where's your sister?"

"Helping Pop-Pop grab the duck out of the deep freezer. We're having duck tonight."

"He makes the best duck." My mouth watered, anticipating tonight's dinner.

"Mom, do you like Mr. Rome?" Despite him telling them not to call him Mr. Rome, the girls still called him that.

I found it cute and funny all at the same time. "I like him a lot, May." I refused to deprive my girls of seeing their mother happy.

I wanted them to witness this side of me. Things were different with Rome than they were with their father. My feelings were deeper for Rome, and I felt like I could really let down my hair and be myself. Rome knew all the good and ugly about me, so I didn't have to pretend around him.

"Who is that?" Mayven snatched the picture of my mother from the top of the laptop.

"She's my mom."

The girls knew nothing about my mother because I refused to acknowledge her. She didn't deserve to live on through my words. As the girls became older and more curious, I couldn't continue to lie to them about it. I wanted an open-door policy with my girls that made them comfortable enough to talk to me about anything. How would they feel that way when I hid my life from them?

"You have a mom?"

I giggled. "Of course I do. I promise I will tell you and your sister about her one day . . . okay?" I pinched her cheeks and scooped the picture out of her hands.

"Okay . . . promise."

"A double pinky-winky promise." I held out my pinky, and Mayven looped hers through mine.

"Where are you going?"

"Mommy has an important lunch with an old friend. When I return, I want to take you girls to surprise Mr. Rome. We can bake him some cookies."

Mayven rolled up her sleeves. "It's a good thing I'll get some practice with Ms. Marie."

"Learn all you can, okay?"

She nodded, and I grabbed the journal and picture to head out the door. I finally stopped beating around the bush and called Dr. Thompson. She was all too thrilled to hear from me.

As much as the lunch was a nice moment to catch up on life, I wanted answers to the dozens of questions swirling in my head. The man that was my biological father was now dead, and I couldn't get them from him. As far as I knew, Clyde was my father. He was the one who stepped up and raised me as his own, so I was his own.

I didn't want to hurt his feelings by going behind his back, but I needed to know. I had to understand why my mother lied to me about who my father was—my entire life. I thought one man was my dad, which was false. Kimba had a bunch of secrets, some, it seems, she was too scared even to share with herself.

I read her journal and felt sorry for her. She wanted to fit in with the popular kids so badly that she sacrificed who she was to fit in. Debra acted like a saint when I was a teen, but she was worse than her son and me as teenagers.

The amount of drinking and drugs these kids did back then should have been illegal.

I mean, it *was* illegal.

It made sense why my mother fell victim to the body. That night she was pressured to drink sent her down a spiral of always having to have a drink or pop a pill before going out to party. The crazy part about it is that she hated herself because of it. She was following the man she thought she loved, who was a raging alcoholic at eighteen.

I pulled into the spot in front of Belle, an Italian restaurant Dr. Thompson suggested. I took a deep breath and grabbed all my things before heading into the restaurant.

The server greeted me and took me to the table where Dr. Thompson was waiting. "Great. You made it." She stood and hugged me.

"Yes. I've driven by this place a few times . . . This is my first time eating here."

There were so many new restaurants throughout Sageport that I needed a guide.

"It doesn't get nearly as much business as those new restaurants on the coast," she scoffed.

"Not a fan of all the new establishments on the coast?"

She rolled her eyes. "Not at all. My husband took me to Pier 3, and I enjoyed the food, but the number of people they packed in there was ridiculous. You can't even enjoy your food over the chatter."

That wasn't Rome's or my experience when we had dinner there. I couldn't really say much since Rome had arranged for us to have the best seat. The food was delicious, and I would go back a second time.

"The food is good."

The waiter came and took our drink orders before handing us menus. I looked over the menu to be sure I knew what I wanted by the time he returned.

"It's so good to see you back in Sageport, Faith. You have no clue how happy I was to see you at the hospital that day."

I smiled and continued looking over the menu. "It feels good to be back. I can't believe all my father has accomplished with his restaurant and coffee shop."

"Carl is resilient. That restaurant is one of the best things in Sageport, along with the coffee. Please tell me you've had a chance to try it."

"Um, I'm embarrassed to admit that I might have an addiction to his chai lattes."

"They're so good." She smacked her lips as if her mouth was getting watery by just talking about it.

"So good. He has me keeping an eye on things while he's recovering, and I have to give myself a pep talk every time I go in there."

"Carl has done good for the community. He donates book bags yearly for the kids' back-to-school event."

"Wow."

"Uh-huh."

As I expected, the waiter came back to take our order. We put them in, and both took a sip of our drinks.

"I found this picture while cleaning Dad's guest room." I handed her both the picture and then the birth certificate.

She froze when she saw the birth certificate. For someone who was a doctor, she couldn't keep a neutral face to save her life. This was some of the emotion I needed that night inside the car fifteen years ago.

"Where did you find this? Kimba said she got rid of it years ago." She spoke more to herself than me.

"Why would she get rid of it?"

She neatly folded the paper and picture and handed them back to me. "I don't know."

"Keisha, please. You were the closest person to her . . . well, Mrs. Atkins too." I dropped the "Dr. Thompson" quickly.

She had the answers, and I wanted to know them. I needed to put this to bed to move on from this chapter of my life. I just wanted to know my mother's reasons for the decisions that she made with not only her life but also with mine.

"Faith, it's better if you don't know. Your mom went to great lengths to ensure you never found out."

"Clearly, she didn't. This *is* my life, and I should know why my mother lied about who my father is."

I wasn't a child anymore and could handle the truth. So much had happened in my life, and I handled that just fine. It felt like God sent me back to Sageport to get a second chance with Rome and closure with my mom.

The amount of hate I felt for my mother through the years wasn't healthy for me. Reading her journal made me feel closer to her than I did when she was alive.

"Richard Blake and your mother were never supposed to happen. He was on the football team, the captain, so you know how that goes." She paused to take a sip of her drink. "Debra Brentwood was in love with Richard Blake ... in love with him. Their relationship was so on and off, and we all knew Richard was off-limits."

"Didn't Mrs. Atkins love Dale?"

"Dale didn't transfer into our school until senior year. By that time, Richard and Debra had been messing around since sophomore year. He was her first. Something happened between the two of them at the spring formal, and Richard called it quits. Not too long after that, she was talking and dating Dale Atkins. Dale and Richard were close friends . . . Apparently, they knew each other from Bible camp that their parents sent them to in Tampa." She took a breath. "They were still thick as thieves even though they both dated the same girl. Once Richard realized how serious Debra was with Dale, he had to make her jealous."

"That's where my mom came in."

"Exactly. Your mom was on the cheerleading team by force. She was good, but we could always tell it wasn't something she would have picked for herself. She didn't date at all and always had her head in a book. Everyone knew Kimba had the longest set of legs, and she was smart. Richard slid in there like the slippery sneak he was." She shuttered, shaking off an invisible ick. "Your mom wasn't used to the attention that Richard was giving her. I don't believe she even truly liked him. I think she was tired of being the girl that didn't have a date, and now she had the most popular guy walking her to class."

"It makes a lot of sense why Mrs. Atkins never liked my mom or me."

"Oh, chile, she hated your mother after that. Debra was furious when she saw they were dating. Richard was terrible for your mother, and I told her that. She started cutting school, drinking, and doing drugs . . . things she never did before. Whenever I tried to warn her, she would cut me off and tell me I was jealous. Typical teenage stuff."

"He's the reason she started to drink," I whispered to myself. Keisha was too deep into the story to truly pay me any attention.

"Kimba and I made plans to get out of this town. We had saved nearly four thousand dollars for our apartment in New York. We got into our dream colleges and were supposed to leave that fall." Keisha smiled. "We planned to go on a road trip in my beat-up-ass Buick. Then your mother was caught snorting coke in the girl's bathroom and was expelled. The school informed her college, and that acceptance letter was out the window. That summer, she didn't care about anything. She lied to her mother about where she was going and spent all her time with Richard."

"She never mentioned any of this."

"Why would she? She was running around with a man who was sleeping with every damn body with a vagina. Debra was angry, but she wasn't stupid. She knew Richard wouldn't make a good husband or father. Everybody in town hated his ass. While Dale wasn't the love of her life, she played it safe. Your mother didn't. She followed Richard around like a puppy. Drinking, getting high, and not giving it up." Her voice croaked.

My heart increased as I held on to every word from her mouth. It was like a Netflix series. I needed to know more.

"She always told me that she knew Richard wanted her for one thing. I used to tell her that she needed to leave him alone. Kimba used Richard because he could always get them liquor and drugs. She didn't have to put out and could drink her problems away. Richard got tired of that, and one night . . ." Her voice trailed off. "He raped her in the back of his truck."

I gasped so loud that the women next to us jumped. "I'm sorry." I quickly apologized. "He . . . He *raped* her?" I whispered.

"Raped her and told her she kept teasing him and to stop crying about it. On the way to drop her back home, they got into a terrible accident. Richard was dead at the scene, and your mother survived. She could crawl out of the car and run to my house." She looked around. "To this day, nobody knows she was in that car."

"Oh God. How did he sign his name on my birth certificate?"

"He didn't. Your mother found out she was pregnant with you a few months later. Your grandmother knew she and Richard were dating, so she signed his name. She refused to let your mother give birth to a bastard. People were already looking at Kimba because she was pregnant. Your mother ended up meeting your father when you were four months old. Clyde was new in town, and he loved your mother. God, that man loved him some Kimba. He legally adopted you when you were six months old."

I leaned back in my chair, trying to digest everything Dr. Thompson told me. While reading my mother's journal, I could read between the lines on some of the stuff. From the first time she mentioned Richard, I could tell he was no good.

My mother hated me because of my father. He raped her and then had the nerve to die, leaving her with a baby. A baby that had *his* blood running through her.

"I remember she would stare at me . . . with such disgust. I always wanted to know what I had done for her to feel that way about me."

"You were only born, baby. Faith, you didn't do anything for her to feel that way about you. Kimba did love you; I know she did. After that accident, your mother had plans to change her life around. She even planned to finish school so she could eventually go off to college. Then she found out about you, and that delayed her plans."

"*Ruined* her plans," I corrected her.

Keisha could say she knew my mother loved me all she wanted; I knew differently. If Keisha had lived in that house with me even one day, she would have been singing a different tune. My mother resented me because my father raped her, and that ruined her life. She was forced to stay back in Sageport while raising her rapist's baby.

Her life would have been different had she stayed clear of Richard before I was even born. Yet, one look at me reminded her of all her stupid decisions, which angered her. This caused her to take solace in the bottle while neglecting her only child, whom she wished was never born.

"Your mother never wanted you to find out. Carl was a great father . . . and he was much better than Richard. He took care of you and your mother."

My father worked hard all my life. He got up every morning, brewed his coffee, and made sure he was out the door to provide for our family. My mother d

idn't wake up until noon. When she did, she would grab a beer from the fridge or a bottle of wine—whichever was closer.

I always knew my father loved my mother more than she loved him. He sacrificed time with his own family to always provide for her and make sure she had plenty. He enabled her when all he wanted was for her to get her act together. I watched a man hold onto the last pieces of his love for the past fifteen years because it was too hard to part with them.

My heart broke thinking of him sitting in that home that once housed his family. It didn't matter that we weren't the typical, close-knit family. We were still his family. He loved us, and we both left him and never looked back.

Mom died, and I moved from Sageport with plans never to return. When my father forced me to leave so I could live my life, I knew he never intended on me ever coming back. He just wanted me to have my own life without constantly being reminded of the mistakes my mother had made in this town.

The rest of the lunch was tense. Dr. Thompson didn't know how to proceed, and she was cautious with her words. Every other sentence, she apologized for being the one to tell me. I didn't blame her. This wasn't her life to ruin, so how could I be angry with her? She was someone who wanted the best for her friend, and that never happened.

Despite going away for college, medical school, and residency, she returned to the same place she had tried to escape to find that her friend had never gotten better.

"This's on me, Faith. It's the least that I can do." She took the bill and slid her credit card into the folder.

"Thank you, Dr. Thompson."

"Girl, you done already called me Keisha . . . Might as well keep it going," she smiled.

This was the first time we both laughed, and it wasn't forced. "I appreciate you being honest with me. From her old journal and what you told me, I understand my mother better now."

"Has your father told you anything?"

"He doesn't know I found the journal. I don't think he even knows that stuff was in there . . . The spare room was supposed to be my mother's sewing room. She never unpacked the boxes in there. My father barely ever went into that room."

"That's a tough discussion. Your father takes so much pride in being your dad."

"It might not be a tough discussion after all," I sighed.

Her pager buzzed. "Shoot. I have to head on to the hospital. This was nice, Faith . . . Please, don't be a stranger."

"I won't," I promised.

I watched as she grabbed her card and quickly shuffled out the door. My mind had a million thoughts swirling after this lunch. Did I expect to hear everything that she had told me?

Absolutely not.

I sat briefly before gathering myself and heading back to my father's house. A quick nap while the girls were away would help this headache I had coming on.

As we headed toward Rome's house, the girls sang along to whatever Kidz Bop playlist I had on my phone. He had texted me that Agnes couldn't stay long today, so he would spend time with his mother. I never wanted Rome to feel like he had to hide his mother from me. If he wanted us to have a life together, she would be a part of that, along with my girls.

On the way over, we stopped at the grocery store and picked up the ingredients for cookies and my famous honey chicken pasta. It was a staple in my home, and the girls requested it at least once a week. After having lunch with Keisha earlier, I truly wanted to unpack this with Rome. He's the only person who knew exactly how I felt about my mother and my relationship. He had witnessed it firsthand, so he could understand how I felt.

We pulled into his driveway, and I killed the engine. Turning in my seat, I looked at my beautiful girls. "Hey, girls . . . So, Rome's mom is sick."

I needed to give them a pep talk before we walked in there. "Should we be visiting if she's sick?" Mayven questioned.

"She's not sick like that." I paused while trying to get my thoughts together. "Um, she has a disease that makes her memory bad . . . So she doesn't remember too much stuff."

I prayed Mrs. Atkins acted right and didn't cuss me out in front of my kids. This was a risky move, but one that needed to be made. We both needed to see how this went to know how to proceed.

"Okay, so, what do we do, Mommy?" Madison, my helpful girl, was always ready to help out however she could.

"Well," I cleared my throat, "just be your normal, respectful selves."

"We can do that!" they both cheered.

"Good. Now, let's grab the groceries to make my honey chicken pasta." I smiled as they both rushed to get out of the car.

Rome opened the door, surprised. "Um, Fay, what's going on?"

"We're making dinner for you and your mama tonight." I held up the bags I was holding.

"And cookies. Mommy said you love chocolate walnut cookies," Madison added.

The smile that came across Rome's face was one I will never forget. It was a mix of being happy and relieved at the same time. "Are you gonna leave us out here?"

Rome opened the door, and the girls filed in, but he stopped me. "Fay, you—"

I cut him off by placing a soft kiss on his lips. "I know I don't have to do anything . . . I *want* to do this."

I made my way into the kitchen where the girls were standing. Rome leaned in the doorway and watched us unpack all the bags.

"Girls, I want you to meet my mama." Rome broke our silence.

The girls put the cookie dough down and followed behind him. I peeked into the living room where Mrs. Atkins was watching television.

"Mama," he said.

She looked up from the TV, and her eyes lit up when she saw the girls. "Who are these beautiful girls?"

He turned and waved for me to stand next to him. I was nervous, but I quietly walked over to where he was standing. "These are Faith's twin daughters."

"You just insist on being with this girl? Are these your babies?" She looked into Rome's eyes.

I was so confused but just remained quiet.

"Mama, be nice. I love Faith. She's my girlfriend, and you need to be respectful to her." He was firm yet gentle with his mother. "These are her daughters."

"Hi, Mrs. Atkins." I decided it was my turn to speak to her.

"Hi, Faith . . . Your girls are beautiful."

"Thank you. Girls, introduce yourselves."

It seemed like Mrs. Atkins was more interested in the girls than me. Mayven was the first to step forward. "I'm Mayven," she spoke super loudly.

"May, she's not deaf," I laughed.

"Sorry."

"I'm Madison, but you can call me Maddie, ma'am."

My girls were so respectful, and it was the one thing that I prided myself on. Raising kids was hard enough, but being able to raise intelligent *and* respectful kids was always the goal.

"They are so precious."

"We're baking cookies . . . Would you like to help us?" Mayven asked.

Rome started to butt in, but I quickly stopped him. "Let her answer, babe."

Mrs. Atkins looked at Rome before returning her focus to Mayven. "I would love that. You know, I'm a pretty good baker." Both girls stood by and held onto her hand to help her out of the chair.

Rome and I sat on his back patio with a bottle of wine and cookies. The girls and Mrs. Atkins were watching a new cartoon movie on Netflix. Dinner went perfectly, and Mrs. Atkins couldn't stop singing my praises about the pasta I had made. Her conversation was all over the place during dinner, but we allowed her to talk.

"You know, she doesn't talk like that anymore . . . It reminded me of the old times when she would talk Allen's and my faces off at dinner," he chuckled and poured us more wine.

"I'm just glad I wasn't called a hussy tonight . . . I will take that as a win," I giggled.

"Thank you for this, Fay. I was scrambling on Uber Eats for dinner, and you just showed up."

"Fay and Girls Catering," I joked.

"Seriously, this means a lot to me. You could have kept your distance after the last time you were around my mom."

"Come on, Rome, your mom has never liked me. I think I would be more scared if she were nice after she caught us having sex. I do know this disease is a lot, and it takes a toll on the caregiver, which happens to be you. If we're serious about being together, then I think this needed to happen."

He took a sip of wine. "You know . . . I read an article that noted that kids being around helps a lot."

We both peered through the window at Mrs. Atkins, laughing with the girls. "I would say that article is correct."

I drank my wine while recounting my earlier conversation during lunch.

"What's up?"

"I met with Dr. Thompson earlier for lunch today."

"Is that why you were being all secretive about where you were?"

"Guilty."

"How did it go?"

I told Rome about the entire conversation and watched him pour us more wine while his eyes widened in shock. I expected anyone to act like that because the news I was told was a lot to comprehend.

"Go ahead and take a sip of your wine to digest."

"Sip?" I watched as he gulped down the rest of his wine. "Babe, why did you come and do all of this after finding that out? I should have been coming over to make *you* dinner."

My father was bummed that we were having dinner at Rome's house but promised to put us up a plate of food. I figured since he and Marie had the girls since they arrived, I would give them a little break to reconnect with each other. Although the girls were a good time, I knew they were a lot at times.

"I wanted to do something for you. Plus, it was a nice distraction from everything."

He bit into a cookie. "How are you going to break this to your father? I'm sure he knows all of this, but how will you tell him you know?"

"I'm not." I polished off the rest of my wine.

"What?"

"Babe, I will break his heart by letting him know that. He doesn't need to know that I know he's not my biological father. As far as I'm concerned, he's my dad."

My father's and my relationship had been estranged over the years, and I was to blame for that. As much as I blamed Ashton for not trying in our marriage, I could blame myself for not trying in my relationship with my father. Despite how distant I was with him, he still made sure to text, call, and visit whenever he was in Georgia.

Growing up, my father provided for me. He was the one parent I knew that I could depend on. Did I wish that he worked less and spent more time at home?

Yes.

I wished he was able to see how my mother really was. Instead, he rushed to work, so he wasn't in the house much. As much as I wanted to fault him for that, he had to provide for us. We were a one-income household, so if he didn't bust his ass, there was no telling where we would be.

"You can't just hold this in, Fay."

"Are we not having a conversation together? I also plan to find a therapist . . . I've been putting it off for a while, and I think it's time. Do I think it would do any good to tell him? No, it wouldn't. This was less about my father and more about figuring out why my mother's and my relationship was so strained."

"Now you got your answer."

"Not one that I would have wanted, but I got an answer nonetheless."

He held my hand. "I love you."

"I love you too." I stared into his eyes.

His eyes differed from those I used to stare into as a teen. He had seen and done so much and experienced so much loss and pain. I can stare into his eyes and see he is tired and drained from life.

I didn't want to leave him again. The days trickled down until I had to pack up the girls and leave Sageport. They seemed to be flying by. I had come here only wanting to be in and out and ended up staying.

Now, I was dreading the day that I would have to kiss him goodbye, with plans to see him whenever he could get away.

"What?"

"I'm not looking forward to having to leave," I whispered.

Sageport had been a forbidden place to me for years. I cut it out of my life like it never existed, and now that I had come back, I had never felt more at home.

This *was* my home.

It had dark memories that I tried to forget, but the people and town outweighed that. Every person I had greeted or run into seemed happy that I was back. Not one person had a bad thing to say about my father and the things he has done for the community.

The small town we all wanted to escape wasn't that small of a town anymore. All the new businesses, restaurants, and the coast were evidence that not all small towns stayed the same.

"Fay, I don't want to talk about it. That shit makes me sick every time I think about it."

I felt the same way.

"Then we won't talk about it," I said, grabbing his face and kissing him. "At least not tonight."

"Not tonight," he confirmed and kissed me back.

Chapter Twenty

ROME

"**W**E SHOULD BE popping bottles or something . . . Why are you so depressed?" Pat flagged over the bartender. "Aye, a bottle of champagne."

"Of course," she smiled, knowing that her tip would be a hefty one if she brought Pat whatever he wanted.

"Shit was hard to do," I replied.

Signing the deal was the hardest thing that I had ever done. The shit felt gut-wrenching and exhilarating at the same time. On one hand, I was sad to be selling something my father had worked hard for. Then, on the other hand, I was excited about my next chapter.

As much as I wanted to keep something that was my father's pride and joy, it was draining.

I could have hired someone to come in and run everything for me, but what was the point? That wasn't what my father wanted when he opened his dealerships. He wanted a family member always to be there to greet everyone. It didn't matter how tired he was. He would make it to each dealership to show his face. That was because this was his passion, which he had always wanted.

We weren't the same. The dealerships brought him so much joy, and they brought me the exact opposite. Every time I pulled into his old parking spot, touched the same door he had touched for years, and sat in his office, I felt sad. It didn't matter how far I had come in my grieving journey. Coming back to the dealerships always brought me back to the day of his funeral.

Since high school, I have been doing everything for everyone. This was my turn to do something that would be good for me. The dealerships were the missing piece of what needed to go, and I was satisfied with my decision. Although it was hard to sign those papers, I knew it was for the best. Living in the past wasn't conducive to where I was trying to go in life. Each time I walked into any of the dealerships, I had flashbacks of how I used to run around with Allen while my mother tried to get a little time with my father. It was a place where our family was whole, together, and happy. I wanted to keep those memories, not the memories where I had forced myself to come into the office every day because I hated it.

The one thing I made sure of in those contracts is that nobody lost their jobs or their titles within the dealerships. Other than the names, nothing would change within the dealerships. I also made them add that they would continue to keep the business relationship with Pat's auto shop as well.

"You never wanted to run your father's shop anyway. He would want you to follow your dreams . . . Don't beat yourself up."

"Trying not to."

The champagne bottle popped, and the bartender poured champagne into our glasses. "What are we celebrating this afternoon?"

"My best friend just became a very wealthy man today." Pat hit me in the back with so much pride and joy.

"Congratulations! Does your friend have a name?" She stared me right in the eye while licking her lips.

"Rome."

"Hey, Rome . . . I'm Kennedy." She shook my hand.

"Nice to meet you."

Someone called Kennedy on the other end of the bar. "Seems like Kennedy wanna spell her name . . . you know," Pat winked.

"Man, you are nasty. I'm not worried about her. I'm a taken man," I proudly stated.

As far as I was concerned, Fay and I were together. She and the girls came to the house every night to cook dinner and watch movies with Mama. Fay was the one that made me realize that I had to stop coddling my mother. She could do things with my help, and I had to stop treating her like a child.

I watched her teach Faith how to make chicken and dumplings the other night. She still wasn't much of a fan of Faith's, but she knew the girls came with her, so she tolerated her. Mama loved spending time with the twins and teaching them about baking.

Pia had come back to work, and she was so happy to see my mother in the kitchen. Now that we have allowed her to bake, she wants to do it all the time. I soon noticed a change in my mother and how she spoke more. More often than not, she talked about current events that she saw on the news. Allen hadn't come up in a while, and I hoped to keep it that way.

"You and Faith made it official?"

"Yeah."

Fay and I didn't need to make it official. We knew this was what we wanted. We didn't know how things would work out, but that was the beauty of life. When needed, you could pivot and figure things out as they came.

Neither of us knew what was next or how things would work with the girls and Mama, but I was excited about the future with her. I had plans to speak to Mama's doctors to see if traveling was good for her. Going to Georgia to visit Fay and the girls didn't sound bad. As usual, Pia was always down for the ride as well.

"I'm happy for you. Sis came back into town, and you ain't even let her get comfortable before you snatched her up."

"I couldn't, man." I laughed and finished the rest of my champagne. "It's like no time passed between us. It's almost like we picked up where we left off."

"That's dope for real. Not every day you get another chance at love with your high school sweetheart."

"Yeah."

"I'm proud of you, Rome. Every challenge that has come your way, you have handled it better than any of us could have. You stand tall and help your mom out every day. Honestly, I think I'm gonna get into heaven just because I'm your best friend."

"You're crazy as hell."

"How did we become friends? You're a saint, and I'm a—"

"Sinner."

"Damn, I was going to say a decent guy."

We both laughed. It was always fun and jokes whenever Pat and I got together. If I ever decided to leave Sageport, I would miss my friendship with him the most.

"You all right."

He shook his head and poured us more champagne. "Dallas asked to move in with me," he revealed.

Dallas was Pat's longtime on-and-off girlfriend. One minute, they were together, and then the next, she was back living in Tampa with her mother. Every week, they seemed like they were going through it. Despite going through it with Dallas, Pat still had fun with the other women he dealt with. But no matter who he dealt with, Dallas was always the one and only.

"She's going to move back to Sageport to be with you?"

"Yeah. She realized I'm not leaving to move to no damn Tampa." He licked his lips while watching Kennedy bend down to get more ice.

"How long is this going to last before she packs up her shit and leaves again?"

"She wants us to take this seriously. I'm always serious. It's her with the foolishness."

"No, she wants you to leave all these other women alone. Come on, get it together. You love Dallas."

He sighed. "When she lost our daughter, shit got too serious. I tried to stick it out, but we were always fighting."

Dallas had a daughter who passed away when she was four months old. They tried to move on and heal from it and even tried to conceive another one. When Dallas got pregnant again, she ended up miscarrying it. The trauma from losing their daughter at four months old and then her losing a pregnancy was too much for them.

I remembered around the time it happened. Dallas would stay out all night drinking and partying. He did everything so he didn't have to deal with the pain. It wasn't long after that that Dallas packed her bags and left him. The two stayed connected and tried to make it work a billion times, but Dallas never returned. She wanted him to follow her to Tampa, but Pat wasn't going for it.

"You were both hurting and instead of trying to heal, y'all were so hell-bent on hurting each other. That was a wild time for both of you."

"For real. I miss her, though."

"Then make it work with her . . . Stop messing around and settle down. You know Dallas is a good woman. You just need to step up to the plate and be the good man she deserves."

"When did you become Steve Harvey? You get a girlfriend and think you got it all planned out." He punched me in the arm.

"I spent a lot of time trying to get it right with the right woman. What you and Dallas had was beautiful, and it could get there again. You both just need to be ready to put in the work. Do I believe she should move in with you?"

Pat read my facial expression and answered for me. "Hell nah."

"Exactly. It's only going to end the same way. You both need to ease into it and moving in isn't easing into anything."

"I agree."

I wasn't a relationship expert. However, I had front-row seats to the destruction of Dallas and Pat. I've witnessed how hurtful they could be to each other and how far they could go below the belt. I don't know how many times I opened my front door at three in the morning, and Pat was there needing a place to lay his head because the police had made him leave their home.

I was someone who believed in second chances, so why shouldn't they have one? I wanted them to make it because when they were good, they were amazing. Dallas made Pat a better man, and Pat made Dallas a better woman. They were powerful together and could be powerful as soon as they healed from losing their daughter.

"I'm rooting for both of you. When is she coming to town?"

"Tomorrow. She wants to spend the holidays together. You know . . . It's the first Christmas we've spent together since Austin passed."

"Damn. An emotional one, I'm sure."

"Yeah, but I'm ready for it. Tired of hiding my feelings from the one person who understands exactly what I'm going through."

"Then stop. How about you bring her to Carl's tomorrow night? Faith is throwing her father a surprise engagement party at the restaurant."

"Word? He gonna have that fried catfish?"

"It wouldn't be a party without that catfish."

"Then you already know I'm going to be there."

We dapped hands and finished the rest of the bottle of champagne. I told Pat I didn't want to celebrate selling the dealerships, and he didn't listen.

His ass never listened.

This was the one time I was glad he didn't listen to me. Despite how shitty I was feeling earlier, I was feeling much better about my decision now. It paid to have good friends around who could pull you out of your head when needed. Pat had always been that person for me, and I was that person for him.

No matter what, we always had each other's back. He had been with me through my darkest times and always managed to hold me up when I was too weak.

I often questioned how I would continue without Allen. He was always my right-hand man, and when he was alive, I could never picture life without him. Pat stepped in to fill the role that my brother played for me.

"Rome?" Faith called out when she entered the dealership.

I had let everyone have the rest of the day off after our party. They all understood why I made my decision and were supportive of me. Half the people here had witnessed me grow from a rambunctious toddler to an adult. They were all family to me, and I would always be here if they ever needed me.

A few of the mechanics who were friends with Carl were heading to the restaurant for the party later. It wasn't goodbye, but a see-you-later. I would still see them around town.

"I'm in my office."

She pushed the door to my office open slightly. "Where is everyone? It's the middle of the day."

"I let them have the rest of the day off."

"Awe, you're such a good boss." She came over and kissed me on the cheek. "What's up? I have a million errands to run for tonight."

"I used to be."

"Huh?"

She touched my face. "You're not having a stroke or nothing, right?"

"Nah. I sold the dealerships," I revealed.

I kept the sale of the dealerships a secret from most, except Pat and Linda. I didn't want anyone else to cloud my decision on what I wanted, and I knew those two wouldn't.

This deal had been in the works before Faith ever stepped foot back into Sageport. I knew I didn't want to live the rest of my life trying to follow in my father's footsteps. As much as that was his vision when he opened the dealerships, he was always so supportive of the things Allen and I wanted for ourselves.

If I told Faith about the deal, she would have tried to talk me out of it. I didn't need her telling me how much this meant to my father and my family. I needed to make this decision because of me and nobody else, and that was what I did.

"What? You sold the dealerships? Why would you do that?" She panicked, still trying to check my face for a smile, grin, or smirk to confirm that I was joking with her.

"This was something that I needed to do for me. I couldn't think what my father would have wanted. He's not here, Fay." I felt myself getting upset.

She noticed the change in my attitude and calmed down. I moved my seat out, and she sat on my lap. "Is this truly what you wanted?"

"Yes."

"Then it doesn't matter what anybody else thinks. You did this for you, and that is all that matters."

She held my head and kissed me on the forehead.

"I needed to let this last piece go."

"And you did that. What's next for you, Rome?"

"I honestly don't know. Guess I'll figure it out as I go."

She smiled. "Well, I guess I owe you a congratulations then."

"I mean, you could give me something else too."

She stood up. "You are so nasty. I have so much that I have to do today before the party. Are you still going to bring your mother to it?"

"Yes. Pia said she would come along for extra help if it's needed. I'm heading there next to shower and get ready."

"See you there." She kissed me on the lips and grabbed her purse, ready to head out the door.

"Make sure you eat something, Fay," I called behind her.

Since I spoke to her this morning, she had been running around like crazy. I wanted her to take a break to eat or sip some water.

"Will do," she called behind her as she headed out the door.

Mama wore her favorite green satin dress that she loved. It looked perfect on her, and for a quick moment, if I closed my eyes, it felt like old times. She only pulled this dress out around the holidays for all the holiday parties she attended.

Pia fastened the pearls around her neck my father gave her for their third wedding anniversary. She reached out and touched the pearls, and I peeped the slight smile on her face.

"You look beautiful, Mama," I complimented.

"You are such a sweet boy." She kissed my cheek. "What holiday party are we going to today?"

Pia and I looked at each other. "Mama, we're going to Clyde's engagement party."

She paused. "To Kimba Stone?"

"No. He's met a new woman, and they're engaged."

"Good for Clyde. He was always too good for that damn Kimba," she scoffed and grabbed her purse, which had nothing but a few old tubes of lipstick in it.

Pia and I decided that we were going to stop lying to my mother. The lying did more harm than good, so it was better to be upfront with her. We hadn't tackled the situation about Allen yet, but that was a battle for another day.

"Are my wallets and credit cards in here?"

"Yeah, Mama," I lied.

Taking control of all my mother's credit cards and bank accounts was the hardest thing. Even being married, she was always so independent and loved to do things on her own. It was a reminder that she wasn't the same anymore.

"All right, let's get out of here. I hate to arrive at a party late," she insisted, and I smiled.

Holding out my arm, she looped hers through mine, and we headed out the door. Other than doctors' visits and quick little trips out with Pia, we didn't take Mama out that often. I was always scared of how she might act or if something would trigger her memory and cause her to have an episode. It was wrong because she deserved to be out and about while enjoying the life she did have.

When we arrived at the restaurant, everyone was there, and more people were arriving. The buffet table had a plethora of different dishes that you could get here, and my mouth was watering. I was trying to get Fay to eat when I hadn't had anything other than a cup of coffee this morning.

"Debra, it's so nice to see you out and about." Dr. Thompson came up to greet us.

"Keisha, you look great," my mother complimented her.

Pia took my mother to find a table.

"It's so good that you got her out of the house. How has she been?"

"She's been doing better. I have Faith's daughters to thank for that. Mama loves spending time with them."

"That's amazing. It's so good seeing both of you out. You know Debra is the Queen of Christmas."

"Sure is."

Mama loved Christmas more than any holiday, and I felt I was depriving her of the good memories. I had been so busy trying to keep her from remembering the bad memories that I had stopped her from experiencing the good ones. She loved Christmastime and watching Christmas movies.

She wouldn't have watched her first Christmas movie the other day if it hadn't been for the girls. The girls were so excited about Christmas that they couldn't *not* talk about it. I wanted to quiet them until I saw how excited my mother was discussing Christmas with them.

"Enjoy the party." Dr. Thompson gently touched my back while going to greet the next person.

I spotted Faith in the corner, ensuring the food signs were correct. She wore a leather maxi skirt with a red cable knit sweater tucked in the front. The thigh-high red boots set the shit off and made me want her more. She looked thick as shit in that skirt.

"Where your man at?" I snuck up and whispered in her ear.

She quickly spun around with that cute little smirk fixed on her face. "I don't know . . . He never asked to be my man."

"Shit, I'm slacking. I thought you already knew I was your man."

"Remind me." She kissed my lips.

"Fay, will you be my woman?"

"Woman? Ooh, I love that."

"Ain't nothing girl about you." I pecked her lips between each word.

"And ain't nothing boy about you." She looked down at my growing member. I had to keep reminding myself that we were at this party.

The minute the party was over, I needed her to myself. Tomorrow was Christmas Eve, and I had a big surprise for everyone.

I was able to rent a big beach house on the coast for Christmas. I didn't know how Mama would act, so Pia and I planned to bring her home if she reacted badly. But I had faith that she would be fine with how Mama had been proving me wrong.

This Christmas was different, and I wanted to celebrate it differently. A Christmas on the coast together sounded like everything I knew it would be. I wanted to surprise everyone with it tomorrow. With the way Carl liked to throw down, I knew that Christmas dinner would be delicious.

"Quit playing like I won't take you in the back."

"Rome, you are forever trying to get us caught. There will be time for that later." She winked and then went into the kitchen.

Everyone got quiet when Faith told them that Carl and Marie were nearby. We all were silent . . . until they walked in through the front door.

"Congratulations!" everyone shouted, although they had been engaged for a while now.

"What in the world?" Carl stammered while Marie busted into tears. Faith quickly made her way to them.

"I wanted to celebrate the two of you," Faith explained while hugging Marie.

A tear dropped from her father's eye as he looked at his daughter. "Faithy."

"Daddy, you deserve this happiness, and I want to be here to witness it all . . . both the girls and me."

The girls hugged their grandfather as everyone clapped for them. While Faith showed them around the party, everyone returned to fixing their plates and enjoying the music.

Mama stuck around and enjoyed everything from the food to the music. I could tell when she was tired, so Pia took my car and brought her home. I sat in the back and watched everyone have a good time. Faith was dancing with her daughters while Carl and Marie were dancing entirely too slow for the music playing.

The girls broke off into their own dance, and that's when Faith scanned the room. She smirked when she spotted me and walked over. "What are you doing over here alone?"

"I sent Mama home . . . She was tired."

"She did so well tonight."

"Proud of her."

"And I'm proud of you." She kissed me.

"I'm so happy with you, Fay."

"Me too." She sat on my lap.

We relaxed and watched everyone enjoy themselves while holding onto each other. Neither of us wanted to let go of the other ever again.

Faith and I belonged together. I didn't get the chance to make her Faith Atkins before, but I damn sure had plans to do it now.

Chapter Twenty-One

ASHTON

"THE POOL IS so warm, babe," Francis cooed while trying to get me to come in with her.

I sat on the lounger with my laptop.

"Not right now, honey. I need to close out all my existing clients before starting this new position."

I accepted the position, although I reconsidered it a few times. It was hard after the girls broke down the way they did. They were eight years old and didn't understand the hard decisions I had to make as their father. I had faith that I would look back when they were older and not regret anything. This was for them and their future. I couldn't let this job pass me by without at least seeing how it would work out.

My mother wasn't happy that Francis and I decided not to stay for Christmas. With how my mother acted around the girls, I needed to get away for a few days. Plus, it didn't even feel right being there without them.

"What is the point of coming here if you're going to wo—"

I held up my finger and answered my phone. "Hey, Roe, what's going on?" I greeted my realtor.

"Hey, Ash. I'm really glad that you and Faith decided to sell. The house is worth so much; you both will have some major dough."

"Roe, what the hell are you talking about?"

"Selling the house . . . Faith called me last week to talk about possibly putting it on the market."

I leaned up and shut my laptop. "What do you mean, putting it on the market? She has refused every time I brought it up."

Faith and I both still owned the home. I allowed her to keep it in the divorce, but if she decided to sell, we both would make money from it. I thought she was holding onto it for a while just to spite me.

"Well, it seems like she had a change of heart on selling. I told her I would use the spare key to take a look and snap some pictures for her."

"Keep me updated, Roe."

"Will do. Happy holidays, bro."

"Same to you and yours."

I knew why she wanted to put the house up so suddenly. It was that new boyfriend of hers.

Faith ripped me a new one when I introduced the girls to Francis and told her I had a girlfriend, and she had the nerve to turn around and do the same thing in my face.

I was livid when I finally made it back to my gate.

I don't know what hurt more, the fact that she seemed happier with him than when we were married or that the girls were so cool with it. I expected them to give her hell like they had been giving me the entire time we were in New York.

What pissed me off more was that she didn't want to provide me with any details of this new boyfriend. She had adopted a nonchalant-ass attitude since we divorced, which always annoyed me.

I mean, shit, act like you cared for me once!

"Our real estate agent called. He said Faith asked him about putting up the house for sale."

"Is she finally going to move out of the house?"

"Seems like she's at least considering it."

"Does this mean we have to look for a place in New York and then help her move into a new place with the girls?"

I didn't like her tone.

If that were the case, I would happily help Faith move into her new place with the girls. She was my ex-wife and had my daughters most of the time, so I wanted to help her.

"You don't have to do anything."

"I didn't mean it like that, Ash."

I stood up. "Give me a minute . . . I need to call Faith."

"As usual," she mumbled under her breath.

Francis went from wanting to be a supportive girlfriend to being annoying. She wanted me all to herself, which was impossible when I had two daughters. It felt like she didn't want me to split my time between her and the girls. Instead, she wanted me full-time.

Taking her away to Jamaica should have made her happy. But no. She complained about me working instead of kissing her in the pool. It was the minor bickering that got on my damn nerves.

Nagging was something that I wasn't used to because Faith didn't do it. She got quiet whenever she was in her feelings or upset with me. Her quietness was louder than nagging. Whenever she got like that, I knew I had to fix it because she could hold a grudge.

"Ash, the girls are on the beach with my father," Faith answered, not even saying hello or greeting me.

"I didn't call for them. I actually called to speak to you." I entered our suite and sat on the couch.

"Oh? What life decisions can I help you with today?" she sarcastically replied.

"Real funny, Faith."

"Sorry. What do you need to talk to me about?"

"Roe called me."

"Figured he would."

"Are you thinking of selling the house?"

"I am."

"Why now?"

"I'm moving to Sageport."

I removed the phone from my ear and looked at it. "You're breaking up . . . I didn't hear you correctly."

"The connection is fine. You heard me just fine."

"When were you going to talk to me about this?"

"After the holidays, but since you called me, I guess we can have the conversation now."

"Why are you moving to Sageport? You've always expressed how much you hated it there, and now you want to move my girls there?"

"I had my own issues with the town. I realized after coming back this is my home and the place I feel most at home."

"Sounds like you are moving there for that new boyfriend."

"I'm moving here because I know it's right for the girls and me. With my father getting older, I need to be here to help with his businesses and so the girls can grow up with him around. My man living here is the cherry on the top."

"So, fuck my parents?"

"The girls live with me, Ashton. When you accepted the position in New York, you knew I would be their full-time caregiver, as I have always been. Your parents can have a relationship with the girls. I've never stopped that."

"Were you even going to discuss this move with me?"

"I was. I'm not you, Ashton. I care about your opinion on things when it comes to the girls. You've been able to live your life and make the decisions you wanted. All I want is for you to give me that same respect and trust that I know what's best for our girls."

Fuck.

I hated it when she was right. All Faith had ever done was do what was right for our family, even when it hurt her the most. She always thought of what would be good for the girls, so I couldn't fault her for that.

"How would this even work out?"

"I've been looking at places here to rent until I'm ready to buy. My father doesn't even know about the move or the girls. I was waiting to talk to you about it before I made any official moves."

"Sageport . . . Why you wanna take them further away from me?" I joked.

"They love it here, Ash. Can you believe they haven't touched their tablet once?"

"For real?"

"Yes. They love helping my father or playing in the yard. Right now, they're looking for seashells on the beach with my father. The wind is kicking their asses, but they are determined."

"Like their mama."

"I'm never going to stop you from seeing your girls. However your new work schedule is, we will figure it out."

"You really wanna do this?"

"I do."

"If this is what you want, then you got my blessing. We'll always be family, no matter where we are."

"We'll always be family."

I smiled. "I'll call the girls later . . . Merry Christmas, Faith."

"Merry Christmas, Ashton," she replied.

"Whenever you're ready, we can all sit down and have a double date."

"Don't push it," she laughed before ending the phone call.

I placed the phone on my lap and leaned back. Having a cordial conversation with Faith was bittersweet. We both tried everything we could, more her than me, to fix our marriage and make it work. Some days, I regretted not putting my all into our marriage and leaving her to do all the work.

Work wasn't something that Faith was afraid of. She always pulled up her sleeves and was ready to put in the work, which is why she deserved my support. If moving back to Sageport was something that she wanted to do, then I trusted her judgment and knew my girls would be fine.

It was already going to be an adjustment not living in the same state as the girls, but now, they would be even further away.

"Everything all right?" Francis asked, coming into our suite and drying her body.

"Faith is moving to Sageport."

"That small town she's from?"

"Yeah. She said she wants to move back with the girls."

"Well, I hope she has her lawyer money. Did you tell her she can't do that without your permission?"

"I'm not going to fight her in court. We both agreed we didn't want to raise our girls in court. I gave her my support to move there."

"What the—?"

It seemed like Francis was having difficulty understanding what a healthy coparent relationship looked like. Faith and I had our moments, and we weren't always perfect when it came to this journey, but when it mattered, we stuck together for the betterment of the girls.

"Babe, what are you not understanding?"

"How you just allow her to walk all over you."

I chuckled to myself. "She's not walking all over me. I want what's best for my daughters, and so does my ex-wife. Just because we're divorced doesn't mean I don't want her to be happy. She sacrificed everything for me to follow my dreams. I asked for kids, and she gave them to me without a complaint. I watched her carry two kids in her womb, lose her figure, sanity, and everything in between to bring those girls into this world. When she did, she raised them and was the best mother to them. Shit, she was a better parent than me most days. So, if she asks for my support on something she wants for herself, I will give it to her."

Francis stood there, unsure of what to do or say next. It was easy to watch on the outside. But she had never witnessed half the shit Faith had gone through. The way she loved and cared for our family, even when I didn't give her that same support back, was admirable.

I don't know if I could have done the same thing.

Faith always put us first, and if that meant that I had to allow her to put her needs first for once, I was going to sit back and allow that to happen. Faith had never taken me to Sageport, but I would be excited to visit and see what my girls' lives were like there once they were settled.

It was the least I could do for her.

"Want to shower together?" Francis sucked on her finger, letting me know that the conversation was over and she wanted sex.

I welcomed the change of conversation. "You already know I do." I stood up, slapped her ass, and followed her into the bathroom.

Epilogue

CHRISTMAS MORNING

*T*HE BEACH HOUSE Rome had rented for us was breathtaking. As soon as you stepped into the sunken living room, the floor-to-ceiling windows gave a spectacular view of the beach. It felt like we were on the beach when we were sitting on the couch. Rome texted me, telling us to pack clothes and meet him at an address. On the ride over, we all tried to decide what could be at the address.

When we pulled onto the cobblestoned driveway, he was standing there to welcome us. The girls were so excited to spend Christmas on the coast. They didn't even wait for us to unpack before they were on the beach. The house had a private access beach entrance that the girls utilized all too much.

Since we had arrived, everyone enjoyed the backyard and the beach. Mrs. Atkins loved sitting in the beach chair in the back with Pia. She would sit wearing her sunglasses and enjoy the cool breeze. I knew Rome was initially nervous to bring her, but I was glad he did. His mother deserved to enjoy this right along with us.

The engagement party went off without a hitch. My father danced until he couldn't anymore. He was so happy that he gave everyone the next day off, which was rare for him. Carl's never closed unless it had to. I love seeing my father so happy. He truly enjoyed having the girls and me here, and it showed. I went from feeling like I had to do it all to having all the help I needed. Marie and my father were quick to jump in to help whenever I needed a break.

"Mommy, we're here." Madison stuck her head into the bathroom; then Mayven came next.

"Yes, come in and lock the door," I told them.

I sat on the lounge couch in the middle of the master bedroom. Mayven locked the door behind her, and they sat next to me, one on each side. It was our favorite way to sit since they were old enough to sit without being held up.

"What's wrong, Mom?" Mayven noticed.

She was always so observant.

"Well, I wanted to talk to you both about something."

"What?" Madison was eager to know.

"What do you girls think about moving to Sageport to be with Pop-Pop and Marie all the time?"

Both their eyes lit up. "Seriously?"

"Yes. How would you feel about that?"

I overheard the girls talking last week about our departure and how sad they would be to leave their Pop-Pop alone again. As much as they felt that way, I felt the same way too. I didn't want to leave my father, Marie, or Rome ever again.

"Don't forget Mr. Rome and Mrs. Atkins," Mayven added.

I giggled while pinching her cheek. "Yes, Mr. Rome and Mrs. Atkins too."

"Would we live with Mr. Rome?"

"Not yet. We would get our own place first . . . and if things go well, then we can eventually move in together."

I had found a rental town house a few streets from Rome's house. It was within my price range and had more than enough bedrooms for us. This was new between Rome and me, and while we knew this would work, I didn't want to rush into living together. We had a lot of things to consider with his mother and me having the girls.

"Mommy, are you in love with Mr. Rome?" Madison asked.

"I am. We love each other very much."

"You are so happy with him, Mom," Mayven added.

It hit differently when your kids could see your happiness shine through. I always put on this fake facade that I was happy and pushing through, and I guess my girls always saw right through it. They had never commented on my happiness when I was with their father or even after the divorce. I never thought they would notice.

"That's because I am happy with him," I smiled.

"When are we going to move?"

"Well, after the New Year, we will return home to start the process. We should be moved to Sageport by February."

"Are we keeping our house in Georgia?"

I shook my head. "No, baby. We're going to sell that house. It's time a new family moved in."

"Good. That means we don't have to pretend to be nice to Lolly." Mayven rolled her eyes.

I remember rocking them in their nursery, scared to let them out into the world. I worried that the world was too cruel and they were too fragile to go out into it.

I didn't have those concerns when it came to Mayven, though. My girl was going to tell you how it was. She wasn't soft, and I didn't give her enough credit for being the strong twin.

She had her moments when she broke down, but that was when Madison tapped in to be strong for them both.

"Girls, I have to tell you both something very important. Can you keep a secret?" I stood up. They both looked at me while nodding their heads. I opened a drawer and pulled out the positive pregnancy test. "Mommy is pregnant," I whispered.

They both quietly squealed while grabbing the piss stick. Luckily, I had sanitized it before calling them in here.

"We're going to be big sisters?" Mayven whispered back.

"Yes. Are you excited?"

"So excited," Madison told me. "I hope it's a baby boy. I want a brother so bad," she stressed.

"Me too. But a little sister would also be cool."

"Whatever God decides to bless us with, right?"

"Yes."

I kneeled and hugged my girls. "I love you both so much."

"We love you too, Mommy," Mayven said, causing me to smile.

I knew my body felt off and chalked it off to the stress of finding out about my mother. However, when I started to feel nauseated, I knew that I needed to take a test. It wasn't like Rome and I were practicing safe sex. We never used any condoms, and it wasn't a thought until I started to feel sick. This baby was a blessing for both of us.

I thought I would have panicked when that test turned positive. Instead, I felt the complete opposite.

Peace.

There wasn't a single worry in my body as the tears poured down my eyes. When Rome knocked on the door to check on me, I lied and said the lobster from last night didn't sit well with me. He gave me space to do my thing while I thought of my girls and how they would feel about all these changes.

The last thing I wanted to do was to uproot their lives and cause them to struggle. Hearing how onboard and excited they were about this new journey was a relief. It was still early, and I knew the girls were patiently waiting for everyone to wake up.

I used this quiet time to our advantage. This felt like the perfect time to tell them about the move and the baby. Rome was still sleeping peacefully the last time I peeked outside the door.

"Should we go sit and wait for everyone in the living room?"

Madison looked at her twin. "Well, Mayven woke up Pop-Pop and Marie." She snitched on her sister.

"Didn't I tell you to wait?" I giggled.

"Well, at least we can get some breakfast before opening gifts." I shrugged and opened the bathroom door.

"Morning, Mr. Rome!" the girls both shouted.

"Rome . . . Please leave the 'Mr.,'" he laughed. "Merry Christmas, girls. Did Santa come?"

"He did, and he ate our cookies. I don't think he liked that soy milk," Mayven snickered.

"We could have given him regular milk, but you have problems with it," her twin called her out.

The girls continued to bicker while heading out of the bedroom.

"Merry Christmas, baby," I kissed him on the lips.

"I think this is the best Christmas morning I have ever experienced. I think it would have been better if . . ." He winked.

"Hmm, how long do you think we have before the girls bust in here?"

He smacked my ass. "They might kick down the door. I think I've kept everyone waiting long enough." He stretched and got out of bed.

"Go ahead and handle that breath."

"It ain't that bad." He walked into the bathroom.

I used that as my chance to grab my gift for him and put it under the tree. Marie and Dad were sitting in the living room while the girls stared a hole through their gifts.

"Merry Christmas, honey," my father smiled.

This was all he wanted for Christmas, so he couldn't care less about any gifts. But I got him the biggest gift that I planned to give him.

"Merry Christmas, family!" Rome came behind me and kissed me on the neck. "I see Mama is right outside in her favorite spot."

Mrs. Atkins and Pia were bundled up, sitting on the back patio. Mama loved being near the water. I made Rome promise he would bring her to the coast more often.

"I brought some coffee and coffee cake out there for them. Pia loves it just as much as your mama," Marie smiled. I allowed Rome to greet his mother while I helped myself to some coffee and cake.

We all sat in the living room, laughing and joking around with the girls. After a quick FaceTime with their father, we gave them the signal to open their gifts . . . and all hell broke loose.

There were so many screams and squeals because of their excitement. They got everything and then some. I had never been hugged so much in one hour.

When the girls were done opening their gifts, they went out to show Mrs. Atkins everything that they had. Now, it was the adults' turn for gifts, and I became nervous.

"Can I give my gift last?" Rome asked.

"Yes, you may." I extended my hands and gave both Rome and my father their gifts.

"A gift? I don't need nothing, Faithy. You have already given me the biggest gift I could have asked for."

"Dad, I wanted to give you more."

"Any order you want us to open these?" Rome asked.

"You open yours first."

I sat beside Marie, who already knew about my pregnancy. She was the first person I told.

Marie didn't realize she was healing the little girl inside me. Her motherly love and comfort meant everything to me. It was something that I never experienced from my own mother, and now I knew why.

It didn't make it hurt any less, but I finally had closure and could stop questioning why my mother didn't love me. I now knew why, and I would close that door in my life.

Rome carefully tore the wrapping paper and opened his box. He pulled out the tiny onesie and stared at me, confused. "Read it," Marie instructed.

"My uncle handpicked me from heaven," he read slowly.

I watched as he picked up the old picture of Allen, him, and me. "Fay, you're not telling me . . ."

"I'm pregnant." I pulled the test out of my pajama pocket and handed it to him.

Rome's eyes became red as tears slid down his face. I watched as he kept looking from the test to the onesie, then back to the picture. "Stop."

"I'm serious, baby. You're going to be a father."

"God is sooo good!" my father hollered. "He's always in the business of blessing us when we need it the most." He stood up and came over to hug us.

"Congratulations, you guys. A new baby to love and squeeze on." Marie hugged and kissed both Rome and me.

Rome finally snapped out of his trance and stood up. He pulled me into his arms and picked me up before spinning me around. "I'm going to be a father, yo!"

I held the side of his face. "Yes, baby."

"Thank you, Fay . . . Thank you." He kissed me repeatedly.

"Thank you, baby . . . I love you."

"We will make this work, I promise . . . Whatever I gotta do, I'm going to do to make us work, Fay," Rome promised.

We shared the most passionate kiss that I think we ever had. Had my father not been in the room, I was sure it would have led to the most amazing sex.

"Dad, open your gift."

He opened the envelope that had a bow on top of it. "All these papers..." he said while looking through them. "A lease... Faithy..."

"The girls and I are moving to Sageport," I announced.

Both Rome and my father looked like they were about to fall out. "You serious, Fay?"

"I'm serious... I leased a town house a couple of streets from yours."

Rome didn't even reply. He just kissed me on the lips. The way he held my face and continued to kiss me was all he needed to do. I could tell he appreciated everything.

It was much easier for us to move to Sageport than for him to follow us to Georgia. I wanted the girls to experience this small town that they have come to love and adore.

"Whew, thank God. Now I can spoil you and that baby with lots of good food. We got to fatten you up and that baby." Marie jumped up like she was about to start cooking a feast now.

"Not too fat. I will still need to lose this baby weight."

"A baby?"

We all snapped our necks to the patio door. Mrs. Atkins was standing there.

The girls must have told her, not expecting her to come in here to repeat it. "Yes, Mama... I'm having a baby with Faith." Rome walked over toward his mother.

We were all nervous.

Scared of how she reacts to the news.

She held onto his hands, and a smile formed on her face. "A precious, sweet baby... You are going to be a father, Rome?" She squeezed his hands.

"Yes. How do you feel about that?"

"I'm happy. I'm going to be a grandmama," she cheered, and we all sighed in relief.

"Congratulations, Debra. We're going to be grandparents!" My father called over from the couch.

"Congratulations, Clyde. I can't wait to spoil this baby. Where's my credit card? I need to head on—"

"Not today, Mama . . . We're going to enjoy Christmas first," Rome told her.

Pia rubbed her back, and she settled down. "Let's get you more coffee," Pia suggested.

Rome walked over with a smile on his face.

"What's that smile about?"

"Well, I didn't know how this would work, but I knew I was determined to make it work for us. It didn't matter if you spent some weekends here or I spent some weekends there. I just knew we would make it work until we knew what we were doing."

"Okaaay . . ." I narrowed my eyes at him.

He pulled out a set of keys from his pajama pocket. "I put an offer in on this beach house, and it was accepted. I want this to be our beach home. A place where we can make happy memories with our families and the girls."

"And now the new baby." Mayven came over and hugged Rome. Madison went to his other side and hugged him.

"Yes, now with the new baby."

It was my turn to be emotional. I sniffled while wiping my eyes. I had no clue that returning to help my father would turn into all this. I was the happiest that I have ever been. My relationship with my father was so much better, and I had rekindled a relationship that I thought was gone forever. We were pregnant with our baby, and now, my girls and I were moving to Sageport.

"Our beach house sounds perfect." I kissed him while the girls hugged us both.

For a while, I doubted if I would ever find true happiness again. I couldn't picture myself building a new life without Ashton.

It was tough.

I couldn't see giving myself to a man again. With Rome, I willingly gave myself to him because I knew the kind of man he was. He has shown me that he's man enough to apologize when he's in the wrong and put in the work.

All I wanted was for someone to put in the same amount of effort that I put into something, and Rome has shown that every step of the way. He has shown me that he loves me and has accepted my girls.

"Remember what you said at Pier 3? How you wanted somebody who wasn't going to run and cower?"

"Yes."

"I'm never running from you again, baby. I put that on everything." He kissed me on the lips.

God told me not to doubt him, and I knew why he sent me back to Sageport. He sent me back here to reconnect with the people I needed most. He sent me back for a second chance.

THE END

*To my husband, thank you for being
my rock throughout the years.
I couldn't do this without you.
I wouldn't want to do this without you.
I love you, Mr. C.*

Acknowledgments

I want to thank my tribe. The Jah Tribe. I couldn't do any of this without the support each of you show me with every release. We are truly a family and have grown together throughout the years. You guys have been riding with me since 2014, and I appreciate every cousin in the tribe. Love you guys!

To Jaleesa, Jaki, and Jaya, I love you guys so much. Thank you so much for being the best siblings ever. I love you guys.

To Quiana and Treasure, thank you for being my sounding board, support system, and putting up with my shenanigans. I love you both soo soo soo deep! With nearly ten years of friendship under our belts, our friendship is compared to wine, it keeps getting better and we're getting finer lol.

Kisha Mills, yes, I went with the real name. Thank you for always being you. For speaking my name in rooms that I hadn't even entered yet. This book wouldn't have been possible if it wasn't for you. When I was at a weird place with my career, you restored that and gave me back the spark I had been desperately searching for. Thank you, Thank you, Thank you.

To my agent, LaSheera, thank you for all that you do for me and my career. You're appreciated so much, and I don't take the work you put in for us for granted.

N'Tyse and the Black Odyssey Media family, thank you for this opportunity. I appreciate you taking a chance and allowing me to be a part of this amazing company that you're building.

WWW.BLACKODYSSEY.NET